- - A DEBT OF DEATH - -

HARRY STARK NOVELS
BY JOHN WORSLEY SIMPSON

Undercut
Counterpoint
Shadowmen
A Debt of Death

-- A DEBT OF DEATH --

A HARRY STARK MYSTERY

By John Worsley Simpson

THE MERCURY PRESS

Copyright © 2008 by John Worsley Simpson

ALL RIGHTS RESERVED. No part of this book may be reproduced by any means without the prior written permission of the publisher, with the exception of brief passages in reviews. Any request for photocopying or other reprographic copying of any part of this book must be directed in writing to the Canadian Reprography Collective.

The publisher gratefully acknowledges the financial assistance of the Canada Council for the Arts, the Ontario Arts Council, and the Ontario Book Publishing Tax Credit Program. The publisher further acknowledges the financial support of the Government of Canada through the Department of Canadian Heritage's Book Publishing Industry Development Program (BPIDP) for our publishing activities.

 Canada Council for the Arts / Conseil des Arts du Canada

ONTARIO ARTS COUNCIL / CONSEIL DES ARTS DE L'ONTARIO

 Ontario / Ontario Media Development Corporation

Société de développement de l'industrie des médias de l'Ontario

 Canadä

Editor: Beverley Daurio
Cover, composition and page design: Beverley Daurio
Front cover image alteration: Joshua James

Printed and bound in Canada
Printed on acid-free paper

1 2 3 4 5   12 11 10 09 08

Library and Archives Canada Cataloguing in Publication

Simpson, John Worsley, 1944-
A debt of death / John Worsley Simpson.
ISBN 978-1-55128-139-1
I. Title.
PS8587.I5475D42 2008   C813'.54   C2008-906294-9

The Mercury Press
Box 672, Station P, Toronto, Ontario Canada M5S 2Y4
www.themercurypress.ca

1968

Rhonda Wilton was seventeen. She had big watery-green eyes and long, naturally blonde hair. Early in 1968, she had escaped from the constriction of her life in Humboldt, Saskatchewan, and made a pilgrimage to the runaways' Emerald City, Toronto, where thousands hung out on Yorkville Avenue, watching the constant flow of tourists and students who came to view the freaks or try to have their way with the loose-moraled, hashish-addled young things in thin, tie-dyed cotton dresses.

Rhonda had escaped not only the boredom of her life on the prairie, but also the physical and mental abuse of her father, a truck driver and farmhand, who had raised her and her brother alone since Rhonda's mother had made her bid for freedom many years before. To quell his demons, Rhonda's father drank, and when he was drunk, he beat his kids. When Rhonda went, he looked for her for three days, perfunctorily, and then washed his hands of her.

Matt Mackey was fifteen in 1968. An only child, he lived with his parents in the small Ontario town of Grandfield, northwest of Hamilton. He was a good student and a dutiful son. Well-liked, he played hockey for his highschool team and acted in the Grandfield Dramatic Society's production of *Our Town*. His mother said he was too young to date, but he was allowed to go to school dances, and he had been with one girl beneath the football field bleachers, albeit with considerably less progress than he later claimed.

Late in the afternoon of a blazingly hot Saturday in July, Matt took a bus into Hamilton and another to Stoney Creek. There, after helping clean the swimming pool behind a huge home, he became a passenger in a bright red, 1966 Mustang convertible with white interior, bought for the teenaged driver by his wealthy father. Matt sat in the rear without being asked. They drove to the home of another teen, a tall, muscular redhead, who got into the front seat.

At a local A&W, they sat with the top down, the humid evening air little cooler than it had been at midday. Exhaust fumes from the rumbling engines of other hot cars driven by testosterone-heavy males wafted over them. They drank root beer, ate Papa Burgers and fries, and ogled the girls who came over to admire the convertible. The teen in the front passenger seat had a bottle of gin he had stolen from his father's liquor cabinet. He put gin in the root beer.

"Jesus, gin and root beer," the driver said. "Save some for the broads. That stuff is panty-remover."

In the back seat, Matt sat fascinated with the banter of the two older boys. If they got only two girls, he'd have to get out, and they would pick him up later at the pool room.

"You're not old enough to go in there, really, but they won't say anything. If we only get one broad, you may as well stay, because if a bird will get in a car with two guys, she'll do a third one, too. We might break your cherry with any luck, Matt. But if it's just two, neither one will want to look like a slut to the other, and they won't want an audience, so a third guy would be out. Sorry. Anyway, we'll tell you all about it, every detail."

After half an hour of flirting and cajoling, the driver got impatient.

"We're not getting anything. Cockteasers. Let's go to Yorkville."

The driver turned to face Matt. "Don't tell my father we went to Toronto. He'll ground me for a month. All right?"

"I won't say anything."

As the engine started, the car suddenly sagged as a fourth youth clambered into the back seat.

"Where we goin'?"

"Ah jeezus, we're not going to get any broads with you along," the teen in the front passenger seat said.

"We've probably got a better chance. He can bullshit anybody." The driver reached behind him and grabbed the hand of the newcomer. "How's it going, Number Two, old buddy."

The new arrival, who was referred to as Number Two—except when the redhead called him Bowel Movement—was never introduced to Matt, who clung to the corner and was ignored by the other three during the drive to Toronto.

Rhonda Wilton didn't like hashish. She had tried it twice and hallucinated both times. She wouldn't drop acid. She had watched a guy on acid try to stop a streetcar by charging down the tracks at it, screaming, and ramming it with his head. She did smoke pot, but she was embarrassed to smoke it in public, and she was afraid of the undercover cops that were practically as common on the street as tourists.

That drippingly hot night, she had gone behind Jesse Ketcham school with a boy called Ralph from Wawa, and they had smoked three joints. The boy wanted to do it with her in the schoolyard, but she had pushed him away and he had left her there, calling her a frigid bitch. Rhonda wondered whether he was right.

She didn't think she was frigid, but she had gone all the way only twice, the first time with a boy in a car in Humboldt, the second time with a man of twenty-two right after she arrived in Toronto, a man who ran a drop-in centre on Gerrard Street and threatened to put her out into the cold and shadowy March night if she didn't come across. She had been fondled and prodded by lots of boys since, but had always stopped short of intercourse. And she certainly wasn't going to do it with a bony kid from Wawa, who stank of sweat and had a face like a gravel road. She had gone behind the school with him only for the solace of the joints.

The Emerald City was losing its glitter. She had had enough of people puking on her in hostels and crash pads. She was sick of Sally Ann soup. But to get off the street, she needed a job, and to get a job, she needed a haircut and some clothes, and a room where she could wash and sleep, and an address. She needed money.

Rhonda wandered back to Yorkville. She sat alone on a wall at the end of the strip, away from the lights and coffee houses and the crowds. The grass hadn't been that good, but she was a little stoned. The hot night air felt thick, although she could feel a slight and welcome breeze, not enough to stir the leaves in the huge oaks overhanging the sidewalk. She'd be able to sleep outside, as long as she could find a place where there weren't any winos. But she was starving, and she had no money, not a penny, and she was filthy. She needed a shower.

"Hi, there."

Rhonda ignored the greeting, pointedly looking away from the car from which it had been called out.

A different voice asked: "You want a drink?" The redhead showed her the neck of the gin bottle, his arm concealing the fact that the bottle was empty. "You ever have a ride in a convertible? Not like this one." The driver revved the engine. "You hear that? You should hear it peel. C'mon, just around the block a couple of times."

"Forget it. She's all strung out anyway."

"You got any money?" Rhonda said, still not looking in their direction.

"What?"

She turned toward them, her eyes down, looking at the car, not interested in the car, but not wanting to look at the boys. "You got any money?" she repeated.

"Money?" the driver said. "Get out of here. She's a hooker, for god's sake."

"She's not a hooker," the teen beside him hissed. To the girl, he said, louder, "You a little short of money?"

"Twenty bucks," Rhonda said, looking up for the first time. There were four of them, not two. One was a lot younger, a kid, in the back seat. He looked frightened, reminded her of her brother.

"Twenty bucks and what?" one said.

"Twenty bucks and I'll go for a ride in the car."

"Hop in."

"Give me the twenty first."

"Yeah, sure," the driver snarled. "And watch you make like a rabbit."

"That's the idea," the redheaded teen whispered.

"Shut up."

"I'm not getting in the car until I get the twenty."

"All right," Number Two said, pausing to take a big gulp from the bottle of vodka he had brought for his own consumption. "Here, I'll give you the money." He stood on the seat, vaulted out of the car and came around to the sidewalk, reaching in his pocket. "Twenty bucks? No problem."

Rhonda looked at him suspiciously. She reached out her hand. Number Two smiled at her. His hand came out of his pocket empty, grabbed her extended wrist and pulled her toward him, wrapping his other arm around her hips and lifting, heaving her into the back seat, where she tumbled over Matt, who scrambled to the far corner, pulling his feet up on to the seat. Number Two leapt in after the girl, shoving her, struggling, to the floor, and holding her down with his feet.

"Go," he shouted at the driver, and the car squealed away from the curb. "Help me," he said to Matt, as the girl fought to free herself, but Matt pulled away. The redhead reached between the front seats and helped hold Rhonda down.

"Jesus, what the fuck are you doing?" the driver shouted over his shoulder.

"Just drive, for Christ's sake." Number Two called out directions over the shouts of the girl. The little energy she had was expended on her voice. Weakened by the effects of the marijuana and months of poor nutrition, she lacked the strength to lift herself from the floor of the car against the pressure of the youths' feet and hands.

"Go right. Put the radio up." He directed them to Rosedale Valley Road, winding between the leafy inclines of a deep ravine. Atop the left slope, the massive brick piles of old money ignored their passage. He told the driver to turn left on the Bayview Extension and after a time, he said, "Okay, turn here and pull in over there. Now, drive in as far as you can." They had turned at Pottery Road, and pulled on to a path that led into the trees flanking the Don River. The sour odour of some upstream-dumped factory's effluent rose from the river, mixing incongruously with the verdant scent of new-mown grass.

"Stop here. We can't be seen from the road. This is good."

Number Two lifted his feet from Rhonda. She tried to climb out of the car.

"Grab her," he shouted at Matt, who shook his head and crossed his arms tight against his chest. "Jesus, kid." Number Two grabbed the girl's long dress and pulled her back. The driver got out of the car.

"Let her go," he shouted. "This is nuts."

"Forget it. Jesus. She wanted twenty bucks, so we'll give her twenty bucks. What's she going to do, tell the cops? Who's going to listen to her? These sluts fuck like minks. She probably blows half the cops on the street anyway. C'mon, I've got a boner that won't go away." Number Two climbed over Matt. "Get out of the way, kid, Jesus." He jumped out of the car, still holding Rhonda's dress. He reached into the car and grabbed her around the waist, and she tried to elbow him in the head. The front-seat passenger clutched her by her upper arms and lifted her slight body out of the car, Number Two pushing her by the buttocks, taking the opportunity to squeeze them. The redheaded teen, who was a weightlifter, proud of his broad shoulders and bulging biceps, raised the girl high in the air.

"Let me go, you son of a bitch," Rhonda shouted, trying to kick him in the groin, but catching him in the thigh, and losing a sandal.

"Jesus, she caught me with a toenail. You bitch." He threw her against the car and she cried out in pain. "All right, let's see what you've got, baby."

He tore open the front her dress, exposing her breasts. "No bra. Not a bad pair. Look at these." He grabbed Rhonda by the shoulders and spun her around. The driver shook his head. His friend said, "What's the matter?

Look at them, nice and round, ooh, and firm." He cupped her left breast in his hand. Rhonda tried to pull away from him, and he pinned her with his body against the side of the car. "Let's see what else she has to offer." He dragged her to the hood of the car, and shoved her upper body down on to it, holding her down with one forearm, and lifting her dress with his other hand. "No panties," he squealed. "Jesus, you don't think she gives it away to all the hippie creeps? She won't even notice two more. Help me with her."

"I'll kill you," Rhonda screamed.

Crouched in the back seat, Matt opened his mouth to protest, but the words stuck in his throat. Tears filled his eyes.

"Help me," the redhead said again. Number Two came around the front of the car; they spun Rhonda around and shoved her face down over the hood of the car. "Okay, hold her down," the redhead said. He unzipped the fly of his jeans and pulled out his penis. He thrust his hips against Rhonda's buttocks and tried to penetrate her. She screamed. "Shut up, you bitch, you love it." The redhead grinned at Number Two and the driver. Rhonda twisted her hips from side to side. "Christ, hold her still." He grunted. Finally he penetrated briefly, before she shook free.

"Wow," he said. "Come on, your turn."

Rhonda kept screaming.

"No, never mind. I don't want to," the driver said.

"You don't want to?" Number Two said, "Are you a suck? We came out to get fucked, and you'll never get another one like this. You want me to tell everybody you chickened out. Come on, do her. Shut up, you bitch." He pushed the redhead aside and pulled the driver behind the girl. Number Two spit on his hand and wiped the spittle on and inside the lips of Rhonda's vulva. He shoved the driver against her buttocks. The driver shook his head, but Number Two grabbed his neck and twisted his face around till it was inches from his. "Do it, you bullshitting rich prick." Finally, the driver shoved against Rhonda viciously, gritting his teeth, displaying not pleasure, but anger, and glaring at Number Two.

"Help me, somebody help me," she pleaded.

"Fuck, somebody's going to hear her," the driver said.

"I'll shut her up," Number Two said. He pulled the driver away from the girl and positioned himself behind her, driving himself into her, his teeth clenched, eyes and mouth agape. He thrust his loins against her again and again. Rhonda screamed louder.

"For God's sake," the driver said. "Somebody's going to hear her and call the cops."

Number Two grabbed Rhonda's hair, raised her head from the hood of the car and smashed it against the hood. She kept screaming. He arched his back, smashing her head again and again. The screaming stopped. He released his grip. Rhonda slid off the hood of the car to the ground.

"She's passed out," Number Two said. He bent over her and slapped her lightly on the face.

"You knocked her out," the driver said.

Number Two put his hand near her nose. He leaned over and laid his head on her chest. He looked up at the other two.

"She's dead."

TODAY

CHAPTER ONE

On a coolish but sunny October day that seemed to hold promise, Harry Stark woke with a headache. After years of waking up that way, he might have expected to be used to it, but the cause of this headache wasn't what had produced most of his headaches in the past: alcohol-enhanced late nights. Stark had woken up with this new headache on most days since he had been shot in the head. Eleven months and nine days before, a woman with whom he had been smitten, a woman who turned out to be a villain, a woman who tried to end his life, had ended the life he had been living. Whenever he thought about her, he could hear his father's voice saying, "There's no conscience below the belt," and his mother adding, "and no brains, either."

That morning, as Stark looked at himself in the mirror, he thought, "I don't look too bad. In fact, I don't look fifty-three. No way. I bet I could pass for thirty-eight." And then he half-sang, half-spoke Johnny Mandel's theme from the movie *M*A*S*H*. "Through early morning fog I see visions of the things to be, the pains that are withheld for me. I realize, and I can see that suicide is painless; it brings on many changes, and I can take or leave it if I please."

Since he'd been shot, it had been a disruptive time for the homicide detective. And Stark liked things to run smooth and steady. But that sure had not been the case in the past year.

The first shock came when they let him out of the hospital, and his landlord Jimmy Yu met him at the door to his apartment above Jimmy's dental practice on Queen Street East in the Beaches. Stark thought it was nice of Jimmy to welcome him home, and Jimmy did do that. But the real reason he had come outside when he saw Stark get out of a cab was to tell him he was closing his dental practice and selling the building in which it was located. The new owner wanted Stark's apartment, and since Stark had no lease, he'd have to go. Jimmy Yu was going to continue to work part-time as a dentist, but mostly he'd be overseeing things at the two Tim Horton's franchises he'd bought.

After receiving that news, Stark was in for a worse shock: both of his local hang-outs had vanished. Sid Holtzman's deli was a real-estate office. Sid had won two million dollars in the 6/49 lottery and had moved to Las Vegas without saying goodbye. Carbo's Bistro had been gutted in a kitchen fire about which there had been some suspicion, since Ulysses, the owner, had been in financial straits before the blaze.

With no focal points left for Stark in the area, he had decided to buy his own place. Beaches real estate was too expensive, so he bought a duplex on Monarch Park Avenue, a leafy street built in the 1920s, that runs perpendicular to the Danforth, as Danforth Avenue is called by Toronto's east enders. Stark's house was a few doors north of the Danforth.

As far as he was concerned, Stark had fully recovered from the shooting, and he wanted to get back on the job, but his superiors had radically different ideas. Union rules meant they couldn't force Stark to quit, but he hadn't been able to get an all-clear from the police service doctor. On the other hand, the doctor was optimistic—at least for Stark's recovery. About his future as a detective, the doctor hinted that if Stark stopped minimizing and even denying symptoms, and complained about them instead, it would be a simple matter to tack a disability pension on to the regular police pension, and then Stark could retire to a fishing cabin on the Saint John River in New Brunswick.

"For God's sake, I don't know anybody in New Brunswick. Why the hell would I go to New Brunswick?"

"It's beautiful on that river, Stark. I spend most of the summer there. The fishing is fantastic."

"The last time I fished, I was seven and didn't know any better."

Stark could have told the doc about the headaches, but he didn't wake up with one every morning. In fact, if he slept seven or eight hours, he'd usually wake up without one, but from years of habit, he couldn't sleep in in the morning. And equally, from years of habit, he couldn't go to bed at a "reasonable" time, but would stay up till two or three in the morning. In the past, many late nights would have been spent at Carbos's or some other bar, or, occasionally, in bed with a woman, all accompanied by liberal amounts of booze and Gauloise cigarettes—except when the woman objected to their strong aroma. But the pills prescribed for him after the shooting precluded alcohol, and the doctor ordered Stark not to smoke. He stopped taking the pills after a couple of months, but he was afraid to start drinking and smoking again. So, now he spent most nights consuming coffee or strong tea and reading nineteenth-century novels. And sometimes watching mindless television talk shows until he fell asleep on the couch.

CHAPTER TWO

In his youth, Dennis Yates had been one of the country's most successful popular singers. His recordings set global sales records, and his face appeared on the covers of magazines and newspapers throughout the world. Unlike most of the antisocial youngsters that formed the big rock groups who built their fame on behaving badly, Yates had presented a public persona of the nice guy: selfless, generous and polite, visiting children's hospitals and old-folks homes wherever he toured. He donated money and time to high-profile charities, and it paid off handsomely.

He remained married to Mary-Margaret, née O'Reilly, whom he had wed in 1973, when they were twenty-three. Now, she was on the plain side, slightly overweight, with a self-effacing public persona that displayed a soft, kindly face. She had been selected for Yates by his manager, Bernard MacIsaac, her features being not unpleasant and her body shapely enough to suggest she possessed the requisite equipment for child-bearing.

Yates had consented to the marriage because his access to a string of discreet carnal partners would be continued. And, after a decent interval, he was to be permitted to divorce Mary-Margaret.

In fact, Bernie couldn't wait for the separation announcement. It was to be brilliant. Dennis and Mary-Margaret would make a tearful declaration of undying love, but confess that their interests and lifestyles and *world vision* had grown apart, that they would continue to raise the children jointly, even vacation together as a family and remain lifelong friends, but, despite their broken hearts, they would reside apart. Yates would immediately make a record called *Too Much in Love to Be Together* that would break all previous sales marks.

Masterful.

But Mary-Margaret would have none of it.

"Up yours, asshole. I'm along for the whole ride, so get used to it."

As time went on, Yates's popularity slumped and his sales went south. The generation that had venerated Yates began using their spare cash for diapers and formula and the occasional meal at the local pub/restaurant in Markham or Kirkland or Burnaby.

Yates and Co. were in no danger of financial collapse, and the two compilation CDs he made sold well for a couple of years before sales fizzled. Bernie's big break-up sentimental blockbuster was never to be. For a few years, club owners continued to book Dennis; his price had dropped, and he pulled in the young marrieds. But eventually the bookings stopped.

Bernie owned the recording company for which Yates was the only really big name, but they had enough other acts under contract to earn more than a decent living for them. The arrangement provided both tax and insurance benefits for the singer. Yates was the owner of a separate corporation, Rocky River Productions, which was listed as providing several functions to Bernie's RR Recordings Inc.: producer, creative consultant, and artists and repertoire. Mary-Margaret had seen to it that she and Dennis had their own lawyer, who had drawn up contracts to protect their interest in the company, and she had hired her own personal lawyer to see that her interests in the marriage/business were equally well protected.

Yates's career carried on in fits and starts; he did a little acting, at which he was lousy; he sang some commercial jingles and he got the occasional club booking. Mostly, he was off the radar, and took to wandering around shopping malls with an inane grin, returning home in a state of euphoria if someone recognized him and asked for his autograph, or terribly depressed if no one approached him.

Years went by with decreasing gigs and growing depression. Bernie paid less and less attention to Yates; the other acts were starting to make good money. For a while Yates went into a kind of hibernation, and then one day he emerged and began to browbeat Bernie into putting him out on tour again, which was when Yates went out on what Mary-Margaret, to annoy Dennis, loved to call the "Wrinklies Circuit"—small-town arenas and native casinos and the like, where the audience came to relive their younger days. Much to Bernie's chagrin, the audience's enthusiasm convinced Yates that he "still had it," and he bugged Bernie incessantly until Bernie finally agreed to arrange a "Remember When" tour of Canada and four cities in the US midwest; he couldn't get any other bookings. Attendance at the twelve venues was reasonable, but not great. When the tour ended, Bernie, fed up with Yates's high maintenance, his delicate ego and inflated sense of his own allure, intended to give the singer and Mary-Margaret the boot. But then Bernie received a strange phone call in Yates's hotel room in Calgary.

The caller was a wealthy and powerful man called Martyn Waterman, who made a lucrative, and what at first seemed to MacIsaac preposterous, proposal. He wanted Yates to be the torch bearer for the Canadian Values Party. He said he could make Yates the next prime minister. Waterman represented a group within the party he called The Compact, which, he said, saw Yates as the perfect candidate: a family man with old-fashioned standards of morality, but with sex appeal, already admired by middle-class parents, a candidate who could boost the party enough to give it a majority. An investigator had found no skeletons in Yates's past. Bernie had done his concealment work well. Bernie was convinced and gave enthusiastic agreement to the proposition before presenting it to Yates with a degree of flattery that would have embarrassed someone who was not a complete narcissist.

Yates was put in the hands of a team of experts that included an acting coach, a public-speaking specialist, two speech-writers, a psychologist, a motion-picture director and a comedy-writer. They turned Yates into a droll, slow-speaking, Will Rogers type—honest, forgiving and never strident. They taught him nothing about politics or economics; he was trained to deflect such questions and turn them into circular arguments. He learned to parry assaults deftly, with a step to the side, letting the force of their vitriol carry them to the floor, like an aikido black belt handling an attacker. The toughest challenge was teaching him French, but six weeks at a private language school in the Laurentians, which included a torrid affair with one of the instructors, rendered him passable in the language.

When the time came, Yates would win the nomination as party leader on the first ballot. Later, a party member in a safe riding would resign his seat in the Commons and Yates would win the by-election in an all-stops-pulled-out campaign designed to showcase Dennis Yates, superstar and statesman. Backroom bribery, threats, blackmail and favours would be ably delivered by the members of The Compact, its six members being among the wealthiest men in the country. They had formed The Compact because they were tired of politicians, even in their own party, screwing things up; they had decided the only solution was to run the government themselves.

The country had been divided into six regions, and each member of The Compact had been assigned a region. Where their influence and effectiveness was deemed stronger in a region than the person assigned to it, they overlapped. Business people were pressured with hints of lost business and promises of increased sales to put their weight behind Yates. They were instructed to do the same thing to their suppliers in turn, stressing that their success would be rewarded and their failure would be punished.

The Compact spent millions on investigations, gathering dirt on convention delegates and key riding-association members, and then had their agents apply the same kind of pressure they used with their business suppliers to extract promises of support and activity on behalf of Yates's candidacy. They eliminated potential competitors that posed any threat to Yates by similar methods, blackmail being most effective against the stubborn, high-minded ones. On one occasion, an Alberta rancher's barn was burned to the ground, and later his horse was shot, before he walked away from the race.

Mary-Margaret's plainness had made Yates appear to be a faithful husband deeply in love with his wife, since, clearly, he could have had all the beautiful women he wanted. To young males, he was no threat. To older men and women, he was a nice boy with a lovely family. And much of his music was sweet and melodic enough to appeal to an older audience. Mary-Margaret's appearance also enhanced Yates's attraction for young female fans, certain that, given the chance, they could woo him away from her.

Mary-Margaret affected a callow, almost vacuous expression in public, holding her mouth in a fatuous smile for so long that her jaw hurt. In private, she rarely smiled. Intense and withdrawn in her relationship with Yates, with her two children, she was open and affectionate. She took her pleasure where she found it, and she found it in a longstanding affair with Bert Bartram, the drummer in Yates's back-up band. Periodically, she also had sex with Martyn Waterman, who had introduced her to Bernie MacIsaac.

Waterman and Yates had grown up together. Never promiscuous and always discreet, Mary-Margaret had nevertheless had intercourse with three boys with whom she had gone steady between the ages of sixteen and nineteen. Waterman had been her first. Matt Mackey had introduced them. She was Mackey's cousin on his mother's side; Waterman was a second cousin on Mackey's father's side. Waterman had approached her about Yates being a candidate for the party, in bed in Waterman's love-nest apartment in the suburban wilderness of Etobicoke, where no one of Waterman's acquaintance was likely to venture.

"His career is in the tank," Waterman had said.

"That's an exaggeration, but you could say his marketability is—waning."

"I have an idea."

"You usually do."

"How would you like to be the wife of the prime minister?"

"He's a bit old for me, Marty, and he's already married."

"I'm serious."

"You, the prime minister? Don't be ridiculous."

"Not me. Dennis."

"Now I know you're kidding."

"He'd be perfect."

"Dennis doesn't even vote. I think you're nuts."

"Look, leave the mechanics to me. I just want to know whether you would support him."

"Dennis doesn't speak French."

"He'll speak French before we're through. Will you stay on the bus, is all I want to know."

"To pull this off, he'll still need me as a prop?"

"More than ever."

"Prime minister's wife, eh? Mmm. Sure. He's getting set to dump me once his career is really flushed down the toilet. He'd spend the rest of a short life snorting coke with his whores, and I'd be stuck in a semi in East York with Bert. This will be like a no-cancellation contract. I want appearance money."

"Appearance money?"

"You need me, Marty. If I'm part of the band, I want scale. More than scale. I want my own income."

Waterman sighed. "We'll work something out."

CHAPTER THREE

It had been almost a year since Stark was shot, but he still thought about it every day. Each morning, a Pollyanna grinned at him idiotically from his bathroom mirror, and Stark would try to paste on the dour mask with which he had always been comfortable. But despite his best efforts at being miserable, the new face would burst through, and remain there until he caught sight of it in the mirrors at his new local hang-outs—Boyd's Best Bagels and Beulah's Bar and Grill—bursting with unfortunate alliteration and both around the corner from his place on the Danforth.

"So, how's retirement, Harry? I haven't seen you in months," asked Boris, the owner of Beulah's.

There once had been a Beulah, but, under the financial pressure of opening such an establishment, and the additional pressure of its not being an immediate success, she dropped dead of a heart attack before her eponymous bar burgeoned. Out of respect, Boris, who had been Beulah's cook and occasional, after-closing, lover, retained the name, even though Boris's Bar and Grill would have been equally alliterative.

Stark was sitting at the end of the bar, beside Roger Sammon, who seemed to spend most of his waking hours on the same bar stool.

"Oh god," Sammon groaned, anticipating Stark's reaction.

Stark's head snapped around, his teeth clenched. He spat the words out.

"I'm not retired. I'm on medical leave. In fact, I've been doing some—private investigator work of my own, but don't tell anybody about that, because—That idiot doctor won't let me go back on the job for another month. I'm sorry, Boris. I'm just—"

"Forget it. I wasn't thinking." Boris nodded, and, taking a step back out of Stark's mirror angle, made a "touched the wrong button there" face at Roger. "So, you're going to return to the police department, then?"

Stark took a deep breath.

"Yeah," he said with a thin smile.

Boris looked at Roger with a question mark. Roger raised his eyebrows and shoulders.

"Well, I'm sure you get tired of the silly questions. Can I buy you a drink, Harry?"

"No, that's fine. I've still got this. Thanks, anyway."

"You still drinking soda water?"

"I'm not supposed to touch booze with these pills I'm on. But don't worry, Boris. You won't have to put the place up for sale. I'll be back to normal in a month or so, and then you'll be able to buy the shoe repair shop next door and expand."

"Just get well, Harry."

Stark gave another weak smile.

Stark had long qualified for retirement from the police service, as they now called it since it had been decided "Force" gave a negative impression. Stark, who had remained single since a short failed marriage when he was young, was terrified of feeling useless, of living off what he had done and not what he was doing now. Far from what the service wanted a detective to be, Stark hated detail work, typing reports, attending courses. He wanted to catch criminals. He never passed judgement. He just liked to catch them, so he was careful in his choice of partners. They would last only a couple of years with him before they got fed up and there'd be a parting of the ways. Stark always picked the smartest, youngest detective in the unit. In fact, often when a plum one arrived, he would throw over his existing partner, which was rarely resisted, because Stark would use their brains and his seniority to make them do the detail work and complete the reports. Stark would just be there for the kill.

He claimed to have solved every case he had ever been on.

CHAPTER FOUR

"Matt Mackey knows."

"Are you sure?"

"Yes. And his book is going to be published right before the election."

"We'll get an injunction."

"Come on, Lee, that's not an option."

Martyn Waterman took a sip of whisky from a large Waterford old-fashioned glass and made a face. He would have preferred red wine, but Johnnie Walker Black was the group's chosen tipple. Seated at the table with him were the other five members of The Compact, whose political and financial reach was that of the global billionaires they were: Waterman sat at the head of the table; on his left, Brian Ball and Norton Fielding, with Ian Covey, Ross Stephenson and Lee Braddock on his right. Braddock's acquisitions alone were so extensive that, in the past month, he had dined in three restaurants he didn't even know he owned.

Braddock said, "What's the book going to say?"

"I haven't read it, but Mackey got drunk at a media awards banquet and told me the book is a series of distorted biographies portraying us as a cabal of evil, rapacious vultures, self-serving capitalists running the country from this room." Waterman scanned their faces. "In some cases, the material may be a little more personal." He took a drink of Scotch. "Mackey also has specifics about our financial involvement, not only with Dennis's campaign, but in the cause of peace, order and good government."

"But we haven't done anything illegal," Brian Ball said.

Waterman leaned back. "Brian, there are things..." He pursed his lips and turned to face Ball. "We would go to prison." As he spoke, Waterman leaned closer to Ball until their faces were inches apart.

"Martyn," Norton Fielding said, "you've made your point."

Braddock raised his hands. "Let's just agree we're in a pickle. How do we get out of it?"

"Let's buy the publisher and kill the book," Ian Covey said.

"Mackey'd just sue and take it to somebody else. Are we going to buy every publisher in the country?"

"He must have a price," Ross Stephens said.

Waterman shook his head with slow finality. "Mackey's not interested in money. He's dying. The book is his—" he waved both hands mockingly "— left-wing legacy. An ultimate gesture of resentment. Our only choice is to wield a mightier sword."

"What's that mean?" Ball said.

Waterman's silent stare took on meaning as it continued.

"Go ahead, say it, Martyn," Fielding said. "You want someone else to suggest the solution you're implying, and then you can say it wasn't your idea."

"Norton, I am waiting for proposals all of us can examine and discuss."

"I'm having no part of violence," Fielding said.

Covey said, "Do you think Martyn's going to sit on him while Brian bashes him with a golf club? Jesus, Fielding."

"He's waiting for somebody to say we should arrange to have the man permanently silenced," Fielding said.

"Don't be absurd," Stephens said.

No one spoke.

Finally Stephens stared at Waterman, his mouth slightly open.

Dennis Yates strode back and forth in Martyn Waterman's office on a floor near the top of BCE Place, overlooking the lakefront and the Toronto Islands. "Your fucking cousin is going to destroy us. My life will be ruined, everything I've worked for. What's he going to get out of it? Money? He hasn't got a wife or kids. He's dying, for christ's sake. What's the point?"

"He's clearing his bloody conscience. And don't call him my cousin." Waterman sat behind a massive French Empire style table that served as his desk. He sprawled on his tilted-back Herman Miller Eames executive work chair, and then suddenly leaned forward, bringing the chair upright, and pointed a finger at Yates.

"Oh, fuck off," Yates said. "What are we going to do? Maybe the cancer will kill Mackey before he finishes writing the book. Jesus, how can you be so sure the publisher doesn't have it already?"

"Matt hasn't finished, and the publisher doesn't have a scrap of paper, not a note."

"How can you be so certain?"

"The man who's working for me is an expert in the field of surveillance and intelligence-gathering. The book exists in only three places. There's nothing on paper; it's in Matt's home computer, it's in his laptop—which he doesn't even leave in his car when he goes into a store—and it's in his head. So, even if we wiped out the PC and ripped the laptop from his hands, he'd just rewrite it. He's fast. Twelve hours a day, he'd have it done in a week. The only thing in our favour is that the publisher only knows that it's a political blockbuster."

"You have to do something."

Waterman smiled wryly. "You make it sound so simple, Dennis. It must be a joy to have a mind like yours. Fix it in the mix, like one of your recordings."

"Well, what can we do? Marty, do you want to go to prison? I sure as hell don't. If something doesn't happen soon, I'm going to drain a couple of bank accounts and disappear."

"I'll have a solution in place very soon. All you have to worry about is your next riding association speech."

CHAPTER FIVE

"Life looks like it's treating you good, Harry."

Stark chuckled.

"You know, Ted, I almost said, 'Can't complain.'"

"What's the matter with that? It could be worse. You might be some kind of vegetable."

"Broccoli?"

"What?"

"I wondered whether they'd give you a choice. I like broccoli."

"You serve broccoli, Bert?" Detective-Sergeant Ted Henry said, addressing Bert Boyd, the owner of Boyd's Best Bagels.

"There's no call for it. The Chinese joint down the street makes a nice beef and broccoli. So they tell me. Personally, I can't stand the stuff. You want a refill on the coffee? How about a nice bagel?"

"No thanks, Bert. I had breakfast, and I've got to watch the calories," Henry said, patting the slight bulge at his midriff.

"Bagels're low fat, you know. Anyway, never let it be said that Bert Boyd tries to force anything on a customer they don't want."

Stark rolled his eyes.

Boyd sneered.

Henry turned and looked at Stark.

There was something. Stark was not the Stark Henry knew. He was too soft, too agreeable, too damned nice.

"Beautiful day, isn't it? I love the fall." That wasn't the old Stark, either. "So, tell me, Ted, to what do I owe your visit?"

"I just wondered how you were making out."

"I'm fine. I'd be back at work now, but..."

"You think that's wise, coming back on the force?"

"Jesus, Ted, you sound like Peters," Stark said, referring to the inspector in charge of Homicide.

"Harry, there's nothing in the way of your retirement. The medical supplement, or however they work the insurance and all that stuff means you'd be better off not working. You'd be set. You could open a little bookstore or something not so goddamned stressful as a homicide detective. Anyway, I'm not sure they'd let you back into Homicide, Harry. I think they'd give you a desk job."

"Peters has tried to squeeze me out before, and I've always been able to call in favours and thumb my nose at the jerk. I guess I shouldn't call him a jerk. At least he lets you run the squad, and he's got his own problems."

Henry gave Stark a puzzled look again. He had never heard Stark say anything like that about anybody, let alone Peters, whom the detective despised.

"Yeah, I guess he does," Henry said slowly.

"So, listen, I'm supposed to be going for a walk. I'm going down to the boardwalk. You want to come along?"

Henry said incredulously, "You're going for a walk?"

"It's a beautiful day."

"I'll pass. I've got to get back. Look, think about it, will you, Harry. Of course, you'll be missed, but at least we've got your protégé now. That's almost like having you there."

"Yeah, Diane made detective, eh? How's she working out?"

"You taught her a lot."

CHAPTER SIX

"We haven't done that for a while," Mary-Margaret said as Martyn Waterman got out of bed.

"You haven't lost your touch, Mary-Margaret."

"You have. I don't think your heart was in it, Marty."

With a little groan in his voice, Waterman said, "Call me Martyn."

"I'm not going to call you Martyn, not in private, you pompous ass. What's bothering you? Are you having a problem with Dennis?"

Waterman nodded.

"What is it?"

"Matt Mackey."

"What about him?"

"Matt's going to blow the lid off that thing we never talk about."

"That's insane. You have protected him all these years. Why would he—"

"Inoperable cancer. His book names us. His parting shot."

"So, what are we going to do?"

"*We* aren't going to do anything. I'm going to do something. The Compact thinks the book is going to blow our cover. It will. That would destroy everything. If Mackey reveals what we've done to make Dennis a winner, it's all over. So we have no choice, as I see it. The Compact is onside, except Norton Fielding."

"That strait-laced dick?"

"He threatened to go to the press if anything happened to Mackey."

"What are you going to do?"

"I'm not sure. But I want you to keep an eye on Dennis. He's unstable. I want him to leave things to me. The other day, he talked about vanishing to some desert island or mountaintop."

"Idiot."

"Control him. He's got important appearances coming up."

"I'll slip some extra dope in his coffee—"

Waterman put his hand over Mary-Margaret's mouth. "And I'll handle Mackey."

After Martyn told Dennis that Mackey was writing the book, Dennis went to Bernie, carrying a shotgun.

"What the hell?"

Yates looked at the gun as if he were surprised to see it. "I'm cleaning it. Never mind. Listen, Bernie, I've got to tell you something." Yates related what Martyn had told him about Mackey.

"Who the hell is he?"

"Martyn's cousin, or second cousin or something. He was with us when that thing went down in Toronto when we were kids."

"So, why is he doing this now?"

"He's dying. I don't know. Whatever the reason is, he's doing it. What are we going to do?"

"What does Martyn say?"

"He went to The Compact—"

MacIsaac's head jerked up.

"And he said Mackey was writing on The Compact and everything. He was trying to get them to—you know—do the dirty work."

"The dirty work?"

"With Mackey." Yates shrugged.

"What do you mean?"

"Jesus, Bernie. The walls have ears, eh?"

"So, what did they say?"

"They said, like, buy him off, stuff like that. The one guy, Fielding—you know Fielding?"

"Of course I know Fielding."

"Yes, of course you do. Well, apparently, he was dumping all over Martyn, saying that Martyn wanted them to—" Yates screwed up his face and lowered his voice to a loud hiss. "Martyn's worried. He said that if Mackey even stubs his toe, Fielding is liable to go to the cops."

"Christ, after all this bloody work." MacIsaac sighed. "Tell me more about Mackey."

CHAPTER SEVEN: 1968

Rhonda was buried in Mount Pleasant Cemetery. She was identified simply as "Rhonda" by other street kids and a couple of social workers. None of them knew her last name, and she carried no identification. Her teeth were so badly cared for the police figured circulating dental records would be a waste of time. They did it anyway, and got no responses. The Morality Squad had nothing on her. She had never been arrested, and therefore never fingerprinted. Her father and brother never found out she died.

After Rhonda's death, Matt Mackey retreated into a world of silence. He stayed in his room, staring out the window. For a while, he did what he was asked to do, as he had always done, but mechanically, without enthusiasm. His grades suffered, but because he did the required work, he got passing marks at first, and then began skipping classes, and his grades tumbled. He resisted all efforts by his parents to break through the barrier that had appeared so suddenly. Eventually, he stopped going to hockey practice, and was suspended from the team. He never went back. He left the house early every Sunday as if he were going to mass, but spent the hour sitting on a swing in Holy Martyrs schoolyard. The priest came to the house, and told his parents, who were embarrassed, but not surprised. The priest spoke to Matt, and elicited a promise that Matt would return to mass, but could get no explanation from him about his changed behaviour. Matt went to church the following Sunday, but after that, he refused to go back. He began to stay out past his curfew time.

One night, the police came to the door. Matt had been arrested for stealing a car. As a first offender, he was given a conditional discharge, but three weeks later, he beat another student so badly the young man had to be hospitalized. Matt was sentenced to three months in a training school and a year's probation. Shortly after his release, he stole money from his mother's purse, and set out to hitchhike to Vancouver, breaking probation. He got as far as Parry Sound before he was picked up and returned to the training school.

Marty Waterman's father had checked the odometer on the Mustang on the Sunday morning after the Toronto trip, and decided his son had defied him and had gone to Buffalo. He grounded Marty for a month, but relented when Marty begged, pleading that he had to have the car because he had promised to take Mary-Margaret to Prudhomme's on the Queen E for her birthday. George Waterman liked his son to go out with Mary-Margaret because she was such a sensible girl and not a "glamour doll," and he wished Marty would get more "serious" with her.

Dennis had trouble concentrating on band practice that Sunday. The other members of the group got on his case. They had a gig the following weekend at a Sweet Sixteen party in Grimsby. Eventually, he got into the music, wailing so loudly he went hoarse and everyone thought he sounded even better, and he twanged his guitar so vigorously he snapped a string.

Number Two went on about his life as if absolutely nothing had happened.

CHAPTER EIGHT

Matt had become a journalist for lust. The summer after his youthful stint as a criminal, he landed a job as a cleaner at the African Lion Safari, a wild-animal park that had opened in Rockton the year before. A girl called Colleen was the driver of one of the zebra-striped pick-up trucks that patrolled the grounds, making sure the wild animals and the human animals driving through in their cars didn't get in contact. Colleen was an attractive girl, a couple of years older than Matt. She had jet black hair, which she wore pulled back severely from her forehead in a pony tail. She had dark, dancing eyes and a wide, glittering smile. Matt was embarrassed to look at her because she returned his look so intently. He looked at the ground, afraid to betray his feelings, fearing rejection and even humiliation because she was older and wouldn't be interested in a kid.

But she was. Matt was wide across the shoulders, had a twenty-eight-inch waist and slim hips. He was tall, with sandy, curly hair and eyes the colour of a summer sky. She had to fight the urge to reach out and lift his chin, kiss his small, pouty lips and ask him to unburden himself of the troubling thoughts she could see always lurking behind his pale, sad eyes.

Colleen was nineteen. She had completed the first year of journalism at the University of Western Ontario. It was her second summer driving the bus. She had been hired by the Kitchener-Waterloo *Gleaner* as a summer intern, but when they told her she'd be working in the "women's" section of the paper, she turned the job down and went back to driving the bus. She added journalism experience to her resumé by reporting for a local weekly. When it became apparent that Matt was never going to make a move, she asked him if he wanted to go to the drive-in with her. Stunned at the invitation, he mumbled that not only didn't he own a car, he didn't even have a driver's licence. Colleen laughed, and he thought she was laughing at him, but she told him she knew he didn't have a car, and that she would borrow her mother's car.

Matt felt a little foolish going into the drive-in with a girl behind the wheel, and he slumped down in the passenger seat. By the second feature, Colleen had persuaded him to clamber into the back seat with her. He had never necked with a girl that old before—a woman, really—and he was nervous and tentative and clumsy, and when Colleen stuck her tongue in his mouth, his eyes went wide. When she put her tongue in his ear, his eyes closed, and he felt weak. After that, they went to the drive-in every Saturday night for the rest of the summer, and Matt became more confident in the back seat. It got so they started out in the back seat, broke for hotdogs and popcorn at the intermission, and watched the second feature in snatches.

"What are going to do if you don't go back to school?" Colleen asked Matt one drizzly day in the Safari lunchroom.

He shrugged. "I haven't thought about it."

"At least you can live at home."

"Mmm."

"You can't just hang around. If you're not going to go to school, then you have to get into something you can build on, work your way up. I like you, you know that, and if we're going to keep seeing each other, you're going to have to get into something that has a future."

There was a flicker of fear in his eyes and his voice broke a little as he said, "Like—what?"

"I don't know—those poems you wrote me are good. Your spelling's a little rough, but that's just practice. I think you could be a good writer."

Matt shrugged.

"Why don't you write a story, and I'll get Mr. Crosby at the *Chronicle* to run it."

"Mr. Crosby won't want stuff from a kid. It's a real paper, you know?"

"What difference does it make? If you can write, you can write."

"But I don't know how to—"

"What?"

"Write stuff an older person would be interested in."

"You're not stupid, and I'll help you. Don't worry about Mr. Crosby. If I ask him to put the story in, he will do."

"One story, what good will that do?"

"You do one, then you do another and another. That's how it works. That's how everything works, Matt."

They wrote the story together, but Colleen insisted that Matt do all the interviewing, take all the notes. The story was about one of the big male lions, who had cut his foot badly on a beer bottle some idiot had thrown against a rock from a car, and how the keepers had to tranquillize the lion and how the vet stitched up the cut and gave the lion an injection of antibiotic. Colleen showed Matt how to use the paper's camera she carried with her everywhere, because on a weekly, you had to take the pictures as well as write the stories. The *Chronicle* ran the feature on the front page, turning inside to a whole page of pictures of the incident.

Mr. Crosby paid Matt thirty-five dollars. His career had begun. He worked for three years for the *Chronicle*, continuing to live at home, where he didn't have to pay for food or rent. At twenty, he was accepted as a mature student in the journalism program at Conestoga College in Kitchener. The following summer, he was hired as a summer student at the K-W *Gleaner*, the same paper Colleen had refused to work for because they wanted to put her in the women's section. Matt was such a good reporter, the managing editor told him not to bother going back to complete the two-year course at Conestoga. At the age of twenty, he was on the staff of one of the finest provincial dailies in the country. When Colleen returned to Western after the Lion Safari summer, she and Matt exchanged passionate letters, and he went to see her a couple of times and stayed with her in her residence room, where he had to remain hidden for the weekend. They made love for the first time, and Matt thought life was beautiful.

Toward Christmas, the tone in Colleen's letters changed. The final one began "My Dearest Matt," and his first love, that had been "for all eternity," came to an abrupt and bitter end.

CHAPTER NINE

"I don't think our problem is that serious, Martyn," Norton Fielding said. They were lunching in the dining room of the Royal Canadian Military Institute, of which Fielding, a former army officer, was a member. Fielding had obtained his engineering degree at the Royal Military College in Kingston and subsequently served his requisite stint in the forces. He enjoyed the discipline and order and the moral strictures of military life, but had found it gave him little scope for chemical engineering, particularly since, in typical military fashion, they had trained him as a commando, providing him little opportunity to apply his engineering knowledge. His service had, however, provided entrée to the Canadian Forces establishment, which had proved eminently profitable and afforded him the base from which he built a business provisioning various countries' military forces with the lethal products of his patented plastics process. Since leaving the regular army, he remained a member of the militia, and now held the rank of colonel.

"So, you don't think it's serious?" Waterman said, munching on a piece of radicchio.

"I don't think we have a problem we can't solve."

Waterman raised one eyebrow.

"I think we should go public."

"What?"

"We hire the best PR man we can find, and we come out of the closet as Dennis's team."

"We don't want to go public. Once the journalistic dogs are unleashed, we'll have to contend with an entire pack of them, not merely one lone sniffing beagle. Some of us could go to prison, Norton. You do realize that?"

"We have the weapon of denial."

"This is a very nice salad."

CHAPTER TEN

Diane Porter sat at her desk in Homicide, studying court documents relating to the first case in which she was lead investigator. It hadn't been much of a murder. A taxi driver had smashed his wife over the head with a large jar of Strub's dill pickles in a drunken argument over the invitation list to their thirtieth wedding anniversary. She had wanted to invite her cousin Buster, with whom (she had once foolishly told her husband) she had had her first "petting" experience—at the age of fourteen. When the first uniformed officers arrived at the scene, responding to the cab driver's 911 call, the man had been sitting at the kitchen table, drinking beer and eating pickles. His wife had been lying on her back, her head in a pool of blood and pickle juice, her right eye agape, a big shard of glass protruding from her left eye.

"What else could I do?" the cab driver had said.

Not much of a case, but Porter wanted to make sure everything was perfect. She had rewritten her report three times and resisted the temptation to ask Stark to check it. She had to pick up her new suit from Holt's, the most expensive piece of clothing she'd ever bought. It cost her more than her wedding dress. That had been a real waste of money. The marriage lasted seven months. She hoped Howard liked the suit. Howard had said that her taupe suit looked baggy on her. Why she worried about her partner's opinion, she didn't know. Howard Case dressed like a colour-blind lumberjack.

Ted Henry came and stood beside Porter's desk. Porter was so intent on her notes that she didn't notice Henry. Finally, Henry said, "What the hell are you doing?"

"I didn't see you there, sarge. I'm going over my report on the Friesen murder."

"Looks more like a goddamned novel."

"I wanted to cover all the bases. I want them to throw this bastard in the slammer and toss away the key. That sonofabitch beat his wife regularly. These reports go back for years. Of course, she would never co-operate with the investigators. Said she fell, or bumped her head on the fridge door. Jesus, here's one where she said she broke her rib by tripping over the cat and falling on the coffee table. Poor bloody stupid woman. So, I want to nail this creep."

"Wow," Henry chuckled.

"Wow what?" Porter looked up.

"Nothing. It's just the first time I've heard you sound like a cop. That's great. Say, listen, we're having a barbecue tomorrow, and I'd like you to come over. Bring whatsisname with you if you want."

"Howard."

CHAPTER ELEVEN

Matt Mackey was on disability leave from the Toronto *Gazette*. To Mackey, the word leave was absurd. It suggested he would eventually return to work. He had said they should call it disability deathwatch. The cancer had progressed too far. Despite the urging of his oncologist, Mackey's research had shown that treatment was a waste of time. It might delay the inevitable, but would mean constant nausea and headaches and exhaustion.

He chose to dull the pain with Scotch and sublimate it with work. He wrote from early morning to late at night, stopping to nap only when the booze knocked him out. Then, when he awoke, he would medicate himself with a pot of strong coffee and half a dozen cigarettes, sitting at his computer. And then back on the Scotch.

The book was essentially finished. He had already done two rewrites and was adding a couple of final chapters. He knew what symptoms would suggest he had entered the final stages. Even then, he would still have several weeks to put everything in order and get the book to the publisher, who had promised to bring it out immediately, whenever it was submitted.

The cover was done, everything was in readiness. The publisher, Magnus Talia, of Newcastle Press, knew nothing of the contents, except that it would blow the Canadian Values Party out of the water. The publisher trusted Mackey implicitly. He had delivered the promised goods in two previous books, and over the years, Mackey had established himself as a pre-eminent muckraking journalist. Not the best writer in the barn, he was a dogged digger with reliable contacts in the highest and lowest places. Among the many plaudits he had garnered were two National Newspaper Awards and a Special Recognition Award from the American Press Institute.

Mackey was seated at his computer, pausing to sip his Scotch, wincing at the pain that wracked his body. He had a Shirley Horn CD cranked up loud. She was singing *Old Country*. He didn't hear the footsteps behind him.

The hand that clasped on his forehead startled him, but he thought he recognized its cold fleshiness as the touch of Gail Corby, the sixtyish receptionist at the paper who had a key to his place and frequently came around to check on him. It was like her to put a comforting hand on his brow.

He opened his mouth to speak, and it stayed open as a long ice pick was driven through his neck below the line of his skull and upward into his brain.

The killer ripped all the cables from the back of Mackey's computer, dumped all the discs from their plastic holder into a large, black cloth bag, and then methodically opened every drawer in the apartment, removed every piece of paper on which notes were written, and put them in the black bag and a matching one. The intruder picked up the computer and left with it and the two black bags, retracing the route taken in entering the building, using the fire-escape stairs, and eventually emerging on the underground garage level.

Norton Fielding arrived on the platform of the Union subway station at precisely the same time every day. As a reserve officer, he spent most weekends and four weeks a year in service. It informed his life. As he did every weekday, he checked his watch at the exact moment that his foot touched the yellow strip that ran along the edge of the station platform. His arrival was timed to be just ahead of the flood of passengers from two GO commuter trains, one from the east, one from the west. He was positioned at the spot where one of the subway car doors would be when the train stopped. The purpose of the exercise was to give him the best chance to get a seat for the trip to his office at Yonge and Eglinton. He looked to his left and into the tunnel at the opposite end of the platform. He could see the headlight of the approaching train. There was a high-pitched shout:

"Grab that child, look out."

The woman beside Fielding was pushed hard by a shoulder. She tumbled into the person beside her, who shoved back defensively. In a chain reaction, others in the crowd were jostled and stumbled and had their feet stepped on. People shouted and cursed.

Suddenly, Fielding was hurtling off the platform and into the track well. The train, pushing a column of air in front of it, whooshed into the station, speeding toward the spot where Fielding lay. The driver hit the brake. The train squealed to a stop twenty feet ahead of Fielding, who had managed to raise himself to a sitting position. He stared at the driver, who was slumped forward, shaking his head.

CHAPTER TWELVE

"Who found him?" Diane Porter asked a uniformed officer.

"Gail Corby. She doesn't live here. The woman in the next apartment is looking after her. She's badly shaken up."

"Who is she? His girlfriend?"

"She looks more like a mother. She's the receptionist at the *Gazette*, where the victim was a big-time reporter. He wrote that racism bullshit about the force a couple of years back, when Hawkins shot that jungle bunny."

Porter glared at the officer. "What's your name?"

"Bertings, sarge."

"Bertings, don't ever use language like that in my presence again, or I'll report you."

"Sorry, sarge. I didn't mean anything. My girlfriend's from Trinidad. It's just that—"

"Never mind." Porter shook her head. "What time was the body found?"

"This morning, at 7:30. She was on her way to work, the Corby woman. She stopped in to check on him. She has a key to the apartment."

"But she's not his girlfriend?"

"No, he was on disability leave. She said he was sick, and she drops by every couple of days to make sure he's all right."

"Anything stolen?"

"The computer. It looks like the wires were just ripped out, and there's a plastic box on the floor there you use to keep discs. It's empty. All the drawers were open. But his wallet's on the desk, full of credit cards and money. He's got a really expensive little stereo set. Just as easy to carry as the computer. I don't think it was a break-and-enter, sarge."

It felt good to be called sarge. As a detective, Porter had a rank equivalent to a uniformed sergeant, a position she never thought she'd reach. She owed it to Harry Stark. The coroner was on his haunches, studying the body draped on the desk.

The coroner, an older man Porter recognized, whose name she thought was Jenkins, looked up.

"How long has he been dead?" she asked.

"At least twelve hours."

"Cause of death?"

"I can't say that here, for god's sake."

"Rough guess?"

"Rough guess is something long and pointed, like an ice pick."

"Ice pick? That's a hitman's weapon."

The coroner shrugged. "Or an amateur's. You know how many people have been killed with ice picks?"

"No."

"Get yourself a cantaloupe. Take a sharp knife and try to drive it in. And then get an ice pick and do the same thing. You'll find the ice pick penetrates much easier and deeper. You're an amateur killer, you don't want to cut somebody, and have him get up and belt you one. It was shoved into the back of his neck and up into his brain."

"That sounds pretty professional."

"The autopsy will be more conclusive. Anyway, these days, with TV shows and movies about mafia killers—they're like visual textbooks, so who knows, but I guess I have to admit it was probably somebody who knew what he—or she—was doing." The coroner struggled to stand, wincing at the pain from an arthritic knee. "Finding out whether it was the mob or his grandmother, my friend, is your part of the process."

Two other homicide detectives arrived. Porter's stomach sank. They had many years of seniority on her, and they were men, and even though she had been given the call, she immediately resigned herself to the idea that they were going to take charge. Instead, they asked her politely to bring them up to speed, and then asked whether *she* wanted *them* to interview the Corby woman. Porter had to stop herself from grinning. She told them that might be a good idea, and added, rather boldly, that they should take it easy on the woman, since she was badly shaken up. They smiled and nodded. When they turned to leave, Porter couldn't suppress an expression of satisfaction. She turned to one of the Identification Unit officers, and asked in a voice that was so bolstered with confidence it sounded just a little demanding. "You finding anything?"

"Like what?" The officer shrugged, and tilted his head to one side. "We haven't found a weapon. There are no cigarette butts to test for DNA. There's only one glass with booze in it. There's no indication the body was moved. The place was taken apart by somebody looking for something. There are no footprints. Entry? No idea."

"What do you mean, no idea?"

"Just what I said. There are two ways you can get in here. Through the door, or through the sliding door from the balcony. Now, it's a nice mild night, so I could imagine somebody leaving the balcony door open and just the screen closed, and that might have made sense as the place of entry if we were on the ground floor, but we're on the seventeenth floor of a twenty-floor building. I think that rules out the balcony, wouldn't you say? Now, what about the front door? It's a dead-bolt, Abloy lock, and it was locked when the woman who found the body arrived. At least, that's what she told the officer. So, either she's lying, or whoever did this had a key."

"Couldn't it have been picked?"

"You can't pick those locks."

"So, wait a minute, you're saying whoever did this locked the door after him when he left? Or she left?"

"I'm not saying anything, sarge. All I do is tell you what's here."

CHAPTER THIRTEEN

Apart from a few bruises, Fielding had been uninjured in the fall. The doctors at St. Michael's credited his fitness with saving him from serious damage. The police were satisfied that the event was a freak accident, the result of an unexplained panic in the dense crowd. Fielding assisted them with his explanation that he always stood rather foolishly close to the edge of the platform and that he simply must have lost his balance. The police said he was very lucky that he fell before the train had proceeded far into the station, giving the driver time to stop. He sheepishly promised to heed their admonition that in future he refrain from standing so close.

Two days after his tumble on to the tracks, Fielding demanded a meeting of The Compact.

"The day before yesterday, the morning after our adversary was fortuitously dispatched... I can't believe this," Fielding said to Waterman. "You are unbelievable." He paused and he and Waterman exchanged glares. Finally, he continued. "As I was saying, the morning after that, I was pushed on to the subway tracks in front of an approaching train." As he spoke, seated at one end of the table, he continued to stare, unblinking, at Waterman, who returned the gaze from the chairman's end, without flinching.

Ross Stephens, the real-estate magnate, said to Waterman, "All right, let's cool this. This is crazy. Anyway, two things: one, Martyn, I think you *might* owe us an explanation. Norton, if you're accusing Martyn of some sort of involvement in Mackey's death and your accident, as you appear to be doing, you're way off base. In the first place, I understood the police said your fall *was* an accident. You're displaying a good deal of paranoia about this. Martyn, can you help us out here?"

Waterman held up his hands. "How?"

Brian Ball, the sporting-goods mogul and former MP, put in, "Martyn, the last time we met, you said something had to be done about this book. You and Norton clashed over the matter. I'm sure this is a bizarre coincidence, but, can you shed any light on it?"

"I can't. There isn't an explanation to give." He didn't look at Fielding. "I'm afraid Norton is displaying symptoms of a persecution complex."

"Crap," Fielding snapped. "I said the last time that you wouldn't put it into words; you wanted somebody else to suggest it."

Lee Braddock raised a hand. "Norton, you've got to admit, you're behaving the same way now you did at the last meeting," Braddock said. "With all due respect, you're being irrational. No one, least of all Martyn, suggested anything violent. Norton, don't you see, it's all very foolish and counterproductive. I think we should count ourselves lucky—in a sad way—that we no longer have to be concerned about Mackey. Now, do we have any other business, because—"

Fielding stood up, noisily pushing his chair away from the table. "I should have known you'd close ranks. I'm resigning. I want nothing more to do with any of you."

"Norton, please," Braddock said. "You're an important part of the organization. I suggest you take a few days to calm down. After that, we'll put this acrimony behind us and get on with the campaign. What do you say?"

Fielding strode to the door, then turned to face them. "Don't worry. Saying anything to the police would be pointless. And doubtless, Waterman *would* sue me—and I have no doubt he would win, since none of you would testify on my behalf. Well, my advice to all of you, which I know you'll ignore, is to disband. You're in league with the devil."

CHAPTER FOURTEEN

"Hold on to your pants, I'm coming." Stark's door buzzer was braying for the third time. Before Stark got the door fully open, Diane Porter burst into the apartment, nearly knocking Stark over.

"Good morning, nice to see you, too. What's going on?" Stark asked.

"That bastard."

"Oh right. I wouldn't dare disagree. Jeez, you might kill me. What's eating you?"

"Peters."

Stark gave a knowing nod. "What's the holy-roller up to now? You've got to hand in your pencil stub before you get a new pencil?"

"Two days I'm on this case, and he takes me off it. Two days."

"I get the time element. What case?"

"Matt Mackey, that reporter. You got any coffee?"

"Yeah, there's a pot. My cup's on the sink."

Porter got a mug from the tree on the kitchen counter. She poured one for herself and went to pour one for Stark in a massive green-and-yellow cup, the size of a soup bowl, but hesitated. "My god, Stark, this thing is filthy. Don't you ever wash it?"

"Just pour. You're pissed off at Peters. Don't take it out on me. Who else have you offended this morning? I bet you used your siren coming here."

"Sorry." She poured the coffee and handed Stark his cup. "You know, I was just getting into the thing, my first, you know, real case, and he takes me off it. But that's not the worst part. Guess who he puts on it instead?"

"Surprise me."

"Bernie Bryden and John Hardy."

"Laurel and Hardy? Jesus. That's like filing it as inactive."

"And it's a big case."

"You know I don't read the papers, Diane. But—as it happens—Bert read the whole thing to me. The dead guy was a big star at the *Gazette*, and he was off writing a book or something. Somebody shivved him in the head? I don't know. Sounds like a hit."

"He was writing a book, in a computer. They took the computer."

"There's a market for stolen computers."

"No-no, listen. The killer ransacked the place, but left the guy's wallet and expensive watch. And they took all the computer discs. So, what do you expect to find in a place where somebody is writing a book?"

"I don't know, Diane, what?"

"No, tell me."

Stark sighed. "Notes, tapes, pictures?"

"Exactly." Porter nodded slowly. "Exactly. Notes. Well I searched the place about as thoroughly as the bad guy did, and, man, he took the place apart. Well, there wasn't a scrap of paper anywhere, no tapes, nothing. Somebody wanted to make sure that whatever Mackey was writing didn't see the light of day."

"What was he writing?"

"I went to the *Gazette,* but nobody knew. The only one who does know, apparently, is his editor, but she was on vacation. She's back today, and I was going to go back there, but then Peters gave me the chop. He put me on another case on which Jimmy Maitland and what's-his-name, Paul Rexton, are leads. A Scarborough drive-by. I'm supposed to be on my way to re-interview some Tamils at a doughnut shop on Kennedy Road."

"Did you tell Beavis and Butthead about the editor?"

"Yeah, but listen. A couple of years back, Mackey wrote a bunch of articles on systemic racism in the department. Bryden and Hardy are about as interested in finding his killer as I am in—" Porter held her hands up.

"So, what are you going to do, Diane? These things happen. Now, I was on a case early on—"

"Wait till I finish."

Stark groaned.

"Here it is: I want you to take over the case."

"Me?"

"I'm serious, if you think you're well enough—"

"There's nothing wrong with me."

"Well?"

"They won't let me go back yet." Stark took a sip of his coffee, and automatically patted his shirt pocket, shaking his head at the remembrance that he no longer smoked.

"Peters is a twerp, but he's not a my-country-right-or-wrong kind of guy. Being popular with the troops is not one of Peters's motivators. In fact, at the risk of insulting you, Diane, it's possible he thought you weren't experienced enough to handle the case. Peters doesn't know from a hole in the ground who's good or bad in the squad. Chances are, he just asked for two experienced officers who were free, and their names were given to him. Did you talk to Ted about it?"

"Henry's in Tuscany."

"Tuscany? He doesn't even like Italians. What's he doing in Tuscany?"

"His wife wanted to go."

"Well, in any case, I'm not going to be able to help you. You must know that, Diane."

"Stark, you can't come back to work until you get the medico's stamp of approval, but that's not what I had in mind."

Stark shook his head. "What then?"

"I want you to take the case privately. What else have you got to do, except hang around Boyd's all day?"

"Privately." Stark chuckled. "Like a gumshoe, a peeper? Where's my retainer? And I don't own a fedora and a trenchcoat. And I don't have a gat."

"A what?"

"A gat, a cannon, a gun. You kids, honestly."

"You've been doing some PI work on the side."

"What big mouth told you that? No, don't bother. I know. But that was a favour for that guy at the CD distributor."

"The one who gives you free CDs?"

"It's not a bribe or anything."

"Never mind. I'm serious, Stark. Why not take the case? You know what questions to ask. You're good."

"I'm the best, Diane. Don't you forget it."

"So, will you do it?"

"It's—not—"

"Why not? I can get you whatever you need from inside. You wouldn't be doing anything illegal. Strictly a private citizen concerned to see justice done."

"Who the hell are you confusing me with?"

"Come on."

Stark sighed. He went to the window and watched a kid go by on a skateboard on tree-lined Monarch Park.

He lived on the second floor of his house. It was divided into three apartments. The main floor was rented to a black jazz drummer and his Mohawk wife. The basement was rented to a retired postal clerk.

Finally, he turned, shrugged and nodded. "Be a diversion, I guess. Might even show these turkeys I'm fit for duty, right?"

"Right."

"No, you weren't, but okay. Wait till I get a notebook."

CHAPTER FIFTEEN

Martyn Waterman was already in his Islington Avenue love nest when Mary-Margaret let herself in with her key.

The instant she shut the door, Waterman shouted at her.

"What the hell were you doing in my apartment?"

She looked at the key in her hand and back at Waterman. "What are you talking about?"

"Not here, for christ's sake. I'm talking about my condo."

"Oh, a couple of nights ago. How did you know?"

"You left your drinks glasses on the bar. You always were a slob, Mary-Margaret."

"I'll just say goodbye then."

"Don't come on with the offended act. You were in there with that drummer twit, weren't you? Or some other low-life you picked up in a bar?"

"I am going to leave."

"Never mind. I apologize. But you have no right to use my apartment for your illicit trysting."

"Can I use this place, instead?"

"Why did you do it? You've never done that before."

"This is ridiculous. You had somebody killed, and you're worried about a shot-spot on your bed?"

"You *didn't* use my bed?"

"Keep your shorts on. We used that nice rug in front of the fireplace. But never mind. What about Mackey?"

"I had absolutely nothing to do with it."

"Right."

"Mary-Margaret, look hard into my eyes. I had nothing to do with Mackey's death."

She studied his face and was struck by his earnestness. She could see fear in his eyes. "Then who?"

"I'm baffled. You know about Fielding?"

"What about him?"

"The morning after Mackey was killed, somebody shoved him in front of a subway train."

"Oh my god."

"He wasn't hurt. The train stopped in time, but he thinks I had Mackey killed and had him pushed to shut him up. I had nothing to do with either thing. Nothing."

"Do you think it might have been—a coincidence?"

"Don't be ridiculous. It had to be somebody else on The Compact."

"God."

"Ball can be volatile, and Stephens is quiet and even-handed, but he's been ruthless in the past. But none of them—" His voice trailed off.

"It's not our problem, and we don't have that *big* problem any more, so that's a good thing."

Waterman sighed. "I hope."

"You told me that no one knows what's in the book, right?"

"Yes."

"Well, then, there's no problem—is there?"

"I'm in the dark about things. I have to rely on my contacts in the police department to keep me informed."

"About what?"

"The killer removed Mackey's computer and discs and notes; whoever did it had in mind to eliminate any reference to—well, if it was somebody on The Compact... In any event, *if* everything has been destroyed, there is no problem. On the other hand—" He held his breath and then let it out. "If the person kept the material, we could be faced with very serious difficulty."

"What can we do?"

"Nothing. We have to wait. If anything is going to come of it, I expect the person will approach me in the near future. I suspect it can be solved with a liberal application of money."

"Blackmail."

They said nothing for a time, and then Mary-Margaret spoke. "Well, if nothing can be done, there's no use fretting, as my mother used to say. We're here. Do you want to do it?"

"We may as well, I guess."

CHAPTER SIXTEEN

Amanda Dworkin was the assistant managing editor at the *Gazette* who had handled Matt Mackey for the five years before he went on disability. She had continued to be the liaison between the paper and Mackey, as well as with Newcastle Press, with whom she had negotiated to run excerpts of what Mackey had promised would be a blockbuster. She had been frustrated in her attempts at getting the journalist to provide her with a first draft of his book, so that she could at least see what she'd be dealing with, work out what parts to run and how to trim and shape them to newspaper size. She'd also wanted to see how much lawyering would be involved and be able to give her bosses and the promotion department a realistic publication date. And co-ordination would be required with the book publisher, Magnus Talia. But, despite fervent appeals, Mackey had remained adamant that not a whisper of the book's contents would pass his lips until he was ready.

Dworkin was devastated on her return from vacation to hear about Mackey's murder. The news knocked the wind out of her. She felt no grief: she had never liked Mackey, resenting that his clout at the newspaper meant she had no real control over him. He had been self-assigning and set his own agenda, leaving messages on Dworkin's voice-mail announcing days off or even vacations the day before he took them. She had complained to her superiors several times about his arrogance and unreliability, but Mackey had been untouchable.

He produced infrequently, but what he did turn out led to criminal convictions, unseated high-ranking public officials and politicians, and, more important, won awards and sold newspapers. In fact, some bean-counter in the promotion department had once worked out that Mackey was worth ten times more to the newspaper than they paid him. What really disturbed Dworkin about Mackey's death was the knowledge that no matter what she said to her bosses, they would blame her for not having been able to cajole from him a single paragraph of his book, not even a hint of its contents. They wouldn't even be able to put a team of investigative reporters on the job to see whether they could weave the threads together to produce a single story on the subject.

Dworkin called Talia. He had told her half a dozen times before, that he, too, knew nothing of the book's contents, that he had no outline; that all he knew was that it involved a highly placed politician; and he certainly had no reason to keep it from her now.

Dworkin then called a contact in the public-affairs department of the police. That woman reported back to her an hour later about the computer's having been stolen, which Dworkin already knew from the news story.

"What about notes, tape recordings?"

"Nothing."

Stark decided he wouldn't be breaking any rules by presenting himself as a police detective rather than a private investigator. In fact, since he wasn't licensed as a private detective, if he had claimed to be one, he would have been guilty of misrepresentation. He had not, after all, he reasoned, been suspended from duty. He still had his badge, although his weapon was at headquarters. He wasn't displeased by that, since he had always hated the thing, especially since on the one occasion he had fired it on duty, a child had been accidentally killed.

At first Dworkin viewed his arrival with the automatic suspicion that everyone at the *Gazette* had for cops, but she quickly realized that he might be her only hope of getting Mackey's manuscript or notes if there were any somewhere.

"It's a terrible thing." Dworkin was sitting at her desk in a glass-walled cubbyhole of an office overlooking the parking lot and the Gardiner Expressway. She had a cadaverous face; sunken cheeks; bulging eyes; thin lips; short, ragged hair. Stark couldn't pin down her age. It could have been anything from thirty-three to forty-three.

"Sorry?" Stark said.

"Matt's death. It's awful."

"Oh, yes, terrible thing. I suppose he had made a lot of enemies over the years, with his exposés and that sort of thing?"

Dworkin nodded. "That's for sure. Listen—do you have any idea whether there might be—"

"Did he get many threats?"

"I don't—think so. I don't recall anything recently. He—had cancer. I suppose you know that. Not many people at the paper knew. He had just a few months left. I was wondering—"

"He was writing a book. Do you know what the book was about?"

"No. That's what I was—"

"I would have thought, with his connection with the paper…"

"We were going to run excerpts." Dworkin sighed. "But he wouldn't tell anyone what the book was about."

"Then, how would you know it was worth excerpting?"

"He was so good that when he said it was going to knock your socks off, it would. We trusted him. I begged him to tell me. He'd never been so close-mouthed before. You didn't find any notes, by any chance?"

"I can't tell you that."

"You did find notes, but you can't tell me you did?"

Stark chuckled. "Wordplay won't do you any good. Even if we found written material, you wouldn't get your hands on it."

"Why?"

"Because *if* we *had* found something, or if we *have* found something, it would be evidence."

Dworkin sighed. "So, you're useless to me."

"Depends on what you have in mind, I suppose," Stark said without humour.

Dworkin gave him a vicious sneer. "I'm very busy."

"Where was Mackey's desk?"

"He didn't have one. He shared an office with Martha Magliore."

Stark grinned and nodded.

"Martha's taken you to task, has she?"

"You could say that."

"She's the best city columnist this town has ever seen. Neither fear nor favour with anyone. Anyway, Mackey had a phone that sat on top of a filing cabinet, where he kept—whatever. He used a laptop, and he mostly worked at home, or in some bar. If he was doing anything in here, he borrowed an empty desk. There's nothing of his in Martha's office, because when he went on sick leave, we had his filing cabinet trucked to his apartment. If there was anything of his here, I'd have it. And you wouldn't get it."

"Bad attitude."

Dworkin shrugged.

Stark sighed. "I don't care what you think of cops, but if you want me to find Mackey's killer, I need some small measure of co-operation. I'd like you to put together a list for me of Mackey's enemies, people he's written about who might bear enough of a grudge against him to kill him. Mostly, though, I'm talking about people who are still out there, people Mackey exposed but didn't quite nail, people he might still be going after. Off the top of my head, I can come up with the mayor as fitting that category. Mackey linked him with that golf club racket, but the mud didn't stick. Maybe Mackey had more on him, or on somebody else in that sort of situation."

"Christ, you're not asking for much."

"Well—"

"I'll put the librarian on it. We'll put together a list."

"Thanks. Look, was he working on any other things beside the book?"

"Not that I know of."

"All right, here's my card. Call me on my cellphone number. And here—" He wrote on the card. "Here's my home number. Call me on either. Don't call the office. I'm rarely there. All right? Say, is Martha in?"

"I saw her earlier. Mackey just kept his files in there. I bet they didn't say two words to each other. She won't be any help."

"That's okay. I sort of know her."

"Her office is in the southwest corner, at the other side of the newsroom."

"Thanks."

Stark strode across the carpeted newsroom, past row after row of reporters and editors staring at computer screens, talking on phones, chatting with their neighbours. They looked young, dressed in casual clothes, some in jeans. He remembered the first time he was in a newspaper office, when he was a kid, in the old *Globe and Mail* building on King Street: the noise, the rattle of typewriters and teletype machines, the horseshoe-shaped desk with the copyeditors bent over sheets of copy paper, wielding pencils. Nearly all of the reporters and editors were men. It was almost the reverse at the *Gazette*. And all the men in the old *Globe* were in dress pants and shirts and ties, and the air was blue with smoke from cigarettes, cigars and pipes. Practically everyone was smoking, and in his recollection, they all seemed to be shouting. Perhaps to be heard over the machines.

Martha Magliore was shouting when Stark reached the outside of her office:

"No, you Nazi jerk, don't yell at me. Go ahead, sue me. I'd love to get you into court, you revolting pig—Yeah, yeah. I'm too busy dealing with humans to waste my time listening to an animal squeal. Goodbye, Adolf." She slammed the phone down. "Jesus," she said with a wheeze.

Stark stepped into the doorway. Magliore looked up. It took her a second to realize who it was, and when she did she let out a scream that turned heads all over the newsroom floor.

"Stark-e-e-e-e-e-y, Jesus, look what the cat dragged in. Starky. How long has it been? *Five* years. Oh my god, it's great to see you. Come in, come in... Wow. Sit down. No wait, let me hug you first." She stood on tiptoes to embrace Stark's upper arms. Her short hair, voice, movements, face and even her dress—jeans and a plaid shirt—suggested masculinity, but the fullness of her lips and something in her eyes gave another message. She had a superb body, if a tiny bit thick at the waist, and her clothes were always a size too small. "Jeez, Stark, it's good to see you. What are doing here, slumming?"

"How are you, Martha?"

"Me, I'm great, I'm cool, yeah. You? Oh jeez, I remember now, you got shot or something?"

"Yeah."

"So how are you doing? I'm sorry, I meant so many times to come and see you. I just—well, I didn't know whether—you know? Anyway, this is great. So, how is it—your—wound, whatever it is. What did happen?"

"It's a long story. Anyway, I'm in perfect shape now, not a problem."

"So—you didn't come to see *me?*"

"Well, sort of. It's about Matt Mackey."

"Poor bugger, eh? It's sure as hell got me locking my door. The world is full of bad people, Stark."

"If it weren't, I wouldn't have a job."

She chuckled. "You always were a cynical bastard."

"Yeah."

Magliore gave him a slightly wistful look and looked at her watch. "Say, let's get out of here. Let's go have a drink."

Stark looked at his watch. "A little early, isn't it?"

"As long as the bars are open, it's not too early. Come on."

Stark drove. She directed him to a mom-and-pop burger joint on Queen West, where it was apparent by the welcome they gave her that she was a regular. She and Stark took a table at the back of the narrow restaurant, and she ordered two beers.

"No, I don't want a beer, thanks. I'll have a soda water."

"Starky turning down a beer? Listen, I'm buying. What, is it because you're on duty, or something?"

Stark nodded.

"Okay." Magliore shrugged. "Never used to stop you. You've changed. I've been looking at you. There's something—what is it?"

"You'd have to tell me."

She held her hands up in front of her, at chest height, as if she were trying to gauge the size of something. "You're mellower," she said. "That's it. The hard edge is gone. Look at you smiling. The old Stark would have snarled if I'd suggested he was mellow. So? Are you on drugs, or Prozac? Is it the—wound?"

"I do take some medication," Stark said. "Maybe, it's just because I'm a little older. Anyway, I wanted to know about Mackey."

"What about him? Somebody must have told you..."

"Told me what? Some woman called Amanda Dworkin told me that—"

"That piece of work. She wouldn't know—What did she tell you, exactly?"

"Just that you and Mackey shared an office."

"Oh. That's all she said?"

"Yeah. She said he really just used a filing cabinet and a phone."

"That's right. He was never there. He worked from home. And then he got sick, poor bastard."

"He was a pretty good-looking guy. Was he straight?"

"Yes, he was."

"Mmm, well?—"

"Ah nice. Thank you. That's more like the old Stark. Do you think I screw everything that crosses my path?"

"Martha, don't be offended. You like to play with boys. I like to play with girls. So if that doesn't make me a—a what? There's no word for it in reference to men."

"Exactly."

"Never mind. Suck up your indignation and tell me. Did you ever have a thing with him?"

"Why do you want to know?"

"It was just a preamble to the next question, which was: how well did you know him. That sounds like the same question, but it's not meant to be."

"What did Dworkin tell you? No one in the office had any idea, least of all her."

"Knew what?"

Magliore shook her head and sighed. "We had a thing. It was more than just a one-nighter. We were never an item, or anything. But we were friends. It hit me hard when I heard about his death. But I have my reputation to think of Stark."

"Of course."

"No, I don't mean that. I mean my reputation as a tough broad. Anyway, we kept it quiet. We saw each other, you know, in that way. Jeez, you wouldn't call it romantic. All right, call it sexual. We got together maybe once or twice a month. He was very good at it, and he had a brain, which—sometimes makes it better. It ended a few months ago, indirectly because of his illness: he went a little, more than a little, depressed with it—and resentful."

"All right, that, you know, doesn't concern me. He was writing a book—"

"Yeah. It was about—"

"Christ, you know what it was about?"

"Eh? Sure. Why?" She looked puzzled.

"Because no one else does."

"He did tell me not to tell anyone. He knew there was no danger of that, because I wanted to keep our thing secret."

"So, what was it about?"

"I don't know much, but it was about something that happened a long time ago, something messy he was involved in, along with some people who are bigshots now."

"Where did this take place?"

"I'm not sure, but I got the impression it couldn't have been here. It was when he was, like a teenager. He didn't grow up here."

"Where was he from?"

"Jeez, I don't know, Stark. I'm sorry. We never talked about it."

"Would it be on his employment records, do you think?"

She shrugged. "I doubt it. That's not a question they ask. Anyway, he only worked two places. Here and the Kitchener-Waterloo *Gleaner.*"

"What's that, a paper?"

"Yeah. He worked there for ten years before he came to the *Gazette.* They might be able to help you."

"He didn't say anything more about the subject of the book, or who was in it?"

"No, he mentioned it once or twice when we were both drunk. The poor bastard was dying from cancer. He had a right to get drunk. He said something like the book would go off like an explosion in the halls of power. Anyway, I didn't ask. I'm only interested in what I'm writing about. I never want to hear other writers prattle on about their brilliant efforts. Most of the time, it's bullshit. And if it's not bullshit, then I get jealous."

"He didn't leave anything at your place, by any chance?"

"We never went to my place."

Stark chuckled. "Why not?"

"His place is a lot closer to work."

"Okay, but he never gave you anything or dropped anything off at your place—or at the office—for safekeeping? Any written material, or discs, anything like that?"

"We weren't that involved. It was just a quick nooner sort of thing. 'Do you ever talk to your husband after sex?' 'If there's a phone handy.' Not quite. We did talk. He was interesting, once you got past the ego. That was a bit of a defence mechanism. Some people are like that." She gave a twisted grin.

"I guess I'm going to Mennonite country, have some food that schmecks. Well, thanks, Martha. You've been very helpful."

"As usual." She leered at him.

"Yeah, right. Well, I'd better go."

"What's your hurry? I haven't seen you in a dog's age. My place is just around the corner. Remember?"

"How could I forget those wonderful nights of throwing ashtrays and bottles at each other?"

"That only happened once."

"Because we passed out the other times."

"We had some good times."

"Another time, Martha. Another time. I'll be in touch."
"You lying bastard."

CHAPTER SEVENTEEN

Bernie MacIsaac was more than just Dennis Yates's fixer. He was Yates's brains, Yates's creator. Without Bernie, Dennis Yates would have been a used-car salesman or an insurance agent.

In highschool, Bernie had played the drums in Dennis's garage band. They called him Bernie the Basher. He made up for his lack of rhythm and musicality by playing louder, which the guitar pluckers compensated for by cranking up their amplifiers until even the soundproofing Dennis's father had jury-rigged in the garage couldn't contain the noise, and the neighbours complained to Dennis's father, who shouted back at them over the din of Bernie's drums: the complainants were just jealous of his son's musical ability.

Bernie wasn't stupid: he was never going to succeed as a drummer. One of his talents was in recognizing potential, and Dennis had great potential. He possessed a distinctive voice, and he could carry a tune. Dennis's voice had a husky quality, mature for his age. There was something special about Dennis, because when Dennis sang ballads (what they called slow songs), girls would get teary-eyed and stare at Dennis wistfully.

One day, Bernie went into Hamilton to a hair stylist and paid sixteen dollars for a cut that would make him look "business-like, professional, really sharp." He bought a blue suit with a faint grey stripe at Eaton's, a shirt, tie, executive-length socks, and black dress ankle boots. He went to a printers on Locke Street and had business cards printed that read Bernard MacIsaac, Talent Agent. He bought a vinyl attaché case to complete the package, and the following day, he set out on the Grey Coach bus for Toronto, where he visited record companies, one after another. The band had already had professional publicity photos taken, which Dennis's father had paid for. Bernie had bought a rock background record, one that you could sing over. He had spent two days taping Dennis singing the lyrics until they were just right.

At the first couple of record companies, Bernie couldn't get past the receptionists, who would ask him whether he had an appointment. When he said he didn't, they told him he could leave the demo tape and his card and the pictures. He knew instinctively that there was little chance anyone would even listen to the tape.

He decided on a different approach. He phoned the next company on the list, lowered his voice and said that he had some material that "one of your people is expecting. But—I'm sorry—we've lost his name. I know he's your key talent person—yeah, that's it, Mr. Bertings. What's his first name?—Lance, Lance Bertings. Thanks."

Ten minutes later, Bernie called back, changing his voice, and said he was in town from New York for a few hours, and he was making time to see "Lance." "Does he know me? Of course. We met at a cocktail party last year."

"Just a minute please," the receptionist said, and put the phone on hold. She clicked another button and said, "Mr. Bertings. There's some kid on the phone pretending to be—something, I don't what. He didn't get around to that. He says he met you at a cocktail party a year ago. I thought you might want a laugh—"

Bertings decided he would have a laugh, took the phone call, and fifteen minutes later, a nervous Bernie MacIsaac was sitting opposite him in Bertings's Danish modern office—its walls hung with gold records and performers' autographed pictures—crossing and uncrossing his new-suited legs. Bertings was impressed with the kid's chutzpah and especially impressed with Dennis's husky, melodic voice. He played one piece on the tape over and over. Within a week, Yates came in for an audition, and a week after that, he was signed to a contract.

CHAPTER EIGHTEEN

The Kitchener *Gleaner* is housed in a fortress-like building. It has long had a reputation as, pound-for-pound, one of the best newspapers in the country. It has been the training ground for many of the superstars of journalism. Its staff is split between eager youngsters on their way up and oldtimers who have chosen to remain in a town big enough to have its own symphony orchestra and philharmonic choir, and enough meaty news subjects to satisfy many journalistic appetites, while small enough that you can be anywhere within the city limits in fifteen minutes.

Don McCardle, the managing editor, was one of those who had stayed. When Stark had spoken to him to make an appointment, he had been struck with McCardle's erudition and articulateness, and his sense of humour.

"Of course I remember Mackey," McCardle said to Stark in McCardle's small, simply furnished office. The newsroom was a fraction the size of the *Gazette's*, but it looked much the same, the same array of computer terminals and reporters writing their stories and talking on phones. But it seemed brighter and more relaxed. People seemed to be enjoying themselves.

"No one who ever met Matt could forget him. We were reporters together. He was here for—what? Ten years, I guess. I never thought he'd leave. I've never met a guy with so many women on the string. He'd go out with three different ones on a weekend. He was amazing. We used to drink together after work. That is, I'd have a beer, and go home. Mackey would have three beers in the same time that I had one and then carry on for the whole night, end up in some floozy's bed and still be in for work on time the next day, looking as fresh as a cool breeze. He was quite a guy. I was really disturbed when I heard about his murder. Terrible thing. Do you have any idea who did it?"

"I can't tell you that, I'm afraid."

"No, of course not."

"You said you didn't think Mackey would ever leave here?"

"He drank an awful lot, like someone trying to kill some bad memory. But he started here so young, you'd wonder what he'd have to forget. Anyway, eventually I got the idea that he drank because he was afraid to test himself. I know he was self-conscious about not having a university degree. He used to call people with degrees 'trained journalists' or 'professional journalists.' He called himself an amateur. It was when he was in his cups, of course, being sarcastic, but the fact that he'd mention it suggested it bothered him. Matt was making a career out of avoiding work, doing as little as possible. I know he changed when he got to Toronto. The *Gazette* made such a big deal out of him, he was finally convinced that he could cut the mustard. To us normal people, he was infuriating. He'd do one story when we did three, but his one story would sing. To be accurate, he was a great journalistic writer, but not a great writer. His stories lacked colour, and I don't think he knew any words longer than two syllables. But he could get people to say things, he could draw these amazing quotes out of them, and he had so many contacts, he could make two phone calls and produce a twenty-inch story in half an hour, start to finish. Finish was the operative word. He did everything in a hurry. He used to cover breaking news, fires, murders, anything like that, because he could do a wham-bam-thank-you-ma'am job and be in the pub with two beers down him before the first edition had hit the street. And he still managed to win three Western Ontario Newspaper Awards, and got an honourable mention in the NNAs—National Newspaper Awards. The funny thing is, I know he became just the opposite of this when he went to the *Gazette*.

There, he took months to do one story, and then it would be a lollapalooza. And there, of course, he did win a couple of NNAs."

"So why did he go to the *Gazette?* Did they make him an offer?"

"Are you kidding? They made him five offers. He turned them down. He didn't want to go. I really think that despite the fact that they came after him, he was afraid he'd be out of his depth in the big city. No, it was his sex life that finally ran him out of town."

"Oh yeah?"

"He was having it off with a cop's wife, and the cop caught them at it. Matt could handle himself with his fists, and he floored the cop with one punch. A week later, he was walking home, and somebody took a shot at him. Matt left town the next morning."

Stark chuckled. "Damned cops, eh?"

"Wasn't quite so funny. The cop eventually shot his wife to death and blew his brains out."

Stark sighed.

"I don't know whether this is helping you. I'm running off at the mouth here, and I'm not sure what exactly you want to know, or if there's anything useful I can give you."

"Did Mackey ever write about politics?"

"I'm sure he did the odd political story. It's a small staff, and if somebody's on holiday, you pitch in, but politics wasn't his bag. Too much of a continuing subject. Matt was strictly a quick-hit man."

"Okay, look. I'm going to have to tell you this—it's confidential, so—"

"Wait. I can't guarantee that if you tell me something newsworthy I'm not going to—"

"It's nothing specific. It's just that we believe something that happened in his youth—probably before he got here—that might have had some connection with his death."

"In his youth?"

Stark shrugged. "That's all I know. And that it might have involved somebody who's in politics now."

"Sounds like a good story."

"Please. There's not enough there—"

"Don't worry. You're right."

"And the theory might be way off base. You didn't grow up with him?"

"I didn't know him till he came here. I was here a couple of years before he arrived. I'm not even sure where he was from. For some reason, I think it was somewhere down by Hamilton. I should be able to find out, though."

McCardle dialled a number on the telephone. "Hi, it's Don McCardle, Gloria. Oh fine, thanks. You? Good. Listen, could you check the records for me on Matt Mackey...Yeah, he was a reporter here for about ten years, and he left here about ten years ago... Okay, thanks."

While they waited, McCardle and Stark talked about Kitchener-Waterloo. Stark said he didn't know the twin cities at all, that he had only driven through on his way to the Shakespearean Festival at Stratford.

"It's a busy little burg," McCardle said. "Nothing like Toronto, of course, but—"

The phone rang. "Oh, great, thanks. Yeah I've got it. Thank you. He was from Grandfield," McCardle told Stark.

"Where the heck is that?"

"I'll show you on the map."

Before he left, Stark asked McCardle whether there was anyone else on the staff who might have hung around with Mackey.

After thinking for a time, McCardle said, "He didn't run with the staff much. I mean the lifers are all sort of square like me, with families. I guess he drank with the odd young one, but they've all moved on, anybody who would have known him. Mostly, he was a loner as far as the people at the paper were concerned. The one guy he did share a lot of bottles with drank himself to death. Sad story. Matt pretty well stuck to seedy bars and seedy people. I think he had more than one social disease in his time. Nobody here today would be able to help you."

CHAPTER NINETEEN

Grandfield, population 1,100, sits at the confluence of Grandfield Creek and Waymere Creek, which combination runs for a short distance as Grandfield Creek, feeding Fairchild Creek, which empties eventually into the Grand River, which enters Lake Erie at Port Maitland. Grandfield exists because the merged creeks, much too small for any sort of navigation, provided ample water power to run a grist mill.

It's a pretty town with most of the houses now owned by young professional families that make their living in the nearby city of Hamilton. There's a day-care centre and talk that somebody might be converting the old Baptist church into a Montessori school. There's an auto-repair garage that specializes in small, foreign cars. There's a small restaurant that used to be called Bert's Grill, but is now the Café Olé. The farmers these days have their apple pie and coffee at the restaurant attached to the Petro-Canada station down the highway.

Fern Berntwhistle saw the tide changing, took a course in Cambridge, and opened a pet-grooming studio in her basement. Grace Paynter's bakery sells out of bread and peach pie by nine-thirty every Saturday morning. George Yu and his family bought the convenience store and expanded it to sell groceries and fresh vegetables, locally grown in season. There's a weekly newspaper, the *Chronicle;* a unisex hairdresser that few of the newcomers patronize; a feedstore; an appliance store, which in recent years has added a sizeable stock of woodstoves; and a pharmacy.

Stark figured the best place to ask about the Mackeys would be the pharmacy. It was a high-ceilinged, brightly lit place that smelled of hairspray and soap. The front portion of the store was given over to gifts and greeting cards; another substantial section was devoted to glass cases filled with cosmetics and watches and jewellery. Stark missed the drugstores of his youth, which smelled of medications and mildew, like the one he rode a delivery bike for, on the corner of Sammon and Donlands, R.E. Young's Drugs, where Robert Young, a tall man with a Clark Gable moustache, mashed pills in a mortar and pestle, always with a Buckingham cigarette stuck in his mouth, a long ash dangling dangerously over the mortar.

The Grandfield pharmacy was staffed with young girls in pink-flowered smocks. Stark approached one of them, a tall, thin girl who kept her mouth nearly closed when she spoke, in a futile effort to conceal the glittering scaffold that was intended to close the gap between her front teeth. He addressed the girl: Carly, according to the nametag she wore, a tag that offered customers her help.

"Excuse me, can you tell me where the Mackeys live, please?"

"The Mackeys? I don't know," she said vacuously. "Just a minute. I'll ask Mrs. Bingham." The girl walked to the back of the store where the dispensary occupied a small corner. Stark followed. "Mrs. Bingham, do you know where the Mackeys live?"

"The Mackeys?" said Mrs. Bingham, a little woman with red-tinted, tightly curled hair.

The pharamacist, a grey-haired man with shaky hands, gave the answer. "Elm Street. Just a minute." He pressed some keys on the computer terminal. "Number thirty-two. Thirty-two Elm Street. Why do you want to know?"

"There's a man..." The girl turned, and for the first time realized that Stark had followed her. "... sorry. This man wants to know."

The pharmacist lowered his head to look at Stark over his glasses. "You're asking about the Mackeys?"

"That's right."

"There aren't any Mackeys. There's *a* Mackey. Cora Mackey, the wife, she died a few years back. Peter Mackey, the husband, he's still there. Is it something to do with Matt, the boy? That was a terrible thing, or do you know about it?"

Stark nodded. "Yes, I do."

"Terrible thing, tragic. Now he's all alone, poor Peter Mackey. They only had the one child. She couldn't have any more. Yeah, he'll be there, I imagine. He's been retired for years. Used to run the feedstore."

"Thank you. Where do I find Elm Street?"

The druggist smiled in anticipation of his joke. "Same place it's always been." He chuckled, and Stark responded in kind politely. "Sorry. It's just down Main Street, that way, north, one block. It runs west. You can't miss it."

Stark nodded. "Thanks again."

Main Street, Elm Street. The millers and farmers and merchants who founded towns like Grandfield in the nineteenth century were busy, practical men with little time to waste on thinking up fancy street names. There were no elms on Elm Street, not that Stark would have known an elm if one had fallen on him. There *had* been many elms, but they had all succumbed to the Dutch disease and were cut down and uprooted. There were still plenty of trees: oaks and maples, some beech.

Thirty-two Elm Street was a large brick house with a wide porch. It was surrounded by tall trees that must have kept it completely shaded throughout the summer. The leaves that would have created the shade, the leaves that had fallen in October, had formed a sodden mat over the front yard. The trim on the house was in need of paint. The eavestroughs sagged in places, and the roof was roughly patched in a couple of spots.

Peter Mackey took a long time to get to the door. Stark rang the bell twice. The second time, the old man shouted that he was coming, that Stark should hold his horses. Stark thought about the expression, one of those that people say all their lives without thinking about its meaning. He thought about people saying, "Home, James, and don't spare the horses," and his uncle who thought he was witty modernizing it as, "Home, James, and don't spare the horsepower." When Mackey finally opened the door, Stark was hit with a wave of alcohol fumes. He blinked involuntarily.

"Yeah?" the man said, glaring suspiciously.

Stark showed him his identification.

"Another cop." Mackey sighed. "You here about Matthew, are you?" He brightened slightly at a possibility that struck him. "They find who did it?"

Stark shook his head.

"No, I didn't think so. They'll never find him. Some paid killer, some wop from Montreal. You'll never find the bastard. So, what do you want? You'd better come in, I guess."

The old man was short. His legs were bowed, his shoulders had a slight stoop, and he shuffled. The house smelled of booze and dampness and cheap cigars, old couches and rugs and dusty drapes and cat pee. Three cats suddenly appeared. A big grey one hissed at Stark, the other two rubbed against his legs till one flopped over on its side and pawed at his foot. A plant was drooped over dead in a Chinese pot in the hallway. It had been like that for years: there was a thick layer of hardened dust on it.

The elder Mackey led Stark into the kitchen, at the back of the house. It was a big room, high ceilinged, lined with glass-fronted cupboards, everything in olive green. It was lit by a single, grimy, white globe that hung from the centre of the ceiling and sunlight filtering through two tall, grimy windows.

"Sit down," Mackey growled, and Stark took a chair at the formica-topped table, with a wide, grooved, chrome strip along its edges, the chairs matching. It reminded Stark of the cheap, serviceable furniture that had been in use in his parents' house when he was a boy, the kind of stuff poor people used to be able to pick up for a few bucks at a used furniture store, but which now commanded extortionate prices as "retro" pieces in stores along Queen Street West. "You want a drink?"

"No thanks."

"I think I'll have a waker-upper. You want a Coke or something? I don't know whether I've got any."

"That's all right. Nothing for me, thanks."

Mackey poured himself a half a tumbler of Wiser's Special Blend. "So, what do you want? The provincials were here after he died, eh. They asked a bunch of questions. I told them everything I knew, which was nuthin'. How the hell would I know anything about Matthew. I haven't seen him in months. He comes about twice a year, at Christmas and sometimes a couple of times in the summer. He used to come more—not much more—when Cora was alive, my wife. She died seven years ago. Cancer." He shook his head.

"Mr. Mackey, I was hoping you might be able to tell me something about Matt's life as a teenager."

"What the hell do you want to know that for? What's that got to do with somebody killin' him now, for god's sake?"

"I'm not sure it has anything at all to do with it, but he was writing a book at the time he was killed that dealt with his adolescence, and I'm the sort of investigator who likes to tie up all the loose ends, you understand? I want to see whether there might be any connection between the book and his death."

"What's it say in the book?"

"I'm afraid I can't tell you."

"Why the hell not? I'm his god-damned father. You can't tell me what my own son wrote in a book?"

"I'd like to, Mr. Mackey, but I'm afraid it's part of the investigation, and I know you wouldn't tell anybody, but something might slip out, and you wouldn't want it to be used by some sharp defence lawyer to get the accused off, would you?" Stark realized he was talking to the old man as if the fellow were a child. He was at once embarrassed for both of them, but forgave himself on the recognition that it was also the way one speaks to a drunk.

"Shit, you're talkin' as if you was actually goin' to arrest somebody. You're not goin' to catch him." Mackey downed the whisky and poured himself another ample measure. He gave Stark a defiant look, which could have been in response to his anticipation of Stark's disapproval of his drinking habits, or to underline his contention that his son's killer would never be found.

Stark gave him an indulgent smile. "Well, Mr. Mackey, I hope that you might be able to give me some information that will help make your prediction not come true."

"About when he was a kid?" Mackey sneered.

"Yes."

"Christ." The old man shook his head.

"Mr. Mackey, listen, just for a minute. Tell me this: can you recall anything that happened to Matt as a youth that stands out as—well let's call it a major event."

"He got a grand-slam to win the township baseball championship," the old man said snidely.

"That's not what I—"

"Well, Christ. I don't know, do I?" Mackey sighed, ran his hands over his face, turned and looked hard at Stark. He got an expression that suggested he was going to ask a question, opened his mouth slightly, and then shut it and the expression changed as if a light had gone on in the catacombs of his mind. He nodded slowly, deliberately, coming to a decision, and then he spoke: "Yeah, there was something. There was something." He nodded faster. "I don't know what good this'll do ya."

Stark smiled. "Tell me what you're thinking about?"

Mackey stared straight ahead, and then leaned back in his chair and looked at the ceiling for a time before he started to speak. "When he was about fifteen or sixteen, he—well, something happened." Mackey lowered his gaze to stare at Stark. "We never found out what. He went to stay at his cousin's in Stoney Creek one weekend, and when he came back, everything was different."

"How so?"

"I dunno. He just—he was always a good boy, you know, a good boy. Worked hard at school, played sports. He always talked a lot to his mother and me—especially his mother. I mean, kids are like that aren't they? They talk more to their mothers, eh. Well, anyway, he clammed up. Right then, right after that weekend. I don't know what happened. We couldn't pry it out of him. He just shut up like he was dumb. I mean, couldn't speak kind of dumb. He spent all his time in his room, wouldn't eat his meals. His schoolwork went all to pot. Somethin' happened that weekend, somethin' changed him, and he was never the same. He started gettin' into trouble, I mean with the police, like. He was arrested. He stole a car, they let him off, but then he beat some kid up, and then he stole from his mother. Anyway, they sent him to one of them training schools, eh. And after that, he pretty much straightened out. They must have done him some good, or something, because he was good again. He went to school and everything, Conestoga, up in Kitchener, and well, you know, he did all right."

"But he never told you about that weekend, about what happened?"

"Nope. Never. To be honest with you, we never asked him afterwards. I guess we didn't want to know." The old man paused. He was looking into space across the reaches of time. He spoke quietly. "Tell you the truth, I say he straightened out, but he never was the same as before, you know. Didn't talk much, hardly spoke. Said please and thank you, all right, but you couldn't get more than a flick of a smile out of him."

"Did the police, back then, ever question him about anything that happened that weekend?"

Mackey shook his head. "Not that I know of."

"So, who was this cousin? What was his name?"

Mackey didn't answer. He was lost in thought.

"Mr. Mackey?"

"Mmm?"

"His name? What was the cousin's name?"

"His name? Marty. It was Marty. Marty Waterman. But he doesn't live there any more, if you're thinkin' about talkin' to him. No-no. He went into television. His old man owned a TV station in Buffalo, eh, and the kid took it over when he died, well before he died really. He's got some big job in TV now. I don't know what it is. I was never interested in that shit."

"Where is he now? Buffalo?"

"Naw, I think they sold that station. I think he's in Toronto. I'm not really sure."

"I'll look into that. Now, is there anything else you can think of that happened to Matthew that was, in the same way, a serious event?"

Mackey shook his head slowly. "No, that's the only thing, the only thing." He looked at Stark. "Like I say, he was a good kid, a real good kid before that, eh."

Stark left the old man sitting in the kitchen with his whisky. The cats ambushed Stark in the hallway again, and repeated their leg-rubbing pursuit till he got to the door. He bent down to stroke them, and the nasty cat suddenly appeared, hissing, its back arched and tail swishing. Stark hissed back at it, and it ran off. Stark smiled.

He heard a sound from the kitchen. The old man was crying.

When Stark got back to his car, an attractive, middle-aged woman in jeans and bulky pink roll-neck sweater swung her slender figure out of an ancient Ford Tempo parked behind the slightly battered black police Chev that Porter had organized for Stark.

"Excuse me," the woman said, smiling brightly. "Are you the detective from Toronto?"

Stark nodded. "Guilty," he said, and smiled.

"You're looking into Matt Mackey's killing?"

"I'm sorry, your name is?"

"Colleen McLean."

"And, Ms. McLean, were you a friend of Matt Mackey's?"

"I was, yes."

"I see. Do you want to go have a coffee somewhere?"

"Why don't we go to my office. It'll be more private. It's on Main Street, the *Chronicle*."

At the newspaper office, the woman unlocked the door and held it open for Stark. It was a tiny, one-room affair, the walls hung with framed posters attesting to membership in various organizations, among them the Better Business Bureau, the Canadian Community Newspaper Association and the Grandfield Chamber of Commerce. There were several front pages from bygone days. Stark looked closely at one that seemed to be the most ancient. Its banner read, *Grandfield Herald*. The date on the folio was September 12, 1888.

McLean said: "The *Herald* was the first paper. Beside it there is the first page of the first edition of the *Chronicle*, 1893. There were two papers here for seven years, and then Horace Bildworth, the *Chronicle* owner, bought out the widow of Milton Grandfield. The Grandfields were the original settlers. There was a Major William Grandfield, who was a militia commander in the War of 1812. He was given land here in gratitude for his service to king and country. Let's see, it would have been one-hundred-and-fifty-six years later that I started working for this paper, my first newspaper job. It was 1968, and I was eighteen. I went on from there to an illustrious career at the London *Free Press*. When Sun Media acquired it, I quit, and bought the *Chronicle*."

"Big staff you have here," Stark said, smiling.

"Yeah, I'm it. Publisher, editor, reporter, ad salesperson."

"Salesman, you mean."

"Oh, you're one of *those*."

"It just came out. Boorish. I'm sorry."

"That's okay. I know where you're coming from. I've had lots of old-fart editors in my time."

"Thanks."

"I'm pulling your leg. Let me get you that coffee. I live in the back here and upstairs."

"No, don't worry about it. I gave up smoking, and coffee always makes me want to have a cigarette. So, you knew Matt Mackey?"

"Oh yes. In fact he was a summer love of mine. He was a couple of years younger. I was a cradle snatcher, a worldly woman of nineteen. We both had summer jobs at the African Lion Safari. He was seventeen. I started him in his career. His first article appeared in the *Chronicle*. And then he got a job as the paper's reporter and editor. Joe Crosby, the owner at the time, also owned the appliance store, so he had people putting the paper out for him. Matt worked here for three years and then he went to Conestoga College and got a job at the K-W *Gleaner*. And the rest, as they say, is history. I'm afraid I threw Matt over when I got back to university and got caught up in the social whirl. I saw him a few times years later, nothing romantic. By that time, I was married to a lawyer. We're divorced. That's where I got the money to buy this place. But that's all the money. If the bastard weren't a lawyer, and a hell of a lot smarter one than mine was, I wouldn't have to freelance to make ends meet. Okay, so back to Matt and his horrible murder. He was a favourite son here, so we're interested in anything that's happening with the case. I've run a couple of stories, but I can't get anything much out of the Toronto police, but now you're here." She took out a notepad. "So, please, what can you tell me? Any developments? Any suspects? How is the case developing, anything you can tell me."

Stark chuckled. "I think we're at cross purposes."

"Oh?"

"You see, I was hoping to interview you about Matt. *You* want to interview me."

"Of course. I *am* a reporter."

"I'm afraid there's nothing I can tell you. You can't use my name. It's—well, I don't want my name used, Okay? In fact, I don't really want you to run a story at all."

"Oh, I'm going to run a story."

"Okay, but I'd appreciate it if you wouldn't make reference to the fact that I was here in town. It could compromise my investigation."

McLean sighed. "Here's the deal. You give me something I can write, and I won't mention that you were here."

Stark sighed. "All right. How's this? Our inquiries have eliminated a number of possibilities and we are narrowing the investigation to certain specific areas. We are developing several promising leads, and we hope to have a resolution to the case in the near future."

"Gobbledygook."

"Well, I can't be more precise. I'm sorry. That's all I'm going to give you. Now, I must be going."

"Okay, wait. Was it a professional killing?"

"I can't tell you that. For one thing, we don't know."

"So, I'm going to say you haven't eliminated the possibility that it might have been a professional killing."

Stark shook his head. "Look, I really have to go."

"Could the killer have been somebody he knew?"

"I'm not telling you any more."

"All right, so what were you going to ask me?"

"I had nothing in mind. You approached me, and I thought you might have something to offer."

"I told you, I haven't seen Matt in years. I wouldn't know anything."

"No, well, then I'll—" He turned to go, stopped and turned to face her again. "Wait a second. You say you knew him when he was a teenager."

"Right."

Stark looked at her. He knew that in order to ask his question, he was going to give her information that she would put in the article she was going to write. But then, it *was* the Grandfield *Chronicle,* hardly common reading matter for anyone on the force.

"Matt's father said that when Matt was about fifteen something happened to him that produced a big change in his behaviour, that he ended up in trouble with the police, in fact. Do you remember anything about that?"

"Why would you want to know that?"

"Do you have to answer every question with a question?"

"I'm a reporter, for god's sake."

"Just tell me whether you recall Matt behaving oddly about that time."

"I didn't know him at that time."

"Fine, then we have nothing further to discuss. I'll say goodbye again." Stark turned toward the door once more.

"Wait a second," McLean said. "There is something I might be able to help with."

"Oh, yes?"

"Mmm. But look, quid pro quo."

Stark sighed. "Ms. McLean, I told you, I can't give you anything. Besides, if you're going to answer a question in return for information, then I wouldn't be able to trust your answer, would I?"

"All right... From the time I met Matt, I knew there was something bothering him. He'd get morose, moody, distant. One time, he came to work looking like a wreck. You could see he'd slept in the clothes he was wearing, and he stank of booze and vomit. I made him go home. If the boss had seen him, he'd have been fired. I covered for him, I said he'd come in, but had the stomach flu, and was bringing up, and I told him to go home. That got me into shit, but it worked. Eventually, I got Matt to open up a bit, a lot in fact. He would never give me the details, but apparently when he was younger, he had been involved in some sort of incident in Toronto. It was something about a girl, some girl that he and his cousin and another guy had picked up. Something happened to the girl. He wouldn't say what, he wouldn't be specific, but—I think the girl died. Maybe a drug overdose or something. Anyway, apparently, they left the girl, didn't take her to the hospital, or get any kind of medical attention for her. He was ridden with guilt. We talked about it a lot, and I think I managed to ease his pain. I convinced him that the past was past, that he was too young to be responsible, to get on with his life—that sort of thing. It seemed to work. I was really pleased with myself. In fact, I actually thought about switching to psychology after that, but I didn't. Okay, so that's it, that's what I know and all I know. But what does that have to do with Matt's murder? Or does it?"

"What about the cousin? Did you know the cousin, Marty somebody other other?"

"You knew about this?"

Stark shook his head. "Not as much as you've told me, no. Do you know anything about the cousin?"

"No. I didn't even know his name."

"What about this other guy?"

"The other one who was with them? No idea. Why don't you ask Mr. Mackey."

"He and Matt didn't get along too well?"

"Matt cut himself off, you know. But I think they've been closer since Matt's mother died. I've seen Matt in town."

"I thought you said you hadn't seen him?"

"I haven't spoken to him. I've seen him driving by. He was here a couple of weeks ago."

"A couple of weeks ago? Are you sure?"

"Yep. I saw Matt and Mr. Mackey together. Why, didn't Mr. Mackey remember?"

Stark rarely told one source of information what another had told him. He kept to his rule by answering with a twist of the lips and tilt of the head.

"Mr. Mackey drinks quite a bit these days, and he's getting older. He probably is confused about the time."

"Okay. Well thanks. If you think of anything else, give me a call." He took out a business card and wrote his home number on it. "Call me at this number, not at the office. I'm never there." He smiled.

"Okay. But why did you want to know about Matt's past problem? Now come on."

"Thank you, Ms McLean. Thank you very much."

The woman watched Stark's car drive out of sight. She picked up the phone and dialled a number at the Hamilton *Spectator*.

"Newsroom, Highsmith," a voice answered.

"Christopher, I have a story for you. It's Colleen McLean."

CHAPTER TWENTY

"Do you believe him?" Bernie MacIsaac asked Dennis Yates.

"Martyn?" Yates shrugged. "He swears he didn't. But Christ, he wouldn't do it himself."

MacIsaac shook his head. "Don't put it past him, Dennis."

"It's too physical."

"Don't forget Mackey was dying, and he must have been on a cocktail of drugs, and on top of all that, he was a drunk."

"How do you know?"

"I checked. You know Bernie. If he needs to know, he finds out. So, what's happening with the fly in the ointment?"

"What fly?"

"Fielding."

"He quit the group."

Norton Fielding sat in front of the computer in his Avenue Road condominium penthouse. His trousers and underpants were around his ankles. On the screen was a video it had taken much trouble to obtain. Fielding was masturbating.

CHAPTER TWENTY-ONE

Inspector Wallace Peters, head of the Homicide Unit, looked solemn. A lay preacher in a fundamentalist church, Peters saw life—and especially the pleasures that make it bearable—through dark glasses. At the moment, he was peering over the top of those glasses at one of his errant sheep.

"I find it most regrettable to have to take to task an experienced officer, and especially one who is recovering from wounds sustained in the line of duty. What could you be thinking?"

"What is it I'm supposed to have done?" Stark asked.

"There's nothing *supposed* about it. You're working as a private investigator."

"I'm not."

"You deny it?"

"I do deny it—*sir*. Who's my client?"

"Tell *me* that."

"I don't have one."

"Don't add prevarication to your—"

"Transgressions?"

"Stark, this attitude of yours is unacceptable at the best of times. This is a very serious matter." Peters picked up a copy of the *Gazette* and tossed it across the desk to Stark. "It's in the paper. You claimed to be working on the Mackey murder. You've been questioning people. This is not your case; you're not even on duty. You weren't acting as a police officer. For a police officer to take money to conduct an investigation is an infraction of the Police Act."

"Inspector, no one is paying me."

"You're doing this as a hobby?"

Stark gave a dry chuckle. "I'm telling you—*sir*—I'm not employed by anyone except the Toronto Police Service."

"You're on sick leave."

"But I'm not on suspension."

"This borders on insubordination, Stark. What are you trying to pull here? Why are you doing this, then? Did you know this Mackey person? I wouldn't be surprised. Another in your long list of undesirable acquaintances."

"He was a journalist."

"He was a muckraker who wrote scurrilous, destructive articles about the service."

"Is that why you assigned Beavis and Butthead to the case?"

"Who?"

"Bernie Bryden and John Hardy."

"How did you know that?" Peters snapped.

"I'm still a part of this unit, sir."

"Who told you they were on the case?"

"I can't remember."

"Stark, you are not on the case. And that's an order. And what's this—" Peters picked up the paper, and read: "'The detective was conducting interviews in Grandfield because police suspect Mackey's murder is linked to an incident that occurred in the victim's youth. Stark declined to comment, but did not deny that that was the purpose of his visit to Grandfield.'"

At least, Stark thought, she hadn't included anything about the thing in Toronto.

"An incident in his youth?" Peters said, throwing the paper back on the desk. "I want a full report from you, every detail."

Stark shrugged.

"Stark, I'm warning you. Now, I'm hereby issuing a direct order, and I'm going to put it writing, and you will sign it: you are not to carry on any further inquiries concerning the murder of Matthew Mackey." He picked up the phone and dialled a number. "Marilyn, come in here, and bring your pad." Peters pointed a finger at Stark. "Before you sign this order, you will go to your desk and complete a full report."

After Stark had left the office in an exaggerated hang-dog shuffle, with Peters fuming and contemplating throwing a paperweight at Stark, and after Marilyn, the department secretary, had come in and then gone back out to type up Peters' order to Stark, Peters' phone rang.

"Martyn. How are you?—Sunday? Yes, we'd love to. Wonderful.—Yes, I am sorry.—Stark was definitely not assigned to the case.—In Grandfield? No, I have no idea what he was doing there. The man was shot in the head. Perhaps you remember? In any event, he was working as a private investigator.—Private.—I don't know who's paying him. What he doesn't know is he's not coming back to work. I'm going to see to that. But that's not your concern.—I agree with you entirely. It's a matter of deploying our scarce resources where they are most needed.—Yes, this man Mackey was no friend of the service.—Oh yes, the church is most grateful for the donation.—Of course.—No—no, I won't forget. The chief is delighted with the idea of the helicopter. It's a perfect compromise.—No, Stark's not going to have anything more to do with the case.—We have to investigate fully every killing whether we like the victim or not, but—Yes, we'll see you on Sunday. Thank you, Martyn."

While Peters was having his telephone conversation, Stark quickly found Detective Bernie Bryden's brief report on the Mackey investigation in Bryden's desk. The report began intelligently enough, then deteriorated into nonsense, telling Stark that the first part had been copied by Bryden from Diane Porter's report, and that the latter part had been added by Bryden.

Stark photocopied the report, along with some pages from one of Bryden's reports on another case, and stapled them together. It wasn't the first time he'd pulled this stunt with Peters, and he was confident that the man wouldn't read this "report" any more than he'd read similar productions in the past. Marilyn, plump and forty-something, came and handed Stark a sheet of paper on which she had typed Peters's order that Stark was barred from the investigation into Matthew Mackey's killing.

"The old fart says you have to sign this, Stark," Marilyn said, rubbing Stark's shoulder. "How's the head?" She pulled his head back against her ample bosom.

"The head's fine, Marilyn, and so am I, seeing your gorgeous frame once more. You've brightened my day." He signed the order and handed Marilyn the photocopies of Bryden's report. "Give this to Peters, will you? It's my report."

Marilyn took the signed order and the stapled sheets to Peters. He looked at Stark's signature and then glanced at the report, seeing the name *Mackey* in several places. He nodded and put both documents in a desk drawer, smiling with satisfaction.

"Is that booze, Harry?"

"No, Roger. Not yet, but soon."

"What have you been doing with yourself?" Roger Sammon said from his usual perch at the end of the bar in Beulah's.

"This and that, here and there—Jesus Christ." Stark clutched at his left eye; it felt as if a needle had been shoved through it at an angle and up into his brain. He doubled up over the bar.

"Harry? My god." Roger jumped down from the stool and held Stark's upper arm. "Boris," Roger called out to the bar owner, who was flirting with a waitress. Boris saw what was happening and went to help. Roger was behind Stark, his arm around the detective's shoulders. By the time Boris got there, Stark was sitting up straight again, shaking his head.

He gave an embarrassed chuckle.

"I'm okay. Thanks, guys. Sorry. It's just a pain I get. Rarely. The sawbones said it would go away. Soon. Yeah, jeez. Hey, back to your post, Boris. Thanks, but really. It's nothing."

"Stark, are you sure," Boris said. "There's a big chair in my office that tilts down flat. Why don't you go in there and lie down for a few minutes?"

"It goes as quickly as it comes. It's just this quick sharp pain, and then it's over. Reclining chair that lies flat? What's that for, Boris?"

"Eh? Oh, sometimes for a little rest. I work long hours, you know, Stark?"

"It's just for you then, is it, the chair?"

"Of course it's just for me. Stark, Stark. You're very naughty."

"Does you wife know about it?"

"His wife bought it for him," Roger said snidely. "I think she was hoping he'd use it and not bother her."

Boris scowled at Roger and went back to the bar.

"Asshole," Roger said.

"Roger, you know you love him."

"Like I love the bubonic plague. Oh, look, here's that nice young colleague of yours."

Stark and Diane had arranged to meet at the bar. Porter took a stool beside Stark's, and put a hand on his shoulder affectionately.

"How are you? I heard about the Peters thing."

"Right."

"And I read about the thing in Grandfield, wherever the hell that is. Why did you speak—"

Stark silenced Porter with a raised hand. "It was an honest mistake. I don't make many, but I made one there."

"Why would you talk to a reporter?"

"She wasn't a reporter."

"Oh. *She* wasn't a reporter."

"The woman owns the local weekly paper. I needed information from her, and I traded very little information to get it. I thought she was just going to run a piece in her paper. Nobody in the real world would have read it. But I was stupid. I didn't think about it until Peters showed me the article in the *Gazette*. She gave me the clue, and I missed it. She said she freelanced to make ends meet. She must have sold the story to the *Gazette*."

"No it said 'CP' on the story, Canadian Press. And it had Hamilton as a dateline."

"Placeline," Stark corrected her pedantically. "Datelines appeared in papers in bygone days, because it might take days, or even weeks, to transmit the report from where the incident happened."

Porter sighed. "Whatever. She strung you a line. So, why were you there? The article said Mackey was born and raised in Grandfield. Where is it, anyway?"

"Between Hamilton and Cambridge."

"That doesn't help."

"Diane, there's more to the world than Bloor and Yonge."

"I think you'll find I've seen a hell of a lot more of the world than you have. That's not booze in there, is it?"

"That's what I asked him," Roger put in.

Stark glared at the piano player. "Do you mind not eavesdropping on police business."

Roger nodded. "He didn't take his medication." He stood and lifted his cigarette pack from the piano top. "I'm going for a smoke." He grimaced at Stark.

After Roger had walked away, Porter put a hand on Stark's arm. "All right, Stark. Grandfield?"

Stark told Porter what he had learned about the book and Matt Mackey's youthful difficulties.

"You think the cousin might be involved?"

"Well, it's all based on the premise that somebody killed Mackey and took his computer to prevent the publication of the book he was writing. But suppose it wasn't the book the killer wanted to suppress? Suppose it was some other story Mackey was working on. That would be in the computer, too. Although Mackey's editor told me he wasn't doing anything except the book. So, I *think* we're on the right track."

"Who is this cousin?"

"I've got it written down." Stark took out his notebook. "He's in television, the old man said. Although, that could mean the guy owns a stereo store. Here it is, 'Marty Waterman.'"

"Marty Waterman." Porter said. "It couldn't be Martyn Waterman. I guess there's more than one."

"Wait a second, Martyn Waterman, the TV network guy?"

"That's what I mean. It couldn't be."

"Do you know where he grew up?"

"No idea."

"Well, put somebody on it."

Porter took out her cellphone and punched in a number. "Who's this? Okay, Jones. This is Detective Diane Porter, Homicide. Yeah. I want you to look something up for me—"

Stark tapped Porter on the arm and signalled that he was going out back. In the alley behind the restaurant, Roger Greenwood stood against the wall, holding the lapels of his jacket closed and dragging on a cigarette.

"It's too late to apologize," Roger said.

"I didn't come to apologize. I came to arrest you."

"Probably."

"What do you know about Martyn Waterman?"

"The media mogul?"

"Yeah."

"Not much, why?"

"I thought you might know him. You get around a lot."

"Wait a minute. I played at his place once, a long time ago, some big house in Forest Hill. He had a short little wife who was a real bitch, kept complaining that I wasn't playing soft enough, or loud enough, or I was playing the wrong tunes or something. I think she wanted Elton John. I never spoke to him, but he seemed like an absolute prick. He wouldn't have noticed an actual person making the sounds that were coming from the piano. Yeah, I remember now. Dumped that bitch of a wife eventually. Why do you want to know?"

"That cigarette is going to burn your finger, Roger."

When Stark got back to the bar, Porter said: "*Who's Who* says Waterman was born in Stoney Creek, Ontario."

"That's where Matt went to visit his cousin."

"A coincidence?"

"Be a hell of a one if it were. But, my god, that old man must be really spaced out. I mean, he said the cousin was 'something in TV.' How could he not know what Martyn Waterman is?"

Porter shrugged. "Now what? Interview Waterman?"

Stark shook his head. "What am I going to ask him? I'm stuck. Listen, can you get me in to Matt Mackey's apartment?"

"Sure."

"Is everything still there?"

"Except what ident took away, which isn't much. You're not going to find anything."

"You never know. Anyway, I want to look at the scene of the crime."

"Yeah, maybe you can figure out how the killer got in and out. The door was locked, and it has to be locked with a key. It's an Abloy lock, so you can't get keys made for it. The apartment is on the seventeenth floor. And he had to carry the computer, and, we imagine, notebooks away with him. So, the thinking is it was somebody who had a key to the place. It couldn't have just been someone he let in, because, as I say, you have to lock the door with a key, and he was hardly in a position to lock the door after the killer left. Mackey still had his key in his pocket."

"Maybe he had a spare key on a hook, and the killer found it."

"Well, the woman who came in to see him every morning, the switchboard operator at the paper, she said there were only two keys, and he had given her one."

"Mmm."

"But, Stark, listen. Are you sure you want to carry on with this thing, because if Peters finds out, you're really toast. Maybe it's not worth it."

"Diane, have you ever known me to give up on something? The only reason he found out that I was in Grandfield was because I opened my mouth to the press, and I won't make that stupid mistake twice."

"If you're sure... After Mackey's apartment, what next?"

"It might depend on you."

"Me?"

"What I'd like you to do is a tall order. Have you got somebody you can trust you can put on it? Because you can't put somebody on it who's going to be asked by a superior what he's doing and have him say, 'I'm doing this job for Detective Porter, right?'"

"What are you talking about?"

"When this thing happened that was so big a deal it changed Mackey's life, and was so big a deal that he was writing a book about it, and was so big a deal that he may have been killed to keep him from exposing it, when this thing happened, it was the summer of 1968—unless I've figured it out wrong—but I don't think so. So, here's what I want you to do. Get somebody to go over all the serious incidents in summer, 1968, involving a female: make it a young female, because I'm pretty sure it would have been. What we want is something unsolved that was so egregious that it would destroy the reputation even all these years later of somebody who was exposed as being involved in it."

"That's not going to work."

"Why not?"

"Because, Stark, what constitutes *egregious?* I mean, falling off buildings on an acid trip, overdosing on heroin, jumping in front of a streetcar?"

"For now, stick to rape and murder."

"It might not be that."

"Anything else, they could talk their way out of."

"I'll ask Howard to do it."

"Howard. The leading light of the Intelligence Unit: sure."

CHAPTER TWENTY-TWO

Norton Fielding worried Bernard MacIsaac. Bernie didn't like loose ends. He had spent his life tying them up or nailing them down. He had made a career of protecting his meal ticket from blindsides. He had mopped up, straightened up and covered up for his charge, successfully kept Yates's many transgressions from the prying eyes of press and public, and had committed as many transgressions himself to protect the singer and then the politician, a man who had slurped, snorted, smoked, stroked and shafted as much as the most notorious of the head-banging rockers. And now a rigid, starch-collared military type was threatening to upset the apple cart. Of course, Fielding didn't know anything about Waterman's real concern, his fear of being identified as participating with Dennis in the thing they never spoke of, but Fielding could easily decide to expose the existence of The Compact and its nefarious activities, and that alone would be enough to destroy Yates's career, and Bernie's along with it.

So Bernie was contemplating dealing with the Fielding difficulty by committing another in a long line of sins. Bernie was sitting in his office at the rear of the third floor of the Yates's flat-roofed, art-deco, twelve-bedroom Post Road mansion. His office overlooked the flat-roofed, art-deco, five-car garage. He had selected that room for his office because he had not wanted to overlook anything that might distract him. In contrast, Yates's room (Mary-Margaret had her own), faced the pool and the guesthouse on the other side of it. Yates supplemented the views offered through his binoculars of female guests and staff with the scenes broadcast on several special channels on his closed-circuit security network, channels fed by cameras concealed in the ladies' dressing room and the four guest apartments.

MacIsaac had all but decided on a course of action when Yates entered his office.

"What ho, Bernie," Yates called out. He had never read a line of P.G. Wodehouse, but some slightly more literate acquaintance who had been a guest at the house had spent that weekend tiresomely addressing MacIsaac as if MacIsaac were Jeeves's master, Bertie Wooster, except he kept calling him "Bernie Wooster," and since then, Yates sometimes used the greeting, with no knowledge of the allusion. He might have said, "Why the elongated visage? You seem distrait, old bean," but his knowledge of the lexicon ended with the *what ho!* Instead, he said, "What's happening, bro? Christ, you look depressed. Take a pill, buddy. Everything's cool."

"You stupid asshole. Nothing's cool, for chrissake. You're going along as if nothing's happened. A guy who was going to blow us away has been wasted, and if the cops do their business right, Marty's going to be nailed for it, and when he goes, we go. But even if the cops are really stupid, or we're really lucky, as long as that loose cannon's rolling around out there, we're still seconds away from destruction."

"What loose cannon?"

"Fielding."

"Marty's not worried about him, so why should you? Marty'll fix everything, Bernie." Yates's ebullience had been chemically engendered. He had a television interview in a couple of hours, and MacIsaac would have to make sure Yates smoked nothing else until then.

MacIsaac leapt to his feet, startling Yates.

"Marty, Marty, Marty. What the hell's the matter with you, Dennis?" He tapped his chest. "I fix things, Dennis, not fucking Marty. I'm the one who saves your ass over and over and over again, you stupid jerk. Jesus."

"Yeah, okay. I know. I'm just saying Marty isn't worried. All right?"

"Dennis, did he tell you he's not worried?"

"Yeah."

"Naturally he'd tell you that. He doesn't want you going off the deep end. Neither do I." MacIsaac shook his head. He'd better pull back on his own concern. He shouldn't have moaned to Yates like that. He'd follow Waterman's lead. "Look, Waterman means *you* shouldn't be worried. *You* concentrate on the nomination. *I'll* look after things. Never mind Marty. Now, go get something to eat, drink some coffee. Don't smoke any more dope, for god's sake, please." He looked at his watch. "Your interview is in one hour and fifteen minutes. Have a shower, get dressed."

CHAPTER TWENTY-THREE

Porter had been right. Mackey's apartment told Stark nothing. He had always left forensics to the experts. He was a people man.

The apartment told him that Mackey had had little imagination. There wasn't a single piece of art in the place. The only things hanging on the walls were a clock and a calendar. The calendar was marked with appointments, mostly for medical treatments and examinations. Some notations meant nothing to Stark. The books in the single bookcase were almost all non-fiction: unauthorized biographies of politicians and businessmen; exposés on corporate corruption, environmental and human-rights abuses, and the like; journalism texts; several true crime books, at least a dozen on organized crime; and some single-volume encyclopedias and reference books. The top shelf, thick with dust, held a row of science fiction and pulp crime fiction. The place smelled, like Stark's own apartment, of dirty socks and bedclothes, but staler and with thicker dust because Mackey's had been closed and unused for several days. There was no sign of blood. There wouldn't have been much bleeding from a single icepick wound to the brain.

Stuck behind the phone on the kitchen wall were take-out menus for Pizza Pizza, Holee Chow, and a local Greek snack bar. Empty pizza boxes and food cartons, and an all-but-empty fridge that reeked of sour milk suggested that Mackey cooked rarely, if at all. The bedroom was neater than Stark's. There was no pile of clothes on the chair, and the bed was made. Since he'd been on leave, Stark had made his bed most days, but not since Porter had put him to work. Mackey must have had a much more active sex life than Stark, judging by the fact that the box of condoms in the night-table drawer was a large one, and half its contents was missing. "Take me ten years to go through that," Stark thought, "maybe more."

The sliding door to the balcony was unlocked. Stark went out and looked down. The edges of the balconies were flanked with smooth sheets of metal with drain holes in the corners. There were no handholds. Stark leaned out and looked up. There were three floors above. He went back into the apartment and studied the desk at which Mackey was sitting when he was killed. The keyboard and the monitor were there, the computer box missing. On the top edge of the monitor, scrawled in black marker, was "@Backup Machine No." and eight digits. Across the left-hand corner was written the word "dirt" and below it "digger." Stark took out his notebook and wrote this down.

He took a last look around the place, turned over the pillows on the couch, groped in the crack between the bed of the couch and the arms and back. He found nothing. He went out into the hall, locked the door behind him, saw the emergency exit door directly across the hall and went through it into the stairwell. He climbed three flights to the door giving access to the roof. He tried it. Locked. There was a new-looking steel plate bolted to the door beside the handle. The steel door frame was dented and scratched beside the plate. Stark rattled the door. It was solid. He walked back down the stairs without holding the handrail. On Mackey's floor, he emerged into the hallway, turned and looked at the emergency door, and then at Mackey's door. He took the elevator to the main floor, found the button on the intercom with "Superintendent" beside it. Buzzed and waited.

"Yeah?"

"This is Detective Stark with the Toronto Police. I'd like to speak to you."

"Just a minute." The accent was Russian.

The man who met Stark in the lobby was tall and stoop-shouldered, in his forties. He looked as if he had been sleeping. Stark showed him his badge.

"Some trouble?" the man said.

"I'm investigating the murder of Matt Mackey."

"Who? Oh, the tenant in seventeen-twelve. There were many cops here before. They took pictures, everything. You want to go in? They told me not to go in and not let anybody in, but you're a cop, so I guess it's okay."

"You have a key?"

"Sure. I got key, unless he change the lock." He held up a master key. "They're not supposed to. Sometimes they do when they split up with husbands and boyfriends. When I find out, I get pissed off. So, you wanna go in?"

"No. I just want to ask you a question. The door to the roof. It's been altered. There's a steel plate bolted to it that looks like it was just put on. What's that about?"

"Two days ago I find it open. Some kids broke it with crowbar or somethink. They do damage all the time, smash things just for no reason, goddamned kids. Go on roof and take drugs. I fixit the door myself. Put plate. They not open so easy next time."

"Take me up there. I want to have a look."

"Whadyou want, take fingerprints, somethink? You won't catch kids, what do you think?"

"Come on. Let's go."

On the roof, Stark found nothing helpful. Not that he had any idea what he was looking for. It was a regular tar-and-gravel roof, with no indication that anybody had ever been up there.

"Your teenagers seem to have cleaned up after themselves," he told the superintendent. "Very neat."

The man shrugged.

Stark went to the edge of the roof over where he thought Mackey's apartment was. He looked over.

"Careful," the superintendent said. "It's a long way down."

"You ever have any break-ins?" Stark asked.

"Just in the cars in the underground garage. They just wait till a car goes in and sneak before the door closes. But not in the units. Special locks. Last year, we had a woman raped in thirteen-nine, but that was because she let the guy in. You can't break in. Swedish locks. You have to get keys from company."

"How come they put such expensive locks on the apartments?"

"Lawsuit. Long time ago. Burglars. Shitty locks. Judge said fix. So they put. He just raise rent to pay for, I think."

"Do you see people come and go? Visitors?"

"Sometimes, sure."

"Did you ever see anybody go to Mr. Mackey's apartment?"

He shook his head. "I only see him two three times. I don't know him."

"Okay. I've seen enough."

CHAPTER TWENTY-FOUR

Just around the corner from his place on the Danforth, Stark passed a *Gazette* box. He bought the paper. The headline said, "Restaurant king shot dead." Stark stood in the street and read: "Multi-millionaire Lee Braddock, reputed to be the biggest private owner of restaurants and hotels in North America, was shot to death last night as he stepped from his chauffeur-driven car at his North York home. Police say Braddock was struck in the head by a single bullet they believe was fired from a distance by a high-powered rifle…" The piece went on to record comments from family, friends, colleagues and neighbours, all of whom expressed the usual shock and horror and puzzlement, with the exception of one unnamed "source close to the victim," who suggested obliquely the death might have something to do with attempts to unionize Braddock's biggest hotel, the Miranda Chinook, in Calgary, which was followed immediately by an irate union president's denial of any connection and threatening to sue at any such suggestion. The article concluded with a brief biography of Braddock, noting that he had been a leading light in the Progressive Conservative party, but had in recent years transferred his support to the Canadian Values Party.

Stark's cat, Powder, greeted him at the door to his place, rubbing vigorously against his legs.

"You can't be hungwy, you dirty girl, because I fed you this morning. Ah, she's a naughty girl," Stark said in a whining voice he would never use in public. Even when a former girlfriend had stayed there, he had avoided speaking to the cat in this high-pitched baby talk his mother and her mother had used with their cats. Stark scratched the animal's head. "You wanna drinky water. Okay." He went into the bathroom, the cat a white blur running past him in the hallway to position herself on the edge of the bathtub.

The cat spent much of her time in a closet (all the time if anyone besides Stark was in the apartment); she refused all nourishment except the cheapest brand of dry cat food; and she would drink only one of two ways—either by dipping her paw into her water bowl and licking the water from the paw, or by lapping at a thin drizzle from the bathtub tap. Stark adjusted the flow from the tap until it was a fraction past the drip, just at the beginning of the drizzle. Powder couldn't time her tonguing to catch drips, and she couldn't handle a stronger flow.

The phone rang. It was Martha Magliore.

"Jesus, Stark, you must be the only person in the hemisphere who doesn't have an answering machine, or call answer. What the hell's the matter with you?"

"I cancelled it."

"Why?—Never mind. When Amanda Dworkin couldn't reach you, she called Homicide. They said you were on disability leave."

"Shit. Did she tell them I'd interviewed her?"

"I don't think so, because to me she said, 'You're a friend of Stark's?' I said, 'Yeah...' She said, 'He wanted this list, and now I've got it, but I can't get him on the phone.' I told her to give me the list, and I'd get in touch with you. How come you're on leave? Did your head start acting up or something?"

"I'm not really on leave."

"Oh. Anyway, I've got this list. Why don't I bring it over? And I've got something else to tell you, too."

She arrived at Stark's apartment in half an hour. Uncharacteristically, she was wearing a suit, navy, with a white blouse, its top three buttons undone. The skirt was well above her knees. She saw Stark's gaze take her in.

"Lunch with the publisher." She made a face.

"Did you bend over a lot?"

"What?"

"Well, your blouse is undone down to your navel. I thought you might have been trying for a raise."

"Jealous?"

Stark chuckled. "So, what did you want to tell me?"

"I want to whisper sweet nothings in your ear, but I get the impression something has made you deaf. I could murder a Scotch."

Stark shrugged. "Sorry, I don't have any."

"Well, what *have* you got? Beer?"

"Tea, coffee, diet Coke."

Magliore was sitting at the kitchen table. She stood up and looked around. "I'm sorry, I must have come to the wrong place. I thought this was Harry Stark's apartment. Have you taken the pledge? No sex, no booze. You going into the priesthood?"

"It has to do with my—" He waved a hand. "I got shot in the head. Now, with the medication I take, I'm not supposed to drink."

"Stark, you've been doing things to your body all your life that you're not supposed to do."

"You get shot in the head, it changes things," Stark said. "You should try it."

"Yeah, right. Okay, have you got real coffee?"

"Instant."

"Jesus. All right, make me a fucking instant then. I guess I had enough wine at lunch."

"So, what did you want to tell me?" Stark said as he plugged in the kettle and checked the insides of two mugs for relative cleanliness.

"There was an intruder in my office."

Stark looked at her, slightly puzzled. "Oh," he said. "Well, I don't do that sort of thing, Martha. Did you call the cops?"

"No, Stark, listen. They weren't looking for my stuff. It was somebody who looked like a mail guy with a bunch of envelopes in his arms. He asked somebody on the floor where Matt Mackey's office was, not my office. Both our nameplates are on the glass, so he'd see the office was shared. My desk is easy to spot. It's got bits of me all over it. And Mackey had a nameplate on his desk so people would know where to leave stuff for him. There was hardly anything of his left in the office, but all his desk drawers had been pulled open, and everything in the drawers and in the trays on the desk, every bit of paper was taken."

"Christ. Why didn't somebody call me?"

"Dworkin tried, for Christ's sake. You've got no fucking answering machine."

"She could have called my cellphone…"

"Yeah, I tried your cellphone, and it's either turned off or the battery's dead. Anyway, your pals in Homicide think you're still on sick leave. Mind you, if you're still up to your old tricks, you won't be in the office any more than if you were on sick leave."

"Well, I'm off it now. But—do me a favour, please. Don't tell anyone else that I'm back to work, all right?"

"Why not?"

"Just—do me a favour, and don't tell anyone, please?"

Magliore shrugged. "So what do you think?"

"About the intruder? Dworkin had been through everything, looking for anything to do with Mackey's book, so I assume she didn't find anything relevant. But the fake mail guy wouldn't know that. Shit. Who saw him? Did he or she say what the guy looked like?"

"I asked them that right away. But these are newspaper jerks, Stark. They're all fixated on getting the paper out. I could walk through the office nude and they wouldn't notice. Three of them saw him. One said, 'He looked like the mail guy... Charlie.' One of the other two said, 'Charlie wouldn't have asked where Mackey's office was,' but he had no idea what the guy looked like. And the third guy said he thought it was the new kid, whoever the hell that is."

Stark poured boiling water over the instant coffee. "You want cream? It's actually skim milk."

"Black."

Stark handed her the cup. "So, what's this list?"

Magliore gave Stark a wry look. "Stark, you asked Dworkin for a list of anybody that Mackey had been doing pieces on who might bear a grudge or want to silence him or something. Remember?"

"Right. So, you have the list?"

"Not exactly."

"Which means?"

"She got one of the librarians to put the thing together, and she couldn't figure who to leave out, so there's just a list of everybody Mackey has done stories on in the past five years, and then Dworkin asked me to help, so we added all the names we could remember of people he had been looking into, but hadn't written anything on yet. I think I know all of them, because he pretty well trusted me not to try to scoop him. And, you know, I know—" She made a motion with her hand, "where a lot of the bodies are buried in this town, and who buried them. So whenever he was working on something, he would pump me for information. I often gave him really useful leads. So we added all those names to the list. Here." She handed Stark a manila envelope. It contained a thick sheaf of computer print-outs of Mackey's articles.

"What's all this?" he said.

"That's what the library produced. They're the first pages of print-outs of all of Mackey's stories for the past five years. They just give the subject and the information in the cutline—if there was a picture with it—and keywords. At the end of that bunch is our list of names."

"That's great. Thanks. And thank the librarian." Stark wondered whether he should put Waterman's name in front of her. He quickly quashed the notion. If a "stringer" in Grandfield had blown his cover, Magliore would have Waterman's name smeared all over the front page. He remembered that when he was bedding her, she told him nothing was off the record unless she agreed to it, not even pillow talk. She said that if he didn't want to see it in the paper, he shouldn't tell her.

"Is that what you wanted?"

"Oh yeah. Martha, thanks for bringing this over, eh. That was terrific of you." He grinned at her awkwardly. He wanted her to leave so he could look for Waterman's name in the material, but he didn't want to seem to be using her; he didn't want to appear ungrateful. "So—uh, more coffee?"

Magliore shook her head. "I can't stand it," she said. "It's pathetic. I don't know whether to laugh or cry. What's happened to you, Stark?"

"What do you mean?" Stark said a little defensively.

She made a what's-the-use face, reached out and patted Stark on the arm. "Okay. I'm going. Thanks for the coffee. This is a nice place, by the way. You're still messy. I'm glad to see that hasn't changed. In fact, if the place had been neat, I'd have just handed you the papers and left, because I'd know you'd either lost it altogether, or you were living with a woman. You're not, are you?"

"No."

As soon as Stark had seen her out the door, he began looking through the pile of print-outs. It took him half an hour to get to the final page, the list that Magliore and Dworkin had produced. There was no mention of Waterman. He had recognized many of the names, but he dismissed the idea of following up on any of them. For the moment, Waterman seemed the only useful possibility. He tossed the papers on the kitchen counter.

The phone rang. It was Diane Porter. She told Stark to stay put. She was coming over. She was at the door in fifteen minutes.

"Get your coat. We're going to interview a guy called Ian Covey."

"Who's he?"

"I don't know. He owns some company, Paige-David Industries."

"What's that?"

"No idea."

"And, why are we interviewing him?"

Porter saw the *Chronicle* on the kitchen table. "You read the article about that Braddock guy who was shot?"

"Yeah, I did."

"That's what we're going to talk to this guy about."

"I'm not working, Diane, I'm just doing this Mackey thing. You can't take me on all your cases. What the hell?"

"Waterman."

"What about him?"

"That's what this guy wants to tell us."

"What do you mean?"

"Ted Henry spoke to him on the phone."

"I thought Ted was in Italy?"

"They cut their trip short. His wife got really sick on some bad smoked salmon."

"Milly? She must be really pissed off."

"No, she's in seventh heaven. It's Ted who's pissed off."

"Why?"

"Their tour people had arranged all the meals, and of course, they were worried about being sued, so they refunded the trip money and gave them five grand on top of that, and offered to take them anywhere they run tours for nothing. Ted likes the dough, but he's pissed because Milly says they're going to take the European gallery and museum tour in the spring."

Stark chuckled. "So, what about Waterman?"

"Ted talked to the guy, and the guy told him that Waterman was involved in the shooting of this Braddock."

"What?"

"Yeah, I know. So, get your coat."

CHAPTER TWENTY-FIVE

The head office of Paige-David Industries occupied an entire floor of the TD Centre. Ian Covey had a vast corner office that overlooked the harbour. Stark figured the office would come close to matching the area of his apartment. Stark and Porter were led in by a secretary so tall and thin, and with such a long neck she reminded Stark of Polkaroo. "God, I'm watching too much television," he thought. "I've got to get back to work."

Covey was sitting behind an immense, crescent-shaped desk with a top of thick glass that stood on a sort of free-form arrangement of small steel I-bars, as if the girders of a half-finished building had been toppled by a tornado and were leaning against each other. Covey was a small man, with a mean, mirthless face. A brass and glass bar occupied one corner of the room. In front of the bar were two couches on either side of a low, wide table that imitated the bar in construction. There were four bar stools. The corner arrangement constituted all the furniture in the office, apart from four oddly twisted leather chairs facing the desk, which Stark figured must have been products of the same diseased mind that had conceived the desk. He chuckled to himself at the thought that this Covey probably paid a fortune for this stuff, and the movers who brought it in probably protested that it was in that condition when they picked it up, that they hadn't damaged it in transit. The walls were bare, each in a different jarring colour, one a sickly lavender, one lipstick red and one in bright green and blue oblique stripes. There was no art, the single object hanging on the walls being a framed cartoon that showed a King Cole-like character sitting on a throne that looked like a child's car seat, letting gold coins drip from his fingers into a small treasure chest on his knee and grinning evilly. Stuck in the grass that surrounded the throne were four tiny crosses, each with a baby's rattle hanging from it. Recognizing the cartoon, which had appeared in the *Chronicle,* Stark recollected who Covey was: the owner of a company that made car seats for kids. The cartoon had appeared after the seats had been implicated in the deaths of four children in four separate accidents. The fact that the cartoon was displayed so brazenly in Covey's office told Stark a great deal about the man.

"Sit down," Covey ordered the detectives. "Your names are?"

Porter introduced herself and Stark.

"I'll be brief. I have a meeting to go to. I regret the necessity for this, but I believe I have no choice. One of our number—When I say *our*, I refer to a group that meets from time to time in support of a particular politician. I insist on discretion in this matter. What I am about to tell you could damage the reputation of this gentleman and others unnecessarily. I realize it will have to become public knowledge during the course of a trial, but until then, no good can be served by its dissemination. Do I have your undertaking?"

Porter gave Stark a quick nervous glance. She nodded at Covey.

"Wait a second," Stark said. "What's going on?"

"It's okay, Stark. Relax. All right, Mr. Covey. We are in accord. Now, what is it you wanted to tell us."

"Well, it strikes me that your superior, Detective Sergeant Henry, I believe?—"

Porter nodded.

"He must have told you what I told him. Summarize it, and I won't have to waste time going through everything again."

Porter sighed. "I'm sorry. He just got back from Europe, and he's jet-lagged. He said you spoke quickly and he had trouble following what you were saying, except that it had something to do with the murder of Lee Braddock and that the killing was connected with Martyn Waterman, the television-network owner."

"Damn." Covey looked at his watch. "All right. Lee Braddock was a member of our little organization."

"What is this organization?"

"That's not important."

"With all due respect—"

"Wait. I want to do this quickly and painlessly. If I have to go into detail, I'll never get through it. We can deal with those issues later. Why was Braddock shot? I have no idea. But I'm sure it has to do with recent incidents connected with the group. One of our members is Martyn Waterman. He alerted us to the journalist Matthew Mackey's book about our group. Public knowledge of our existence and the assistance we have been giving to a certain person with political aspirations would not be helpful, and, in fact, might seriously harm his chances of election. Another member of our group, Norton Fielding, accused Martyn of suggesting obliquely that we should arrange for Mackey to be—to be eliminated. Fielding was being absurd, and we dismissed his concern—until Mackey *was* killed. That shook us rather badly, and then the day after Mackey's death, Fielding was pushed in front of a subway train."

"What?" Stark said.

"I don't remember that," Porter said.

"The train stopped in time, it was reported as an accident, and we all wanted to believe that it was both an accident and a coincidence. Martyn is persuasive, and we were eager to be convinced that he had nothing to do with either event. But now that Lee has been killed—well, these happenings must be connected..." Covey clenched his hands and shook his head. "I can only surmise that Martyn has lost his mind."

"Why does it have to be Waterman?" Stark asked.

Covey looked at Stark. "It couldn't be anyone else."

"Why not?"

Covey held his breath for an instant, and released it audibly. "Martyn is the driving force; he drew us together. He's the planner, the leader. The rest of us are—troops, I suppose. We wait for his instructions and we act on them."

Porter said: "It could be someone outside of the group, could it not?"

"I don't think so."

"Who else knows about the existence of this group? Who is this politician?" Porter said.

Covey hesitated. "I suppose it has to come out—Dennis Yates."

"He was a singer, or something, wasn't he?" Stark said.

Both Covey and Porter looked at Stark as if he were from another planet. Porter turned to face Covey. "Yates is running for the leadership of the Canadian Values Party, so I assume he knew about the group?"

Covey nodded.

"Who else?"

Covey shrugged. "His manager and his wife, but Martyn always insisted they were the only ones who knew, and they had a deeply vested interest in keeping the group's existence confidential."

"Why kill this guy Braddock?" Stark said. "I can see the path between Mackey and this fellow Fielding, but why Braddock? And why didn't Fielding go to the police about this group after he was pushed in front of the subway train? That would have added credence to his allegations."

"He said he couldn't prove anything, and Martyn would sue him and win. Then Fielding resigned from the group and told us we were in league with the devil."

"But he had threatened to go to the police earlier?" Porter said.

"Not in so many words, but we all understood the implication."

"And Braddock?" Stark said.

"I have no idea."

"I'd like to back up to the Mackey killing. Are you saying that Waterman proposed that Mackey be killed so the existence of this political group of yours wouldn't be made public?"

Covey hesitated. "I'm not prepared to make any further comment on that. And I didn't say that Martyn suggested that Mackey should be killed. That was Fielding's inference. I am simply saying that in light of subsequent events, questions have to be raised."

CHAPTER TWENTY-SIX

"I'm fucked." Dennis Yates burst into Bernie MacIsaac's office. MacIsaac was reading the paper at his desk. He rotated his chair slowly and looked at Yates over his glasses. Yates paced in the centre of the room. "I'm getting out while I still can."

"What are you ranting about?"

Yates pointed at the desk. "Christ, you're reading the paper. Lee Braddock, for god's sake. First Matt, then Fielding gets pushed in front of the subway and now Braddock is *killed*. It doesn't make sense. Unless Marty figures he's got to kill anyone who can link the Mackey murder to him. He's going to take us all out."

"Don't be ridiculous."

"Well, what then?"

MacIsaac raised his hands. "I don't know, Dennis."

"I'm not going to sit here and get murdered, I'll tell you that."

"Dennis, why the hell would anybody murder you?"

"Why did somebody murder Lee Braddock? It's got to be Marty."

MacIsaac leaned toward Yates. He said slowly and deliberately: "That doesn't make sense."

"Not if he's gone off his fucking rocker, it doesn't make sense, no."

"He hasn't gone off his rocker. And stop that goddamned pacing."

"I can't. What the hell's the matter with you, Bernie? How can you—"Yates made a frustrated gesture. "The campaign is dead. We can write that off."

"Why?"

"As soon as they put Braddock together with the grou~ murder, the whole thing is blown."

"Why should they connect Braddock's death with be different if they knew what Mackey was writir going to tell them? Now, listen, I don't want t Braddock. But if you think Martyn Waterman is s out all the members of the group and think th protect him—Dennis, if he puts a dent in one of whole bunch would rush to the cops, and he'd protecting himself by killing Braddock, he'd b self. So, it's not Waterman who's doing it."

"That's worse."

CHAPTER TWENTY-SEVEN

"Waterman looks like our guy for Mackey," Porter said. "I can't figure the Braddock killing, though, or the Fielding thing."

Stark shook his head. "What did the Braddock killing look like? You were there. Any forensics?"

"They haven't found anything. And where Braddock was standing, the way he was hit, the killer must have shot from a long distance. The shooter could have been on any of three hills opposite Braddock's place. Braddock's driver said he had the radio on and didn't hear the shot. Braddock had just got out of the car. One bullet right in the side of the head. There must have been two shots. The driver said he saw Braddock duck and turn to his left, as if he thought the shot had come from that direction."

"I thought you said the driver didn't hear the shot?"

"Well, no, but he figured it out as soon as he saw his boss's brains splattered over the side of the car. I didn't go to the autopsy. Carl Matisse is supposed to be lead on the case, but he's wrapped up in that little girl's killing, so Ted asked me to interview Covey. I guess they'll pass me the file. I'll get the coroner's notes."

"How far away are these hills?"

"About five hundred metres.

"Do you realize how difficult a head shot is from that distance?"

Porter shrugged, and said a little sheepishly, "I haven't done much work on that sort of thing—"

"This guy's a crack shot, believe me. At that distance, if he were using a high-powered rifle, the bullet would drop—I'd guess about five feet. I'd guess the reason Braddock ducked and turned to his left was that the first shot missed him on that side. Travelling at supersonic speed, the bullet would create a sonic boom as it passed Braddock that would sound like a being fired at right angles to the actual source of the shot. He turned, iper adjusted his aim, and pop. So, we've got two killings by pros, or Somebody as good as this guy or these guys would be expensive. in this little cadre of capitalism, I suspect, would have the finan- ithal to afford a quality hitman. We're going to have to inter- owns on this list Covey gave us."

lready think Waterman is the culprit?"

Henry and give him the list. Tell him what Covey told detail some officers to speak to these guys, all but im."

"The police investigated my subway accident, and that's what they determined it *was,* an accident. And I concur. Did you not read the report?"

Porter shook her head. Fielding looked at Stark, who was looking around the high-ceilinged room. It would have been an unusual room in a modern house—a vestibule—but they weren't in a modern house. They were in a house built in the early part of the twentieth century in the Annex. It was a large house, three storeys, solid brick, with a large square veranda, on which Fielding had left them standing while he studied their identification. The vestibule was about the same size and shape as the veranda. Along its walls were six doors. Stark had been in a house like this before. He knew the single door on the south wall near the entrance was to the cloakroom. Straight ahead were two doors, one to the stairs, one to the hallway that led to the kitchen. On the north wall, the first door would lead to the library or study or sitting room at the front of the house, the second to the living room, the third to the dining room. The whole room was in oak. Stark studied the photographs and military medals that hung on the south wall. Fielding cleared his throat. Stark turned quickly.

"Sorry—" He smiled weakly. "Who was in the forces?"

"I was. I asked whether you had read the report. Judging by your age, I would imagine you're the senior officer. Your junior has just indicated that she hasn't read the report on my accident. Have you read it?"

"No, sorry."

"Then what, may I ask, are you doing here?"

"Actually, Detective Porter is in charge." Stark turned toward Porter. Fielding's eyes followed his.

"Are you aware of the death of Lee Braddock, Mr. Fielding?" Porter said.

Fielding looked from one to the other. He took some time before he spoke.

"Who sent you?"

Porter looked at Stark. "Well, we—had a conversation with a Mr. Ian Covey, who gave us certain information that has led us here."

"Speak clearly."

"We were told that you were a member of a a political group, and that the journalist Matt Mackey was writing a book that would embarrass this group and interfere with its efforts to get Dennis Yates elected leader of the Canadian Values Party. Mr. Covey told us that you accused Martyn

Waterman of arranging Mackey's murder. And also of attempting to kill you by having you pushed in front of a subway train. That, sir, is why we are here."

"I've never heard such crap. Covey has always been a bit hysterical."

"He didn't seem hysterical," Porter said.

"It was an accident. Some child got loose from its parents, they were trying to grab it, and there was a commotion. I always stand very close to the edge of the platform. In the confusion, someone bumped against me, and I fell. It's as simple as that. Rather careless on my part. And as for accusing Waterman, that's absurd."

"Are you saying that Mr. Covey is lying?"

"No, that he's confused. Covey lives in an entirely artificial world of finance. Life goes on around him, and he's unaware of it."

Porter looked at Stark. She was hoping her mentor would help, but Stark just smiled. Porter glared back.

Fielding went on: "I did have words with Martyn about the Mackey business, but that was just normal interplay, debating action that should be taken, if any, in the face of a perceived threat."

Stark spoke rapidly: "Covey thinks Waterman had Mackey killed. He thinks Waterman had you pushed in front of the train to shut you up. That job was botched. Covey thinks that Braddock was next on the list. He's afraid for his own life. I think you should be afraid for yours."

Fielding stared at Stark, his expression at first defiant, becoming appraising and finally thoughtful, and he turned away. After a moment, he sighed, having seemed to have come to a decision. "We'd better go in here," he said, indicating the door Stark had thought was the library. It was. Two walls were stacked with books, most of them, it appeared at a glance, with a military theme. A third wall was arrayed with military artefacts: cavalry swords and the like. The fourth wall was mostly occupied by a row of four long, narrow, leaded windows. Stark chuckled to himself. The room was a cliché, a movie set of a library: ancient leather chairs; dark wood; wrought-iron, curlicued standard lamps. Fielding took a straight-backed wooden chair behind a leather-topped writing table. He gestured to the leather chairs. Porter sat in one, sinking into it and losing all authority.

Stark remained standing, leaning against the back of another chair. He leaned harder when he was hit with a wave of weakness, followed by a sharp pain stabbing at his left temple. He closed his eyes, and his knees bent slightly. He sat on the arm of the chair. In seconds, the pain had gone. Neither of the others had noticed the bout.

"I need a drink," Fielding said. He pressed a button in the wall, and after a short time, a woman in a blue smock appeared. "Get me a Scotch, Sandra. Do you want anything?" he asked the detectives, who shook their heads. After the woman left, Porter started to say something, but Fielding raised a hand to silence her, and signalled that they should wait. They sat in silence until the woman returned, carrying a heavy crystal glass with an ample amount of liquor on a silver tray. After she left, Fielding took a drink of the Scotch, and, looking from Porter to Stark, he said, "All right, what else did Covey tell you?"

Porter waited for Stark to speak. When he didn't, Porter said, "I think we've told you all we care to tell you about what Mr. Covey said, sir. We would like to hear your account of things."

"What I mean is, did he tell you about the group?"

"Yes, Covey told us that there was a political group working to get Dennis Yates elected."

"That's all he told you?"

Stark was getting fed up. "Look, we're investigating a murder—two murders—we haven't got time, nor the inclination, to play twenty questions. If you think you can tell us selectively what you want to tell us, you're very wrong. Now, either give us straight answers to *our* questions, or we'll take you to the station."

Fielding glared at Stark for a long time before turning to Porter.

"I will tell you what I know that is pertinent to your investigation, and I will tell you what I suspect, which may or may not be of any value. I had already decided to tell you when I asked you to come into the study. I was and remain reluctant to say anything that might in any way reflect badly on all except one of the members of The Compact. The one member I am not concerned about is that pretentious demagogue Martyn Waterman and his high-handedness. I think he is responsible for the death of Matthew Mackey. He implied as much."

"What did he say?"

"I don't remember the words. Essentially, he suggested that Mackey was going to ruin us all, and then he dismissed every proposal made by members of the group to influence Mackey not to publish his book. Waterman was waiting for one of us to suggest that Mackey be killed, and I said as much. Waterman immediately responded that it was clearly not his idea. I had already told the group that he was waiting for someone else to offer the solution so that he could deny responsibility for it. I wouldn't be surprised if he had taped the proceedings. Waterman, you know, had the most to lose from

Mackey's book—" Stark and Porter looked at each other. "—because Waterman is the king of dirty tricks. I have intelligence that he has committed criminal acts, bribery, extortion. Not directly, of course, but through his agents. Dennis Yates is Waterman's stooge. He offers Waterman the only chance he has to become the prime minister of this country. Martyn spent a fortune grooming the man. Yates now operates like an automaton. You throw the switch and he performs: 'Dennis, press conference': he springs into action, thwacking questions like a tennis pro. 'Dennis, debate': he turns his opponents into bullies and smart-ass know-it-alls. But once he's off the stage, one on one, he's a blithering idiot. If he had an idea, he'd be dangerous. Getting him elected is everything to Waterman. I do think he had me pushed on to the tracks. I didn't see what happened; a body lurched against me."

"And Braddock?"

Fielding raised his hands. "That—is bizarre. I have no explanation for that. It has to be Martyn. I know Lee Braddock very well, and I can assure you there is nothing in the man's background that would lead to this, no shady dealings, nothing like that. He and I both, I might add. We have certainly done our parts to further Yates's political career, I'm somewhat embarrassed to admit, but our purpose *has* been more honourable than Waterman's, and we have not committed the scurrilous acts that some of the others have been guilty of. But wait, I shouldn't be saying that. The organization's motives have been commendable. Everyone, except Waterman, has had the interests of the country at heart. Don't persecute the group. Go after Waterman."

"What do you think would motivate Waterman to kill Braddock?" Porter asked.

"I can only think that Lee might have challenged Waterman in private, following our last meeting. I quit the group and warned them about continuing to collaborate with Waterman. Lee was the kind of man who would not want to embarrass Waterman. He might have spoken to him later and said that Waterman should do the right thing, or he would have to break silence."

CHAPTER TWENTY-EIGHT

After Stark and Porter left Fielding, Stark said he wanted to go to the scene of Braddock's killing.

"Why do you want go there?" Porter asked.

"I want to see for myself."

There was nothing at Braddock's sprawling ranch-style home to suggest it had been the scene of a violent death. Stark and Porter stood at the spot in the forecourt of the triple garage where Braddock's body had been. A long driveway led to the area at the side of the house. They had parked on the road and walked up the driveway. Someone had parted the curtains in the front room of the house and watched them. As the detectives studied the scene, a woman came tentatively around the corner of the house.

"Excuse me," she said, a little timidly.

"Ma'am?" Porter said.

"Who are you?"

"Oh, I'm sorry. We're police, ma'am." She showed her identification.

"They told me the police wouldn't be coming any more." The woman was not as old as she had first appeared to Stark. She was tall, with a self-conscious stoop. She was wearing a long, pink housecoat and slippers. She had put a sweater over her shoulders. Her arms were folded. There was a chill in the air. The sky was an unbroken ceiling of slate grey. If it had been another month or so later, a sky like that would have been threatening snow.

"I'm sorry," Porter said. "We won't be here long. There's no need for you to be out here, Mrs. Braddock. We won't have to bother you."

The woman nodded uncertainly and retreated.

"Did you interview the wife?" Stark said.

"Somebody else did. They got nothing."

"They didn't know what to ask."

"Do you want to talk to her?"

"I don't think so."

"So, what did you want to show me?"

Stark pointed into the distance. "Those are the three hills?"

Porter nodded.

Stark shook his head.

"What's the matter?"

"Well, I started thinking about this, and now that I'm here—remember when I told you that in five hundred yards, a bullet will drop about five feet."

"Yeah. Wait a minute: how do you aim at something when the bullet isn't going to go where you're aiming it?"

"Puzzling, isn't it. You know, if you were at a thousand yards, the bullet would drop almost thirty feet. In fact, if I remember correctly, three hundred and thirty-five inches or twenty-eight feet."

"How do you know this stuff?"

"I had to work on a case a few years back where a sniper was taking people out at random."

"So, how *do* you aim?"

"Well, first you look through the scope at the target. If you know the relative size of the target, there are dots in the scope that you compare with the target and that will tell you how far away it is. Then you use these knobs on the sight to adjust the the crosshairs to compensate for the bullet drop and to correct for wind drift."

"How do you figure that out?"

"I don't know. Listen. Once the correct elevation is dialled into the scope, the shooter aims directly at the target and fires. If his calculations are correct, he gets a hit. If not, he makes a quick adjustment and tries a second shot. If he hasn't got time for that, he squeezes off another shot right away."

"Complicated little devil, isn't it."

"And we're talking about a fairly stationary target. Braddock gets out of the car, pauses to close the door—. But the question is, why."

"Why what?"

"Well, why go all the way up there—" Stark pointed at the hills, "to shoot him down here?"

Porter shrugged. "They didn't want to be seen."

"You think there was more than one?" Stark said archly.

"All right, he or she didn't want to be seen."

"There's something wrong with this picture. If this guy was a pro, he would be very expensive. He'd be like a European assassin, or something."

"Waterman could afford that."

"Yeah, but wait. A pro is paid for results. He's probably going to have only one chance. A pro resorts to this kind of long-distance business only when you can't get close without getting caught—because of heavy security, around a head of state, for instance. That didn't exist with Braddock. And with Fielding, they couldn't get any closer. They pushed him."

"They?"

"Don't you agree there's something odd about this? In the final analysis, despite all his skill, in reality the shooter was bloody lucky to take Braddock out. Especially with a head shot. Pros don't rely on luck, Diane. This thing doesn't add up."

CHAPTER TWENTY-NINE

The apartment was daylight bright, belying the fact that it was after midnight. All the clothes the man was wearing were new, paid for in cash in a store where he was not known: a hat, a navy blue suit, white shirt, blue-and-red-striped tie, long black socks, gleaming black wingtips, shiny new shoes. He was only wearing the clothes for that night's business, and dispose of them. His hair had been recently cut and was closely cropped, well above his ears, and perfectly parted. He walked stiffly erect, proud and correct, a small smile of satisfaction reflecting a job well done. An incongruous element about his person was the Remington 870 pump-action shotgun dangling from his right hand. He slipped the gun into the brand new hockey bag he had bought for the purpose. It was blue, with a Maple Leafs logo. He paused at the door. He looked around, even though he had brought nothing with him he was not taking away. He had nothing in his pockets, no wallet, no identification, no keys. He opened the door, and left. Behind him, in one room of the apartment, was a dead man.

CHAPTER THIRTY

"You've been slacking off." Bert Boyd was chewing on the unlit stub of a cigar as he polished the deli counter.

"What are you talking about?" Stark said. "You're not going to attract much business from the girls in the insurance office with that thing stuck in your gob."

Boyd's hand shot up, yanked the offending item from his mouth and put it behind his back as he turned toward the door. "Jesus, don't scare me like that."

"Well, don't take the chance."

"They don't come in now. They come in on their way to work, and then they don't start coming in again until about ten o'clock."

"Well, that cigar end could blow it all for you. Destroy your image, Bert. Diane, have you had one of Bert's new flax muffins?"

"Flax?"

"Oh yeah, flax. And multi-grain, fat free. He's got all the crunchy stuff now, Bert has. Very healthy, very trendy."

"I'm impressed," Porter said.

"Up yours," Bert growled.

"Say, you know, the other day, a bear came in here," Stark said.

Boyd's head tilted to one side, his expression saying, "Wait for it."

"A bear?" Porter said.

"Yeah. Apparently he had heard about Bert's new line. He came up to the counter and said, 'I'll have one of those flax.................... muffins.' And Bert said, 'Why the big pause?'"

Porter chuckled. Bert looked from one to the other.

"I don't get it—ah, big paws. That's not funny, Stark." Bert waved a hand at the two, who were both laughing loudly. He walked to the end of the counter, sat on a stool and noisily opened the *Racing Form*.

"Bert's kind of sensitive these days," Stark said. "Probably been eating too many flax muffins. Hey, Bert, what did you mean, I've been slacking off."

"Forget it."

"No, really."

"I meant you haven't been in, so I figure you haven't been doing your walking routine." He affected a look of mild admonishment.

"I've been busy."

Boyd waved a hand as if to say, "Don't say I didn't warn you."

"I guess we'd better not ask for a refill," Porter said.

"Let's not push our luck." Stark sighed. "So, what do you think?"

Porter shrugged. "We have to talk to Waterman."

"Why?"

"Well, we'll probably make it harder to get anything if we talk to him, but, if he's the one doing this stuff, we might save lives by letting him know we've got our eye on him. If only we had some physical evidence."

"We haven't got *any* evidence."

"Maybe we have to find Mackey's friends. We went through his place with—" Porter hesitated, "a fine-toothed comb. Here's a guy who makes his living with words, and he's got an apartment that's totally wordless—"

"Words? There *were* words. Christ, I forgot I wrote it down."

"What?"

"On the computer."

"There was no computer."

"On the what-do-you-call-it, the screen."

"Like a sticky note or something? We didn't see anything like that."

"No, no. On the—right on the box of the thing, the plastic part, there was writing."

Porter gave a dismissive shake of the head. "We saw that. 'machine number something or other.' So what? He probably had the thing in for repair and they wrote the invoice number on it."

"Maybe, but—humour me." Stark got his notebook out. "Yeah, here. Okay, let's call Bobby Payne and ask him what he thinks."

"Who?"

"Our computer techie wiz. Here's his number."

Porter sighed.

"All right." She took out her cellphone and phone book and dialled the number of the information-technology department at headquarters.

"IT, Payne."

"Just a minute," Porter said, and handed the phone to Stark with an irritated look. Stark glared at Porter and snatched it from his hand.

"Bobby?"

"Stark? Is that Stark?"

"It is I."

"You back from leave? How are you feeling?"

"Well, I'm not exactly back from leave. But listen, I want to ask you something."

"Shoot," Payne said.

"On the top of a computer, on the rim of the monitor, actually, I found this writing—" He read the notation. "Got any idea what that means? Oh yeah—" He gave Porter a look and kept looking at her as he said, "in front of the part that said machine number and all the numbers there were the words @Backup, and there were also the words 'dirt' and 'digger.' What do you think, Bobby?"

"It could be a user name and a password," Payne said. "Yeah, I'm pretty sure I know what it is. I'll just ask somebody to make sure. It shouldn't take me long. Be back to you soon. Are you upstairs? Stupid question. You never are."

"No, call me on my cell. You have the number?"

"I got it, Stark. I'll be right back at ya."

Stark handed Porter the cellphone with a self-satisfied smile. "He's checking. And what the hell were you playing at? Why didn't *you* talk to him? If the word gets back to Peters—"

"He's in Calgary on a convention."

Stark looked down the counter to where Boyd was standing. "Bert, you miserable old bugger. Sorry, I mean, you gentleman among gentlemen, could I trouble your good self to pour two mugs of your finest Arabica."

"Get it yourself."

Stark turned to Porter.

"I like a man who doesn't sulk. Get the coffee. You're younger. And I'm sick. Oh, and you're a woman."

Porter raised her eyebrows, went behind the counter and poured the coffee.

"Anything else, sir?"

"Don't be stealing any goddamned doughnuts," Bert said. "And by the way, for your information: one of my customers for flaxseed bagels? He's sitting right across the counter from you there." Bert pointed at Stark with his *Racing Form*. Stark's phone rang.

"Stark."

"Stark, it's me."

"Yes, Bobby?"

"Okay, it's an outfit in California that lets you back up your data online. You set up an account with them, and every day they connect with your computer and copy all the new stuff that you have arranged for them to copy. They do it automatically. There are lots of outfits like that."

"Jesus."

"Is that good?"

"It might be incredibly good. Can you get me their phone number?"

"I'll get it for you, but what are you trying to do?"

"I want to get some stuff that I think a murder victim might have had them store for him."

"You might have trouble. No, you *will* have trouble. They have all kinds of privacy things, you know. But listen, that 'dirt' and 'digger' thing might be the way into the stuff. I guess I'd better—well, where are you?"

"I'm at a deli. Why? What have you got in mind?"

"Well, I want to get you to a computer, and then I'll come and try to get the stuff for you."

"Yeah, Okay. Meet me at my place." Stark gave Payne the address.

He was ringing the buzzer at Stark's apartment fifteen minutes later.

"How'd you get here so fast?" Stark asked him.

"I hopped a ride in a scout car."

"You didn't tell them you were coming here, did you?"

"Hey, I've worked with you, remember? I told them to drop me at an address a block away. So, what's up?" Payne nodded at Diane Porter with the slightly embarrassed smile of someone not being introduced to a stranger. He wondered whether she was Stark's girlfriend, but thought better of it: she was too young and attractive to be one of Stark's. Maybe a sister or something?

Porter stepped over Stark's bad manners, and extended a hand to Payne.

"Detective Diane Porter," she said.

"Oh," he said, unable to hide his surprise. "How are ya," the lanky, gosh-darn-it thirty-five-year-old said, giving Porter's hand an awkward but energetic pump.

"The computer's in the back room," Stark said, leading the way.

It took Payne less than half an hour to connect to the data storage website pretending to be Matt Mackey operating from a new computer, to download the required software, and retrieve all the files that had been previously backed-up by the service.

"There you go," he said, folding his arms and sitting back with a wide grin.

"That's it?" Stark said.

"Good thing you've got the broadband hookup."

"The what?"

"The high-speed cable. Made it a lot faster. I pulled in everything this guy had the service back up. I hope what you're looking for is in there."

"Me, too," Stark said. "Wow, that's terrific, Bobby. I owe you a beer."

"You'll be drinking it yourself then. I don't drink."

"Oh."

"Makes me sick. But you can buy me a Coke any time, and one of those home burgers from the place down the street here. I love those things."

"You got it. Listen, do you mind taking a cab back downtown. I'll give you the fare. It's just that we want to get at this stuff."

"No problem."

Stark handed Payne two twenties.

"It won't be this much."

"Buy yourself a burger."

"I might just do that. Thank you, and good luck."

"Oh, and you didn't see me today, and you definitely didn't see me with Detective Porter. We're doing a bit of, you know, undercover."

Payne made a zipping motion across his lips. Porter saw him out. When she got back into the room, Stark was sitting in front of the computer staring at the list of retrieved files. He turned to Porter with a mocking smile.

"Okay," Porter said, raising her hands in surrender. "You were right, I was wrong."

"I don't know where to look first."

Porter looked over his shoulder, and then said in an ironic tone, "Well, you know, Stark, my best guess would be in the folder slugged 'books,' with the seven hundred and sixty kilobytes."

"Yeah, right. I know." Stark took a deep breath. "Here goes." He double-clicked on the file, and it opened, the page count running to three hundred and sixty-seven. "Lot of reading," Stark said.

"I'll go make some coffee. Do you know how to bookmark the text?"

"No."

"Here, I'll show you. You go under insert …"

CHAPTER THIRTY-ONE

"Where have you been? I've only got the biggest goddamned speech of my career to make and you're out—shopping or something." Yates was expertly applying make-up.

Mary-Margaret looked at her husband as if he were a dog that had just barked at her but had failed to interrupt her thoughts. Because he meant absolutely nothing to her, nothing he said had any effect. "You've spoken to the caucus before. Why is it such a big deal?"

"This isn't the caucus, idiot. This is the party executive, the key members of the caucus and some of the biggest movers and shakers in the country. The Compact arranged it. It's invitation only, no press. It's supposed to be an opportunity to meet the leadership candidates. Unfortunately, somebody forgot to tell the other three idiots about it."

"So, only one idiot will be there."

"Yeah, you."

"What a wit you are."

"That's one up on you, isn't it. For Christ's sake, hurry up and get ready. Where the hell were you, anyway?"

"Why would you care?"

"I don't. But you go wandering off on a day when everything is going to come together. This could be the day I become prime minister, or as good as. Now, I know you're just along for the ride, but this has a big payoff for you, too, right? So get it together."

Mary-Margaret sighed. "I went to see Martyn."

"Jesus, stay away from him. He could be doing these killings."

"Don't be ridiculous."

"Yeah, that's what Bernie says, ridiculous. Well, if it's ridiculous, then who the hell *is* doing it? This tie doesn't look right, somehow."

"Maybe it's like *The Manchurian Candidate.*"

"The what?"

"The movie where the killer has been brainwashed by the Red Chinese to bump off an American politician. Maybe when you make your speech tonight, the same sniper that got Lee Braddock will take you out."

"Thanks a lot." Yates shook his head. "So, what did Marty say?"

"He wasn't there."

"Where was he?" Yates said with a nervous edge to his voice.

"He was probably where you should have been, schmoozing with all these high rollers that are supposed to get you elected."

"No, I'm going to arrive after everybody has sat down for dinner, I make a big entrance."

"Be a really big entrance if somebody shoots you."

"Fuck off. Why did you go see Marty?"

Mary-Margaret shrugged. "I just wondered what he thought about the killings."

CHAPTER THIRTY-TWO

"This is unbelievable." Stark spun his chair around and looked at Porter. It had been easy to find Mackey's book among the hundreds of files retrieved from the remote data storage: it was by far the biggest file; Mackey had titled it *Scabrous*. "Unbelievable. How the hell did he know all this stuff about The Compact. It's as if he had been at the meetings. He must have had somebody inside."

"But why would one of them tell Mackey this stuff? They're all filthy rich. He couldn't buy the information from them. Maybe it was Braddock. Maybe that's why he was killed."

"Mmm. I don't know. Christ, we've got to nail these bastards. The two of them killed this girl and just left her there. We've got to go the office and look this up."

"I got all these files assembled," Porter said, "but I haven't had a chance to look through them." It took less than an hour to find what they were looking for.

"Here it is, Jane Doe," Porter said, flipping the pages in a file folder. "Cause of death blunt-force trauma to the frontal cortex. Vaginal tearing, lots of sperm."

"Would they still have that? Sure they would."

"DNA?"

"First we make sure they've got the sample, and then we go see the Crown."

At the Yates mansion, a pretty female servant paid no attention to Stark. She couldn't take her eyes off Porter.

"Hey, miss," Stark said sharply, "I asked you a question."

She gave Stark a disdainful look. "I told you, they're not here. I don't know when they'll be home."

"You see this?" Stark shoved his identification in the girl's face. "I'm not with the Jehovah's Witnesses. I want to know where the hell they are."

"They don't tell me where they're going."

Porter said softly, "Maybe there's a notation on a calendar or an appointment book?"

The girl smiled at Porter. "Come in while I look."

The detectives stood in the cavernous reception area. Stark watched the girl climb the wide spiral staircase. Porter watched Stark.

"I'd say you're just about fully recovered," Porter said.

Stark said absently, "Oh, yeah, but it's a waste of staring power: she's clearly only interested in you."

Porter shook her head. She scanned the brilliant white walls in the wide foyer that rose to the ceiling of the second storey. In the centre of the exterior wall was a long rectangle of glass bricks. "Look at this place, eh?"

"This is what you get for making ugly noises into a microphone."

"He was a good singer."

"Right." Stark shook his head.

"Look at that plaque over there: he won the United Nations Music for Peace award in 1975. Look at all the gold records, and two Grammys."

"Please, you're making me quiver."

"Your problem is you're hidebound. You have tunnel vision."

"Go on. Surely you haven't run out of metaphors."

"I mean it. You're so convinced that your music is the only music that you refuse to give anything else a chance, just in case you might like it. And that would never do, would it?"

"Here comes the girl."

Stark had a better angle to watch the maid come down the spiral staircase. She ignored him and again stared at Porter, smiling suggestively. She smiled back politely, but uneasily. The maid held out a sheet of notepaper.

"Listen," she hissed in a loud whisper, "don't tell them I gave you this. They'll fire my ass for sure. I found it on her dresser."

Stark stepped in front of Porter and grabbed the paper from the girl. On it was written "Granite Club, cocktails 5:30, dinner 7."

"How do you know this is for today?" Stark asked the maid.

"It wasn't there this morning."

"All right, thanks."

Porter nodded at the maid and beat Stark to the door.

CHAPTER THIRTY-THREE

Two former premiers of Ontario were chatting in the lobby of the Granite Club. As he passed, Stark nodded at them and gave the kind of smile you give to someone who is supposed to know you. They smiled back warmly, and after he had gone by, they leaned closer to each other and spoke, each clearly asking the other who that chap was who had just walked by.

"You know them, do you?" Porter said.

"I like to play with their heads."

The detectives couldn't find their quarry. Stark spotted a woman with a clipboard who looked as if she might be a club official.

"Excuse me."

"Yes, sir, can I help you?"

Stark said, "We're looking for an event at which Dennis Yates—Do you know Dennis Yates?"

"Of course."

Stark would have been happier if she had said no. He looked at Porter, who returned a so-there smile. "We're looking for an event at which he is in attendance."

"May I see your invitation."

Stark showed her his identification.

"Police. Is there some trouble?"

"No, we'd just like to see Mr. Yates."

"I'd like to have some idea of what it's about, to avoid any potential disturbance."

"We just want to have a quiet chat with him. We'll be the image of discretion."

The woman smiled weakly. "Very well, I'll take you to the room." She led them to a black door that bore a sign "private meeting." She looked at her watch. "They'll be having cocktails at the moment. Dinner will be served in fifteen minutes. Now, if you wait here, I'll go in and find Mr. Yates and bring him to you."

"That won't be necessary." Stark gave her a get-lost smile, opened the door, and before the woman could protest, he and Porter slipped into the room unnoticed. The room was filled with men in dark suits and gleaming black shoes, all standing in groups of two or more, all keeping eye contact with each other, all smiling, all with the same confident, erect stance. In each group, the listeners were paying rapt attention to the speaker, politely waiting their turn to contribute to the conversation.

Stark put a hand to his mouth and leaned toward Porter. "There's not a single ADHD type in the bunch. Do you see Yates? I wouldn't know him if I fell on him."

"I don't see him."

"What about Waterman?"

"You *know* what he looks like."

"Yeah, but I don't see him."

"I don't either."

"Well, there's a lectern. I assume Yates is going to make a speech. We'll get him then. It'll be fun. Maybe Waterman will come in with him. Go get us a couple of ginger ales from the bar there. We should blend in."

Porter looked at Stark's baggy green suit. "Yeah, right," she said and went and got the drinks. A woman came into the room through another door. When Porter brought the ginger ales, she said, "That's Yates's wife, Mary-Margaret. They've been married for years. They're supposed to be the perfect couple."

"You know all this stuff. Do you read fan magazines, or something?"

Porter looked at Stark and sighed. Mary-Margaret was circulating, smiling broadly, tipping her head from one side to the other like a ballerina, and offering her hands, palm down, to be held lightly by the fingers.

"She looks like Loretta Young," Stark said.

"Who?"

Stark looked sharply at Porter.

"She's coming this way. What do we do?"

"Nod and smile, for god's sake."

Before Mary-Margaret got to them, the woman who had directed Stark and Porter appeared beside the lectern and asked everyone to sit at the tables because dinner was about to be served.

"What now?" Porter asked.

"Let's sit over there." They went to a table in the far corner in front of the bar. "This is where I would normally sit anyway," Stark said, grinning. The only non-white in the room, a Chinese man of about thirty-five with a haircut that looked as if it had been done with a ruler and a scalpel, joined them at the table, extending his hand and introducing himself as Ken Wong. Porter looked nervously at Stark, recalling Stark's racist joke about two Wongs not making a white. Stark gave a little chuckle.

"Quite an impressive gathering, don't you think?" Wong said. "Who are you two with?"

"Security," Stark said, smiling.

"A burgeoning business," the man said, nodding appreciatively.

Stark shrugged and turned to Wong. "Burgeoning means to bud or sprout. Its current corruption has all but destroyed a beautiful metaphor and turned it into a buzzword."

Wong looked at Stark in puzzlement that turned to disbelief and finally to indignation at the realization that the man had actually corrected his English. Stark returned a smug smile and folded his arms. The servers delivered the food and the three of them ate in silence. As the coffee and dessert was being served, the door Mary-Margaret had used opened and two men came in. The diners rose and applauded. Stark noticed that Wong was particularly enthusiastic. Yates clasped his hands over his head in the champion's salute. Bernie MacIsaac scanned the crowd.

"Who's the other guy?" Stark whispered to Porter, who shrugged.

"Let's get him now," Porter said, "while everyone is chatting to each other and not paying attention to Yates."

"Nuts to that," Stark said. "In the first place, we should hang around and give Waterman a chance to show up; in the second place, I want to nail this hypocritical bastard after he starts talking about Canadian values; and in the third place, we're here, we may as well eat." He affected a toothy grin.

During the dessert course, Yates began touring the tables, shaking hands, trading quips, slapping backs, never letting the smile diminish. He seemed extremely popular. At a couple of tables, he was asked to sign autographs. When he got to the detectives' table, he embraced Ken Wong, who told him in a voice trembling with admiration that he was the only hope for the future of the country. Yates nodded politely to Stark and Porter, shaking their hands. After the walkaround, Yates returned to the head table. While the cognac and port, and cheese and crackers were being served, Bernie MacIsaac went to the microphone.

"Ladies and gentlemen, I was not expecting to be saying anything tonight, but Martyn Waterman, who was supposed to have been our master of ceremonies, has been unavoidably detained, so it falls to me to introduce our speaker. Let me introduce myself—" He went on to describe Yates as a lifelong friend, and to paint a picture of the man as a saint and a saviour, a defender of liberty, a guardian of freedom, a paradigm of decency, a devoted family man, and so on. Yates rose slowly to the exuberant applause, almost as if he were embarrassed by the outpouring of admiration. He paused, blew his nose on a bar napkin and shoved it into his untouched bowl of chocolate ice cream sundae, the folksy, homespun dessert selection. He loped to the lectern, perfectly timing his speech to start before the applause had completely died.

"I'm going to put this country back in the hands of those who know how to run it: you people here in this room." When the applause began to fade, he said, "I'm no economic expert, but I know you are, and I am going to rely on you. I am going to count on you and to trust in you, and together we will take Canada to the greatness it should have. Who here is fed up with being sucked dry by the left-leaning Liberals?"

As the applause broke out again, Stark stood up. Yates acknowledged his support, but gestured politely that he should sit. Instead, Stark, followed by Porter, who scrambled to her feet when Stark patted her shoulder, made his way to the front of the room.

"I see you're eager, sir, but we'll have plenty of time for questions later," Yates said with a nervous chuckle.

When he got to the lectern, Stark took out his badge and handcuffs. In a loud voice, amplified by the microphone, he said, "Dennis Yates, I'm arresting you for the rape and murder of an unidentified female."

As he handcuffed Yates's wrists behind his back, Stark recited as much of the police caution as he could remember. He and Porter led Yates out of the room. No one besides Stark uttered a sound. Both Bernie MacIsaac and Mary-Margaret had stood when Stark had approached Yates, but neither made any protest. The most damning aspect of the event was Yates's reaction. Not only had he not objected to being arrested, but his expression and slumping shoulders gave no suggestion of surprise.

When Stark and Porter got Yates to the lobby, Stark stopped.

"Take him out to the car," he said. "I forgot something." He turned and went back to the meeting room.

CHAPTER THIRTY-FOUR

Late at night, in the parking lot beside Cootes Paradise in Hamilton, a man carried a shotgun, barrel down, held close to his leg, the stock tucked under his arm. In his other hand, he held three green garbage bags, one inside the other, stuffed with something. He hurried along the edge of the water to a point where the trees concealed him from traffic on Highway 403. He listened for a moment, and hearing nothing but the whoosh of tires on the road, he swung the gun behind him and then forward in an arc, releasing it so that it rotated several times before it struck the water and vanished beneath the dark surface. He poked holes in the green garbage bags, found several rocks and put them in the bags, and tied the opening of the bags in a tight knot, pressed the bundle to expel the air and threw it in about the same spot in the water he had tossed the gun.

CHAPTER THIRTY-FIVE

While Bernie MacIsaac had been uncharacteristically stunned by the manner of Yates's arrest, he snapped out of it the instant the door to the conference room closed behind the two detectives. He took out his cellphone and speed-dialled the home number of the lawyer who acted for Dennis Yates Inc., and told him what had happened. One minute and thirty-seven seconds after disconnecting from MacIsaac, the lawyer had reached by cellphone, at a bar on Richmond Street, Ron Simms, one of the best criminal lawyers in the country. Despite his fifty-five-inch waistline, he had arrived at police headquarters seven minutes before Stark and Porter brought in their prisoner.

"Mr. Simms, how are you?" Stark said warmly.

"Tolerably good, Detective Stark, tolerably good," Simms said, removing an unlit but well-chewed Cohiba cigar from his mouth, and bowing.

"Do you know Ron Simms, Diane?"

Porter shook her head.

"This is the maestro mouthpiece, the king of counsels. He loves to eat cops for breakfast, and you can see, and I say this with respect, that he has consumed more than a few."

Simms bowed to Porter. Stark liked Simms. He enjoyed jousting with him, and the challenge of trying to beat him. Unlike most cops, Stark had no personal stake in what he did. He liked catching criminals, and the game wasn't over until the judge passed sentence, but he didn't feel moral indignation if the bad guy wasn't drawn and quartered, and he believed as strongly in the legal system as any lawyer. He recognized that he had the might of the state behind him, and the accused had the right to defend himself against that power. Simms knew all the tricks, had invented a few, and that was perfectly fine with Stark, who never took lawyers' attacks on his character or ability to heart, and frequently enjoyed a drink with them after the case was resolved, no matter what the outcome.

"I would like to speak to my client alone before you begin torturing him," Simms said.

"You'll have to ask Detective Porter. She's the arresting officer."

"Sure," Porter said to Simms, "but let us get him signed in and upstairs first. All right?"

Later, after talking to Yates, Simms gave the door of the interview room a rap, and Porter and Stark came in.

"My client says he has no idea what this is about. I'm impressed by the depth of his tolerance. He has no resentment toward you; he realizes you are meeting the responsibility with which you are charged, but he says it's clear you are sorely misinformed, and are most certainly being made the dupes of his political enemies, who have trumped up some charge in an attempt to destroy his reputation. My feeling is, an obsessive and delusional fan might be behind these allegations. I think we should be able to clear this matter up in short order and then we can discuss the steps to be taken to expunge in public fashion the besmirching of Mr. Yates's good name."

"He raped and murdered a teenage girl."

Yates shouted, "This is absurd. What girl? Where? When? It's insane."

"May 8, 1968, in Toronto. The victim was never identified."

"What?"

Simms raised his hands. He had put his cigar in the handkerchief pocket of his voluminous grey, pinstripe, soggy end up. "Wait," he said. "Nineteen sixty-eight? How old were you in May, 1968, Dennis?"

Yates thought for a second, and said, "I was eighteen. But—"

"Dennis, please." Simms turned to Stark.

Stark cut him off. "I told you, Detective Porter is the arresting officer. Speak to her."

Simms turned to Porter and flashed a quick synthetic smile. "Detective Porter. What evidence could you have that would link anyone, let alone Mr. Yates, to a crime alleged to have taken place four decades ago?"

Porter smiled. "I don't think I'm going to tell you that, Mr. Simms. I think I'll leave that up to the Crown. In the meantime, we're going to take a blood sample from Mr. Yates. You might tell him that we have the right to do that. Now, we'll leave you alone with Mr. Yates, because the evidence we have is compelling, and the blood test will be conclusive. Of course, if we are wrong, then Mr. Yates will be released with our apologies. But I think Mr. Yates will decide to tell you that his past has caught up with him, especially in light of what his partner in crime, Martyn Waterman, has told us."

Yates' head gave a little jerk at the mention of Waterman, but he said nothing.

Porter gestured to Stark and they left the room as Simms opened his mouth to protest, but was lost in the revelation that the media czar was somehow involved.

Porter asked Stark, "Did you see him jump when I said Waterman had talked?"

"That could backfire."

"How so?"

"Because Waterman will not utter a self-incriminating peep. Simms is going to know within five seconds that Waterman hasn't told you squat. The potential danger posed by Waterman as an unknown quantity would have been better to have at hand."

"Sorry—"

"Don't worry. The DNA is the thing we have going for us."

"What if they can't match the DNA? What if the sperm sample is no good?"

"Then, we'll be in shit. I'll meet you at the car. I don't want anybody to see me here. You make the arrangements for the blood and for Yates to be locked up, and then we'll go get Waterman."

Stark had descended into deep sleep in the car, his neck tilted back against the head restraint, mouth gaping wide, when a rapping on the window near his ear jerked him awake. He looked to his right into a vast expanse of grey pinstripe, protruding from the top of which was the smiling face of Ron Simms. Stark rolled down the window.

"I thought you got shot in the head?" the big man said, pulling his lapels together with a beefy hand against a cold wind blowing down College Street.

"What do you think this is?" Stark pointed to the scar at the left corner of his forehead.

"They'll never kill you, Stark. Say, who *is* this Yates guy? His civil lawyer was annoyed when I asked."

"He's a politician. He wants to be the leader of that loony Canadian Values Party. But he used to be some kind of rock singer."

"Canadian Values Party—I've heard that name before. He was a rock singer. Well, I'm not surprised. He's an idiot. I don't think you'll get him, though. I'm getting an order to stop the DNA testing."

"On what grounds?"

"Charter of Rights and Freedoms. There's case law. You have no reasonable grounds to obtain the blood sample."

"Sure we do."

"Well, you're going to have to show it. You lied to him about Waterman. I checked." Simms made a face.

"Ron, good luck with this one. You'll make a bundle out of the case, but the best you can hope for is a deal with the Crown. Anyway, I'm not going to talk any more about it. You'd better get a cab. You're going to freeze."

CHAPTER THIRTY-SIX

Martyn Waterman's apartment occupied half the penthouse floor of a building overlooking the harbour. Waterman had knocked down walls and installed arches so that about half the area, on the lake side, was in a single storey, with about eighteen feet of ceiling height, much of the space capped with skylights. The vast balcony was a garden planted with grass and trees and shrubs and perennials. Obsessed with privacy, Waterman, who had been married once, years before, briefly and disastrously, had no servants. When he wanted the place cleaned, he used the company that had the cleaning contract for his television stations across the country. A clause in the contract required them to have a team of cleaners at his condo within half an hour of his call, and he supervised the cleaning, moving quickly from room to room. His caution was understandable. The apartment was arrayed with more pieces of art than a small city's public gallery, from Jackson Pollock to Van Gogh, from Fra Angelico to a still-life by the Spanish artist Zubaran. There were Henry Moore sculptures and eight seventeenth-century Flemish tapestries.

Waterman had had a sophisticated alarm system installed, complete with video cameras and ultraviolet beams. In the foyer of the building, a security guard employed by the condo corporation sat at a desk facing a bank of video monitors. Most visitors to the building had to be admitted by the guard, who was required to obtain permission from an apartment resident before admitting visitors. Waterman's visitors, however, did not have to pass the guard's scrutiny, since the penthouse residents had a separate elevator, the door to which was opened by a key or by a signal from a resident's apartment.

Stark and Porter learned of the special arrangements for the penthouse suites when they queried the security guard about admission to Waterman's place. The guard was unhelpful, declining to concede that anyone by the name of Waterman or any other name, for that matter, was resident in the building. It was with the delight that such occasions brought him that Stark shoved his face close to the man's and told him he was under arrest for obstructing police, at which point, the guard eagerly gave them Waterman's number and told them about the elevator. They dialled the number several times, but got no response. Stark went back to the guard.

"Take us up there."

"I can't."

Stark loomed over the desk.

"I'm not allowed to leave my post"

"I don't have time for this." Stark spoke calmly, but with increasing menace.

"I'll have to call somebody."

"Who?"

"Another officer."

"Officer? What do you mean, officer?"

The guard shrugged. "Another security guard."

"Call him."

The guard made the call. "He's coming," he told Stark.

Stark shook his head. "Coming from where?"

"He's at the pool. Through the—here he is now."

A short, fat guard, whose uniform was too big for him, came around the corner eating a chocolate bar. He held it behind his back when he saw the detectives.

"What's up, Pat?" he asked the other guard.

"Take over. I've got to go with these guys."

The fat guard looked at Stark and Porter. They were cops for sure. They must have nailed Pat for selling grass. He had warned him to stick to selling to residents, but Pat was greedy, and suddenly outsiders, friends of the residents, and friends of their friends were showing up in the lobby. He knew it would end like this. He wanted to tell Pat to keep his mouth shut, but he was afraid they'd think he was in on it. Stark grabbed Pat by the shoulder to hurry him along. That's it, thought the fat guard, but they went to the penthouse elevator, and Pat used the pass key to open it.

The fat guard called out: "Hey, Pat, you can't go up there. Who are you going to see?"

Stark turned quickly and glared at the fat guard, who raised his hands in surrender and sat down.

The elevator rose rapidly to the penthouse floor. The door opened and they stepped into a wide foyer. A massive crystal chandelier hung from the centre of the ceiling. Long, narrow tables lined the walls, topped with vases filled with silk flowers. Track lights illuminated six large paintings that depicted impressionist reproductions of views of the city and the lake from a vantage point corresponding with the position of each painting. There were four doors in white and gold, three of them single doors; one, facing the elevator, was a double door. The guard led them to that entrance, and then pointed to a button beside the door.

"I hope you know that the instant I press that thing, I'm out of a job."

"As if I gave a shit," Stark said.

"Don't worry about it," Porter said, looking between Stark and the guard. "You're following police orders and have no choice. I'll write you a letter if it comes to it. Ring the bell."

The guard pressed the button. There was no sound.

"These apartments are totally soundproof. The guy in P3 brought in a rock group for a party. You couldn't even hear the drums."

"That must have been a relief," Stark said, rolling his eyes.

They waited, then Stark said, "Ring it again."

The guard did as he was asked, but said, "He probably won't answer. Nobody can get up here unless they're invited, and—"

"Open it," Stark said.

"Jesus. I can't—"

"Now."

The guard shook his head, but produced a pass key and unlocked the door. Stark pushed him aside and opened it.

Stark called out, "Martyn Waterman, this is the police. Come forward please."

The three of them listened. There was no response.

"He's probably out," the guard said.

"You stay here," Stark told the guard. The detectives began to check the rooms, of which there were twelve, not counting storage rooms and bathrooms. Porter went one way, Stark another. The second room Porter tried contained an incongruous combination of shelves lined with books on three walls, and rows of television monitors on the fourth. Each monitor had a label identifying it as carrying the signal from one of the stations in Waterman's network. None of the monitors was switched on. The light in the room was dim. Porter saw the screens and the rows of books first. She jumped when her gaze struck Martyn Waterman, who was sitting in a wingback chair in a corner of the room, staring. Porter's cop training kicked in. She ducked slightly and had reached for her gun before she even realized what he was looking at. She stopped in a half-crouched pose and then straightened slowly. Waterman's eyes were sightless. His white shirt and blue tie were in bloody shreds. Streaks of blood had dried on his face, some from dark spots on his forehead and cheeks, and some from splatters from the massive chest wound.

CHAPTER THIRTY-SEVEN

"What the hell is he doing here?" Detective-Sergeant Ted Henry spit the words at Porter, jerking a thumb at Stark. Porter, looking sheepish, started to answer, but Henry silenced her with a gesture and turned to Stark, who grinned inanely at his superior. "What the hell, Stark? Are you out of your mind? Peters is going to have your head."

"He's away," Porter put in meekly. Henry glared.

"Why didn't you clear out, and leave Porter here? You're nuts."

Stark shrugged. "I couldn't leave, Ted."

Henry shook his head. "After we get this done here, you're going to disappear, through the garage, hiding in the back of a scout car. Somebody told the vultures about this; a pack of them is out there with cameras."

"I don't think vultures travel in packs, do they?"

"Stark, if you don't shut up—Now, what happened?"

Henry rode back to headquarters in Porter's car.

"So, you've been barking up the wrong flagpole."

Porter looked at Henry.

"Watch the road."

"What do you mean?"

"You thought Waterman was behind the Braddock killing?"

"I told you, Mackey's book said it was the 1968 murder—of the girl—Waterman and Yates—"

"I've been blanking that thing out of my mind." Henry sat with his arms folded, looking straight ahead. "I read the note you left me. Very thorough. All about the book and everything." He sighed. "That was Stark's idea, picking Yates up in front of all those high rollers?"

Porter glanced quickly at Henry. "I guess so."

"You know, you need a little—" Henry sighed. "That was Stark's idea of a joke."

"We had the book, which was like a dying confession, I figure—"

"It's hearsay."

"Yeah, but—"

"To get the warrant that you need to extract the blood for the DNA sample, you need sufficient grounds. The Crown is going to have to argue that the book is enough. You did the whole thing backwards, and Stark knew it. You had to go to the judge first, get the warrant, and then pick up Yates."

Henry raised a hand. "It's not too late, but you can't hold Yates and you can't charge him. And we could be in the shitter—god damn that Stark. He knew better. Anyway, we have to get the Crown to argue the grounds to take the sample. If we can't get the sample, we haven't got a case, and then we're going to be facing a lawsuit and god knows what else. This could cost Yates the nomination. That was so dumb, so Stark's little personal agenda—" Henry looked hard at Porter. "You didn't have anything to do with the thinking behind this?"

CHAPTER THIRTY-EIGHT

The Waterman killing was a media event that rattled so many cages that Peters cut short his convention and returned to take personal charge of the investigation, which meant detailed daily reports to his superiors and (more important) standing in front of cameras and microphones and reading meaningless, vague updates. Both the detailed reports and the drivel for the news media were provided by Ted Henry, who was actually leading the investigation, which meant spending most of the day writing reports based on information from a team of detectives and "liaising" with the Crown. (He loved to use the word because it annoyed Stark). But there was little point in saying it now, since Stark was decidedly out of the loop. His role in things had been concealed from Peters, but Henry told him to keep his nose out, or it would mean the end of his career. Henry felt bad using the threat, because he knew Peters and others in the force had no intention of letting Stark return to active duty. They planned to give him a desk job, in the knowledge that that would produce his immediate retirement.

The investigative team found little to go on. There was a tape from a lobby security camera in Waterman's building showing a man in a dark suit carrying what appeared to be a brand-new blue hockey bag with a Maple Leafs logo. The man picked up the phone beside the elevator and appeared to speak to someone, who must have been Waterman, before the elevator door opened and he went inside. The person seemed about average height. There was nothing unusual in his gait or posture. He wore a tweed hat with a turned-down brim that concealed his face, and when he entered the elevator, he didn't turn around while the door remained open. When the elevator door could be seen opening later in the tape, the man was carrying the hockey bag on his right shoulder, such that the bag concealed his face from the camera.

Waterman had been shot from about five metres, and, based on the spread pattern and the plastic wad from the shell and the size of the recovered pellets, the killer had used a twelve-gauge shotgun, with .00 buckshot. At the centre of the pattern was Waterman's throat; pellets had also struck his chest and face.

Forensic staff repeatedly watched the video of the man in the suit; they blew up parts of the video, made prints of the parts that showed the hockey bag and the full body of the man and a close-up of his head, with the piece of cheek and chin and the tip of the nose that were visible. Investigators were assigned to take the prints to the Leafs souvenir shop and to sporting goods stores and department stores throughout the city to see whether someone recognized the bag or the man. When a credit card had been used to complete the purchase, they collected available information on the customers. Each of these customers was investigated and questioned, special attention being paid to any who had a criminal record, or who could not satisfy the investigators that he had a legitimate source of income.

With the assistance of the Ontario Provincial Police and three regional police services, canvassing was also completed of every purveyor of shotguns and shells in the Greater Toronto Area, in addition to every sporting goods outlet and department store. Staff in these establishments were shown the photographs and the gun shop personnel were asked whether anyone had bought three-inch SSG shells in the last month.

None of these queries proved of any value.

The killer had left no fingerprints. The tape ran for six minutes between the time of the man's entering the elevator and his exit from it.

Henry and Porter found this puzzling. The man was clearly somebody Waterman knew, or he wouldn't have allowed him in. It was hard to believe that the murders of Matt Mackey and Lee Braddock were not connected with the killing of Martyn Waterman. The weapons in the three slayings were different, but all three had a professional feel. The original theory that Waterman had hired the killer held together; if he had hired the man, that would explain why he let him in. But then why did the man kill Waterman? If there had been a dispute over payment or some such, one would imagine that an argument would have occurred.

"Unless Waterman was waiting for him with a bag of cash, and the guy dropped it in the hockey bag, took out the shotgun and wasted Waterman, who was the only one who could connect him to the other crimes," Henry said.

"Not very professional," Porter said.

The few prints that *were* lifted from the apartment that did not match those of the victim had been checked against the cleaning staff and eliminated. Fibres and strands of hair were plucked from carpeting and upholstery and placed in polyethylene bags for later examination and comparison, but were not expected to provide any assistance until and unless a suspect was identified.

Every member of The Compact was questioned and probed and prodded as much as was permitted by their political and financial clout. Because he was now being queried about anything he might know vis-à-vis Martyn Waterman's murder and not the 1968 slaying, Dennis Yates was again available for Diane Porter to interview, and under the law, Yates was expected to co-operate and assist the police in their investigation as long as he was not being asked to incriminate himself. But Yates refused to respond to any questions until the mountainous form of Ron Simms had darkened the entrance to the Yates abode and had threatened to spread the arms of one of Ridpath's finest examples of a Thomas O'Brien chair, into which the lawyer had slowly and wheezily lowered himself. Porter wondered whether it was fair for Simms to charge his clients for the time it took him to enter and position himself in a room and to rise and exit from same.

"Let us agree on the ground rules," Simms said, scrunching his rubbery face into an insincere smile. He raised a hand to silence the protest he anticipated from Porter, but they were interrupted by an opening door, and Mary-Margaret entered, followed by Bernie MacIsaac. Both Simms and Porter gave Yates questioning looks. Yates offered no introductions.

"I'm police," Porter said, as if explaining a grown-up situation to children. "Detective Diane Porter. I'm about to interview Mr. Yates about a matter—"

Mary-Margaret interrupted. "I'm not leaving."

"Nor I," MacIsaac said.

Porter looked at Yates, who made no reaction, and at Simms, who shrugged. Porter sighed.

"All right." She rolled her eyes. "Mr. Yates, I explained that I only want to question you about—"

"There will be no questions that connect in any way with the earlier affair," Simms said, "and I will be the final arbiter concerning whether Mr. Yates should or should not answer a particular question. Is that understood?"

Porter glared at Simms. She turned to Yates. "You knew Martyn Waterman?"

Yates made a face. "Of course."

"What was your relationship with him?"

"My *relationship*? He was—a friend."

"And political adviser?"

Yates shrugged. "Yeah."

"How long did you know him?"

"Since we were kids."

"Where was that?"

"Stoney Creek."

"I see. So, Mr. Waterman was helping you with your political campaign?"

"Yes. Does anybody want a drink? I'd like a drink." He looked at Mary-Margaret, who drilled him with her eyes. He made a face at her and turned to Simms, whose name he couldn't remember. "Do you want a drink?"

"I wouldn't say no, I suppose. Perhaps a cognac—"

"Cognac? Wait till you taste this stuff. Bernie, do you know where the good cognac is?"

"Yeah," MacIsaac said without moving. He and Mary-Margaret remained standing. Yates was sitting in a Louis XV reproduction chair, with broad gold and maroon striped upholstery. The room was furnished with a jumble of styles and periods, a few of the pieces antique, and a couple of art-deco items that actually went with the architecture of the house. Mary-Margaret had bought all the furniture, choosing things she liked, based mainly on their high price and colour. The most striking object—and incongruous even in that eclectic setting—was an incredibly ornate Bechstein, George II-style concert grand piano. It stood on six, "Chippendale-style, carved legs, the entire base covered in twenty-four-karat parcel gilt and silver leafed."

When it became apparent that Yates would have to get his own cognac, he went to an art deco liquor cabinet, "designed by Roger Heitzman of Santa Clara, California," found the desired bottle and poured a liberal amount into two Waterford balloon glasses.

"You won't want one?" he asked Porter.

Porter shook her head. "Mr. Yates, I'm told that Waterman was the chairman of a group of people who were working on your behalf politically, a group known as The Compact, is that correct?"

Yates shrugged.

"And Lee Braddock was a member of that group, right?"

"Just a minute," Simms said. He paused for a sip of the cognac. "This is delightful," he said to Yates, who smiled in acknowledgement of the compliment. "I'm afraid I must ask your indulgence, detective. I would like to have a brief discussion with my client before we proceed."

"Look—"

"We're trying to co-operate, but the process must take its natural course."

Porter sighed. "Go ahead."

Simms wanted to chat with Yates because this business of The Compact was news to him, and he wanted to know whether this Lee Braddock was the very wealthy, but dead, Lee Braddock he knew about. That he thought the information important was evidenced by his contemplation of an activity that required him to rise from his chair. With considerable exertion, he extricated himself from the deep cushions and led Yates to the glittering piano, which stood on a crimson-carpeted platform.

"Lovely instrument," Simms said to Yates.

"My wife bought the fucking thing."

"About this Compact—"

Yates was open and frank about the group's existence, membership and activities. He spoke with a resignation and boredom. His political career had come to a crashing end, and his life in the limelight was over. Being a star was all he knew how to do. Marty's death finished everything. Together, they had had a good chance of surviving the accusations of the girl's murder. It was so long ago, and Simms had told him they'd never get a DNA warrant based on hearsay, so they had no case. With Waterman's brilliant mind at work, they could have turned the allegation to their benefit: charges of political dirty tricks and the like, particularly with the *Gazette's* reputation as a super-Liberal paper. Without Waterman, Yates was through. Mary-Margaret and MacIsaac, watching Yates and Simms confer, knew they were through, too. His descent to obscurity would mean their own. The cessation of The Compact's funding would leave Yates without sufficient income to continue their lifestyle. Neither Bernie nor Mary-Margaret would have a function.

Simms and Yates returned to their seats. Simms took another sip of cognac.

"Detective, let me ask you: is your theory that the same person who killed Lee Braddock also did away with Martyn Waterman? And pushed the gentleman—?" Simms looked at Yates.

"Fielding."

"Do you believe the same person pushed Mr. Fielding in front of a subway train?"

"I can't tell you. But, obviously, all the victims were members of The Compact," Porter said.

"We can't see that Mr. Yates has any contribution to make to your investigation. We don't want this to deteriorate into a fishing expedition, do we?"

"I want to know where Mr. Yates was at four o'clock yesterday afternoon."

"Wait just a minute. You assured us that Mr. Yates was not considered a suspect, and now you're asking—"

"It's routine, Mr. Simms."

"I was here," Yates said.

"Did anybody see you?"

"My wife was here. Bernie, too." He looked at Mary-Margaret and MacIsaac, who returned his look. "Come on," Yates said. "Tell her."

"He was here," MacIsaac said flatly.

"Jesus," Yates said, shaking his head.

"Do you think that another member of The Compact might be the killer?" Porter said.

Yates shrugged. "I don't think so. These guys aren't—and what the hell for? It doesn't make any sense."

"Martyn Waterman never said anything to you that might point to one of the other members? He didn't share any suspicions with you?"

"No. He never said anything about it."

"When Fielding was shoved on to the subway tracks and then when Braddock was shot, you must have talked about who could be doing it?"

Yates shook his head as he took a sip of cognac.

"Come on, Yates, the book—"

Simms raised a hand. "Wait. That's an area that we're not going near."

"But listen. There was more in the book than—"

"Detective, please. Don't go near that, or that's the end of our discussion."

CHAPTER THIRTY-NINE

"The black guy at your place told me you might be here. Who the heck is he? Good looking guy." Martha Magliore had slid on to the stool beside Stark in Boyd's Best Bagels. She might have slid off again if Stark's body hadn't prevented it. "Oops," she said. "I'm a little pissed." She had both hands on Stark's nearside shoulder, her breasts sandwiching his upper arm. "Will you buy me a coffee?"

"Bert?"

Boyd looked up from the *Racing Form*. He gave Magliore an appraisal and wasn't impressed. He walked slowly along the length of the counter, poured the coffee and stuck the mug on the counter in front of Magliore, far enough away from her that when she retrieved her hands from Stark's shoulder, they were less likely to knock the mug over. Boyd raised his eyebrows at Stark in disapproval. Stark shrugged.

"Martha... Don't fall asleep. Here's your coffee—it's only two o'clock in the afternoon."

"The new holier-than-thou, sanctimonious Stark looks down his nose at people vulgar enough to get tipsy in the middle of the day, is that it? You never got drunk in the middle of the day yourself? Stark, this Presbyterian Simon Pure schtick doesn't suit you, old boy."

"You're using the allusion incorrectly."

"What illusion?"

"Allusion. Simon Pure doesn't mean priggish; it means the genuine article."

"Fuck off," Magliore said loudly, drawing a censorious look from Bert Boyd.

"What do you want, Martha?"

"I was in the neighbourhood, that's all. You're a friend. And right now I need a friend. You are my friend, right?"

Stark sighed. "Martha. Let's go for a walk."

Magliore wrapped an arm around Stark's arm and gazed up at his face with a little-girl expression. He led her across the Danforth. Jimmy Windsor, Stark's first-floor tenant, hesitated as he walked along the north side of the street.

"She found you."

"Thanks Jimmy. I owe you one."

Windsor laughed and went on his way.

When Stark finally got the star columnist to his house on Monarch Park, he took her up the stairs he'd had built at the back of the house to afford a separate entrance to the upstairs apartment. He had to practically carry her up the steep flight. She was leaning on him far more than necessary. When he closed the door, he turned and found himself wrapped in her arms, with her grinding her loins into his and trying to pry open his mouth with her tongue.

"Martha. Easy." Stark pushed her away. She clenched her fists and stomped her foot.

"Damn it." Her eyes were wet. Her shoulders slumped. "Shit. I'm fragile right now. I'm going through some stuff." She shook her head, made a little gesture of frustration and defeat, turned, walked into the living room and slumped down on the couch.

"I'll make coffee," Stark said. By the time he took her a cup, she was lying back in the corner of the couch, her head tilted up, mouth open, snoring softly. Stark swung her legs around on to the couch, got a pillow and blanket and tried to make her comfortable. He unplugged the phone in the bedroom. While Magliore slept, Stark read *Strangers and Brothers* by C.P. Snow. At five o'clock, he went to Beulah's for dinner. Porter called him on his cellphone.

"I think it's Yates," Porter said.

"I don't care who it is," Stark said, chewing.

"Are you eating?"

"Bread stick."

"You don't care who it is?"

"Not my case, Diane. I'm not going anywhere near it. I want my job back."

Porter was silent, then said, "They're not going to give you your job back, Stark."

"What?"

"They—"

"All I need is a clean bill of health from the medico, and I'm back in the unit."

"Henry let something slip today. He clammed up when I pressed him, but it was obvious. They're going to reassign you to a desk job. They're probably going to offer to promote you, give you more money and more responsibility; but they know you'll quit."

Stark stared into space. Finally, he said, "This is you surmising, right?"

"Not really—"

"What did Henry say exactly?"

Porter sighed. "He said, 'Stark is like my grandmother. She thought that because her brain worked fine, she could still do all the things she had always done. She nearly burned the house down twice and she kept falling off chairs she climbed on to change a lightbulb or something. Finally, we put her in the home. And that's what we're going to do with that old bastard.' That's what he said."

Stark clicked off his cellphone.

CHAPTER FORTY

Bernie MacIsaac cleaned out his office, put everything that was his, and a few things that weren't, in cartons, and carried them to his SUV. It had been a good ride, but he'd come to the end. He wasn't worried: with his contacts and knowledge and ability, he'd get another mount in no time. But this ride was over.

Mary-Margaret knew it was over, too. She was finally admitting the truth. She knew who had killed Martyn Waterman. She was glad Marty was dead, but she'd miss the money—not the sex, though. Martyn Waterman made love the way he lived his life—in control of himself first of all, but also in control of everything and everyone around him. Comparing the lovemaking of Waterman with Bert Bartram, Mary-Margaret's drummer-boy lover: Waterman was like calisthenics; Bartram was like tennis. You worked up a sweat with both, but one was routine, the other was a game. But Berty was going to be a player she couldn't afford. She was going to have to trade him for a less-expensive rookie. And then she was going to have to look for another husband. She had entrée to the right circles; she had aged well; in fact, she told herself she was better looking now than when she was young. And she knew how to pleasure men. She'd be fine in the short term, as long as she watched her spending. The kids were both at school in Europe, taken care of by a trust account administered by the bank. Eventually, she would have to tell them what was going on, but not right away. She knew what she had to do now.

CHAPTER FORTY-ONE

If the killer of Lee Braddock and Martyn Waterman was the same person, and if that person's intention was to destroy The Compact, the attempt was successful. Many lawyers made a great deal of money in a very short time, as the remaining Compact members sought legal advice individually and collectively, spoke to the other members and had their lawyers speak to the lawyers of the other members. These conferences were completed in a continuous series of discussions beginning minutes after the first news flash announcing Waterman's murder, and were conducted so intensely and concluded so rapidly that long before the first police arrived at the first Compact member's residence, all the remaining members had agreed upon and rehearsed what they were going to say. And long before those police arrived, communications had taken place at high political and criminal-justice and law-enforcement levels, and unequivocal orders had been issued that no information on the case was to be given to journalists except by Inspector Wallace Peters, who was himself instructed that he was to impart nothing substantive, and was admonished not to make any mention of a connection between Waterman's death and that of Lee Braddock, and that nothing whatever was to be said about any confraternity of which the dead men might or might not have been members.

The sum total of these efforts was that detectives' interviews of Compact members produced nothing to further the investigation into either killing, and the news media were reduced to quoting informed sources and suggesting alternately that Waterman had been slain by (a) a master burglar, (b) a jealous homosexual lover, or (c) [and this seemed to be given most currency] a male prostitute. About the weapon that killed Waterman, Peters told the assembled journalists, who shouted angry questions at him, only that it had been a gun. The journalists' anger rose with their frustration, and their questioning became increasingly impolite, but Peters kept his cool and his smile, aware that the cameras were recording his every action. In his mind, he projected a statesmanlike image, and he believed these were his shining hours. In fact, he came across as a blithering Pollyanna, who found something to grin about in the death of one the country's leading businessmen.

"Come on. It'll only take fifteen minutes." Diane Porter was speaking to Lorna Bede, the assistant Crown attorney on the Yates case.

"Do you know how busy I am, detective?"

"I really need that DNA warrant."

"When was the girl killed, 1968? Forty years ago, and you're in a rush?"

"My guy could flee."

"Did you tell him you were going for a warrant? That's pretty stupid if he's a flight risk. Anyway, I have to ask around about the circumstances; you'll just have to wait a couple of more days. Or just go to a judge yourself."

"Without this, we've got nothing."

CHAPTER FORTY-TWO

The night before Porter spoke with the assistant Crown, and after Porter had told Stark about the plan to force him into retirement, Stark had returned to his apartment to find Martha Magliore sitting in the kitchen, drinking coffee.

"You're still here?"

"Oh, very nice. Thank you," Magliore said. Her expression changed from feigned annoyance to pouting. "Starky?" she said in a little-girl voice.

Stark groaned. "What?"

"Let's do it the way we used to, Starky. Take me." She stood in the middle of the kitchen with her hands at her sides, fists clenched, a sulking child demanding sweets.

Stark strode to the door and opened it. Magliore watched, puzzled. He was at her side in three strides, grasped her by the elbow and wrist and led her to the door. "Goodbye, Martha," he said, pushing her out on to the landing, closing the door behind her and locking it.

For a few seconds, there was silence, and then Magliore began shouting obscenities and suggesting Stark was no longer a man and other things in that vein, including a threat of revenge. Her diatribe was short-lived, and eventually she stomped down the stairs. A few minutes later, Stark heard footsteps coming up the stairs.

"Shit," he said.

There was a knock on the door. He thought about not responding. The door handle was turned, the knock repeated, and then a voice said, "Stark, it's me, Jimmy Windsor."

Stark hurried to open the door. "I'm sorry, Jimmy. I thought it was—somebody I didn't want to see. Come on in."

"That's okay. I've got my accountant downstairs...That friend of yours who was here..."

"She left. Sorry about the noise. She's—a bit excitable."

"I see. She opened my door and came in. I was with Mr. Geopolous going over the books, and she said, 'That fucking asshole Stark, your fucking tenant upstairs'—she thinks you're *my* tenant. She said, 'He's dead. He's fucking dead.' And she left. I just came up to check—you know."

Stark chuckled. "I'm not dead, Jimmy. Thanks for checking, though. Very considerate."

"Your head okay?"

"Couldn't be better. I'll be back at work before you know it."

After Jimmy Windsor had gone back down to his accountant, Stark leaned his back against the apartment door, staring at the ceiling. After a time, he went into the kitchen, got a glass out the cupboard and put it on the table. Then he fished under the sink and withdrew an almost full bottle of vodka. He took it to the table and sat down, holding the glass in one hand and the vodka in the other. Finally, he said, "This is bullshit." He unscrewed the cap of the vodka bottle, stood up, carried the bottle to the sink and tipped it upside down, propping the neck up in drain. Powder the cat was rubbing against his leg.

"You wanna a drinky water?" Stark said in high-pitched cat talk.

CHAPTER FORTY-THREE

The following afternoon, Diane Porter was in Stark's apartment bemoaning that her Yates investigation was being held up. "How the hell are you supposed to do this job with no resources, eh?"

"Diane, you can't count on anybody but yourself and close contacts. Cultivate those guys and stick with them and don't go through damned procedures because they'll bugger you up. People're not going to help you unless you can make them an offer that will feather their nest. What's the assistant Crown care about a forty-year-old case where the deceased was a god-damned street kid?"

Porter shook her head. "We're only going by Mackey's book. How do we know he didn't have a thing against Yates, and was out to get him with a parting shot he wouldn't have to answer for?"

"Yates's reputation? I don't think we have to worry much on that account any more." Stark smiled.

"You landed me right in it, arresting the guy in front of all those high-rollers. Peters jumped on me with both feet."

Stark held a palm up. "It's your case. I was just along for the ride."

"Right."

"It was worth it to make sure that dick didn't end up as prime minister. And now we have to nail him—*you* have to nail him—for the rape-murder."

"I'm afraid he's going to skip before we get the DNA testing done, *if* we ever do get the blood sample."

"What's the Crown say?"

"Yeah, she thinks the book might be sufficient, a dying confession. She told me I should just go and ask for the warrant myself, but I don't know what the hell to say."

"Yates won't skip. He's going to try to ride it out, and with Simms as his lawyer, he's got a damned good chance."

"Not if we have DNA."

"That will only prove he had sex with a loose-moraled, pot-smoking hippy runaway. He's going to accuse the other two of killing the girl."

"He's still part of the act."

Stark shrugged. "Maybe I can short-circuit your little DNA problem."

"What do you mean?"

"I have a sample of bodily fluid from Yates."

"What?"

"Remember when I went back into the conference room when we nabbed Yates."

"Yeah..."

"When he got up to speak, he blew his nose and put the napkin in his ice-cream bowl. I got the napkin and the bowl and bagged them. I got a guy sitting at the head table to sign the seal, and I got him to sign a piece of paper on which I wrote something like, 'I saw Detective Harry Stark remove a napkin and bowl that had been used exclusively by Dennis Yates on such and such a date.' I have the guy's card. All you have to do is take the bag to forensic."

"Why didn't you tell me?"

"The blood sample would be cleaner. We—*you*—will have to convince Simms that the napkin exists and the sample is valid and so on. Or wait until they get around to testing it. And maybe the sample won't be any good. What we really want is for Simms to plead him. Although—I don't think he will."

"Why not?"

"The case will be so high profile. And I don't think the Crown would make him an offer he'd want. It's high profile for her, too."

"I'm aiming at Yates for the Waterman murder. No one else had the motive he did."

"To get rid of a living witness to the rape-murder?"

"Exactly."

"Don't you think he'd have been better off with Waterman around? The two of them could have ganged up on Mackey, say he killed the girl and lied in the book."

"What if Waterman didn't have sex with the girl? What if his sample comes back negative?"

"Yeah of course, you'll already be doing a DNA comparison on Waterman's blood."

"Maybe Waterman thought he could finger Yates and get a pass. Or maybe he told Yates he was going to give himself up? At this point, there's no one in this thing but Yates."

"So, you figure he killed Mackey? And pushed Fielding? *And* killed Braddock? Christ, was Braddock there in '68?"

"I haven't put it all together yet, but I still say Yates must have offed Waterman."

"No."

"If it wasn't him, then who?"

"I don't know, but you haven't got—*anything* on which to base a charge against Yates. Besides, Yates was at the Granite Club when Waterman was killed."

"Waterman was killed in the afternoon."

"Yates hasn't got the balls."

CHAPTER FORTY-FOUR

The next morning, as he read Martha Magliore's column in the *Gazette*, Inspector Wallace Peters'seyes widened in shock and then narrowed in anger, and finally returned to their normal, hooded, side-to-side-darting selves, and he smiled. He had Stark now. Gross insubordination, unprofessional conduct and lots, lots more. He had him good. He was going to be able to get rid of that smart-ass who thought he was too good to follow the rules, who had habitually disobeyed his orders and undermined his control of the unit. Stark wouldn't be able to rely on friends in high places on the force in this one. He was beyond that. This was the end.

Peters beamed with growing satisfaction as he re-read the piece: "Is there a connection between the slaying of media kingpin Martin Waterman and the murder of Lee Braddock, the high-rolling multi-millionaire hospitality-industry bigwig?" (Magliore had spelled Waterman's first name wrong, and because the star's copy was untouchable, the copy editor who had handled the column had been delighted to let the error stand.) "In his investigation so far, Detective Harry Stark has questioned Norton Fielding, another prominent businessman—" When he had finished the article, Peters put the paper down on the kitchen table, smiled smugly and folded his arms across his chest and gave a nod of finality, as if he had just watched a condemned killer drop through the gallows trap.

"You look like the cat that swallowed the canary," Peters'swife, Pat, said.

"Mmm. Oh very nice, dear. Lovely breakfast."

"I wasn't talking about—"

"Yes, just lovely," Peters said, shoving the newspaper in his briefcase and kissing his wife on the cheek. "Must go. I'll call you later."

Lovely day? Mrs. Peters thought. It was raining.

Diane Porter read the column over the phone to Stark. Stark laughed.

"Stark, it's not funny."

"You know why she wrote that column?"

"I don't think why is the question. The question is how. You must have given her the information. Why did you tell her?"

"I didn't. You think I'm nuts? Careless is what I am. My notebooks were on the kitchen table and the cow must have read them."

"You had sex with her?"

"That's why she wrote the column, because I refused to have sex with her. I had a thing with her a couple of years ago." Stark chuckled. "But I don't remember having sex with her. We were always so pissed, we'd wake up naked in bed beside each other, and I'd assume we had sex. All those times I got into trouble because lust clouded my reason, and now I'm in deep dung because I refused to have sex. It's really funny."

"I don't see the humour in you being drummed out of the force."

"In *your* being drummed out of the force."

"Stark."

"Marilyn called. Peters wants to see me."

"What are you going to do?"

"Well, first I'm going to see the doctor. My head is aching, my stomach is in a knot and I'm sweating like a horse. I'm tired out. After I've seen the doctor, I'm going to go see Peters and quit."

"You're just going to give up?"

"What do you think? You said they were going to squeeze me out. I'd rather go out in a ball of flame than a guttering bonfire doused with Peters'spiss. I'm not going to sit there while the sanctimonious prick lectures me. I'll walk in and toss my badge and gun on his desk and walk out, and that will be the end of it. The end."

CHAPTER FORTY-FIVE

"I hope you're pleased with yourself," Porter told Martha Magliore. They were sitting in her office in the *Gazette*. "You've destroyed the career of the best police officer on the force."

"What are you talking about?"

"That stupid column."

"It was as close to being dead on as I could get without being sued. And I'd be able to get the whole story past the lawyers if a certain policeman *friend* remembered that when a friend does something for you, you're not supposed to return the favour by spitting in her face. And I ruined his career?"

"He's on sick leave—"

"Because of my column?"

"He was injured, and he's not supposed to be doing police work. I asked him to help me out on the Mackey case, because nobody in the squad was putting themselves out to find the killer; they despised Mackey because of the stuff he wrote about cops. When the brass found out that Stark was investigating, they ordered him not to. You write this thing where he looks like the lead investigator on the case, and you put stuff in the column that looks as if it came from him. He's going in to quit today before they can kick him out."

Magliore put her head in her hands. "Why didn't the jerk say something? Damn it."

"If Stark is really a friend, you went to his place on a social visit, not to interview him. And then, when he was out, letting you sleep off a skinful of booze, you stole information from his notebooks. You could easily be charged with obstruction of justice. Do you know that?"

"They'd never charge me. Anyway, I wouldn't have written this if I'd known. Is there anything I can do? Stark's a great guy—not as much fun as he used to be—and I wouldn't do anything to hurt him."

"This great guy isn't the one whose notebooks you secretly pried into and he's not the guy you wrote a column about because you wanted to get back at him when he wouldn't sleep with you? That can't be the great guy, surely."

Magliore slumped back heavily on her chair. She made another fleeting effort to muster indignation, but that fizzled, too. Finally she said, "Is there anything I can do? What if I help him solve the case? Would that get him reinstated?"

"It's my case, not Stark's."

"But if it was going to get him back on the force, then you could give him the collar, or part of it?"

"What do you know about it?"

"It's not so much what I know, but who. I can get the goods on these guys—with your help. If we could work together. Waterman was the biggest fish in the media pond. Maybe Stark didn't tell you he's already interviewed people about Braddock. It was in his notebook."

"So?"

"This is no time to play coy. *I* gave Stark that list. That's how he knew about Braddock."

"What list?"

"Stark didn't tell you?"

Porter sighed.

"It was a list of people Matt Mackey was investigating. Stark asked me for it. People came to Matt with stuff—they come to me the same way—and you take notes, you take names, you make discreet inquiries around the periphery, and then you leave it alone because you've got a bunch of other stuff you're working on. We shared an office, and we bounced names off one another. One name he mentioned a couple of times was Braddock, along with five or six others. I didn't write down what their names had to do with, because I figured if Stark wanted to know, he'd ask me. He never asked, and then I see the names in his notebooks, so I figured he must have known about them from another source."

CHAPTER FORTY-SIX

Stark emerged from the doctor's office on Queen Street in the Beaches with a sardonic smile, but the twist had soon gone out of it. First, he walked down to the boardwalk at Kew Beach and sat on a bench. The smile vanished and he cried a little, looking out over the cold, grey lake. He thought about where he was and how he had arrived there, about what he'd been and seen along the way and what he'd missed. After a few moments, he sighed, slapped himself on the knee, got up and strode off, holding his head artificially high. Feeling the need for strong coffee and inane conversation, he got his car and drove north to the Danforth. Bert Boyd didn't disappoint on both counts. He was in fine form.

"Did you read this article on this old fart in Nova Scotia, sold this painting for a hundred thousand. Can you believe this?" Bert brandished a copy of the *Sun*. "Look at this." He spread the paper in front of Stark. "A kindergarten kid could do better with fingerpaints. Folk art, they call it. Piece of crap is what I call it. Listen: 'Its naïve lack of perspective is its strength. The unrestrained use of bold colours mark it as one of the finest examples of primitive painting by one of its most renowned practitioners—' and so on. And guess what that's supposed to be?"

Stark studied the photograph of a painting briefly. "A duck."

"You read it," Boyd snapped, snatching the paper away. "That looks like a duck?"

"It's got webbed feet and a flat, wide—bill." Stark held a hand up to his mouth, fingers straight and held together.

"The legs on the god-damned thing! It's more like one of those Florida things—a flamingo. Have you ever seen a duck that colour except in a kid's bathtub? It's bright yellow. Give me a break. I've got a cousin owns an antique place on Queen West, I could put my paintings in there and sell them for a hundred grand. I was good at art in school."

"Great idea. You don't mean the one that got busted for fencing copper wire?"

"You always have to throw cold water?"

"No, Bert, you should take up this folk-art stuff. This guy from the East Coast paints what he has lived with all his life. A fishing boat and a seagull up in the sky. I guess you could paint—bagels, maybe the coffee machine. The hat rack in the corner. That would be symbolic, you could have a blue hard hat and a fireman's hat and a nurse's cap, to reflect the eclecticism of your custom—" Stark turned around to find Bert on his stool at the other end of the counter, furiously turning the pages of his paper.

Stark took the subway to headquarters. The doctor had told him not to drive until he had another CT scan, so he thought he'd better look as if he were following the rules. The doctor was worried about Stark's headaches, and there were one or two other parts of the man's machinery he wasn't happy with, including the fact Stark got tired easily and couldn't walk up a short flight of stairs without breathing hard. He had ordered tests.

Stark hadn't been on the subway for years and had forgotten how much he hated it. Stark found most humans a waste of space and oxygen. He liked cats and dogs and kids up to the age of ten. He liked brains, especially in women, and particularly in good-looking women who were generous with their gifts. He could never recall encountering the things he liked on public transit, and today was no different.

At the first stop, a whale of a woman with two shopping bags found it too strenuous to walk ten feet to an empty seat, and instead beached herself beside Stark, crushing him against the panel between the seat and the car door without apology. Stark tried to pull himself away from her fleshy thighs, but they flowed after him, occupying the space he had vacated and pressing him still tighter against the panel. Despite the cool weather, the woman was perspiring, and emitted an odour like onion soup. She had bad breath, and worst of all, she insisted on sharing with Stark what should have been the private details of her family life, starting right in as if continuing a conversation she and Stark had already been in the middle of.

"My daughter, the one who lives with me, is thirty-seven, and I'm sixty-one, but who has to do all the shopping? Yours truly. And with my back. Sometimes the pain is almost too much to live with. How's your back? Back problems are the biggest cause of people taking time off work. Did you know that? They did a scientific study. The only thing worse than back problems is foot problems, and I've got them, too. So, who has to go shopping?—"

At Homicide, Stark marched straight into Peters's office. The inspector looked up with an angry expression, about to dress down whoever had barged into the room without knocking. When he saw Stark, Peters's expression changed to an oily smile.

"You're here. You got my message?"

"I was out."

"Well—sit down." Peters couldn't help a tiny snicker.

"I don't think I will, Wally. Here."

The "Wally" had Peters bristling, but he picked up the envelope Stark had tossed him without comment. Stark waited while he read the brief note from the doctor and reread it. Peters looked up.

"What's this mean?"

"Just what it says. I'm to go on a disability pension immediately. That means right away, now, today. It means you can't boot me out, because I'm already out. So, goodbye, Wally. Don't get up." Stark walked out of the office, leaving Peters with his mouth open, the doctor's note in his hand. Stark stopped in to see Ted Henry and told him the news. Henry said he was sorry and what a great cop Stark had been, and there'd never be anyone to replace him and what a privilege it had been to work with him and other lies. They exchanged hugs and pats on the back, both men awkward and uncomfortable.

"By the way," Stark said, jerking his thumb in the direction of the squad room, "if these jerks try to hold any kind of retirement do for me—not that they would—tell them I won't be there. But you and I will be in touch, I'm sure. I'll see you."

Stark walked out of the department without a glance. He didn't have to clean out his desk. There was nothing in it.

CHAPTER FORTY-SEVEN

Martha Magliore's bread and butter was creeps. Sometimes she exposed them, sometimes she threatened to expose them, sometimes she protected them, sometimes she flattered them, sometimes she even entertained them. She despised them, but she relied on them, and at times she despised herself for that.

The trouble with moving so much among creeps is that your judgement gets wonky. You begin to see everyone as a creep dressed as a sheep, and you begin to make heroes out of people who aren't heroes. The resident of the sagging semi-detached on a dead-end street in the Junction she was standing in front of would never be mistaken for a hero by Martha. In her words: "If you look up 'creep' in the dictionary, you'll find his picture." But this was one of Martha's protected creeps, protected because he was a fount of information on all things perverted and their purveyors and participants in the city of Toronto and environs. He possessed such information because he was a member of this fraternal and sororal netherworld. He was a reliable source; he took a twisted delight in exposing his fellow-travellers, and especially the highly placed ones. Secret lives were, however, generally safe with him because he didn't reveal them indiscriminately, but only when asked about a specific person and only when adequately compensated. Martha had a roll of bills in her pocket.

Terrence Fowland greeted Magliore effusively. He was a frighteningly ordinary looking man. (Martha would have said normal looking.) He had soft hands, with immaculate, perfectly manicured nails. His touch was gentle and caring, and he had a warm and appreciative smile. He was a wonderful listener, someone you felt you could pour your heart out to. He was the kind of man that mothers would leave their children in the care of. Men didn't like him because he was too attentive to their women, who found him highly entertaining, as did children. In Martha, he aroused revulsion. She didn't know if Fowland was a practising pedophile, and she didn't want to know. And she wasn't sheltering him from justice: the sex crimes squad was fully aware of Fowland, rousting him regularly. He had been arrested several times, but never charged. It was, Magliore told herself, possible that he only fantasized about young boys. It was possible. The walls inside the old house were a veritable gallery of depraved sexuality. It seemed to Magliore an anteroom to hell. Photographs, sketches and paintings showed people in a panoply of sexual congresses, many of them acts that Magliore could not have pictured in a lifetime of nightmares. But the images of rubber suits and machinery that distended and pinched and bloodied the intimate parts of the body did not disturb Magliore as much as the simple photographs of angelic-looking boys, smiling innocently for the camera.

"Ms. Magliore, beauteous and brilliant scribe, to what do I owe the pleasure? Come in." Fowland extended a hand, which Magliore ignored.

"You've redecorated," she said, scanning the grimy, peeling wallpaper and the mangy furniture.

"I don't entertain much, so there's just me here to look at it... Perhaps it is a bit—overly retro. Take a pew, or is this just a drive-by? I see you told the cabbie to wait."

Magliore put a hand on the back of a wine-coloured easy chair. Dust rose.

"I want you to look at a picture." The paper's photo department had produced a picture of Lee Braddock outside a meeting of the Canadian Values Party, talking with Dennis Yates. "Here." She handed the computer print-out of the photo to Fowland.

He immediately smiled and, with the lilt of a knowing question in his voice, said, "Oh yes?"

"You recognize him?"

"Which guy? Dennis Yates?"

"The guy with him."

"This one?" He pointed to a man in the rear.

Magliore pointed to Braddock. "Do you know him?"

"That guy?" Fowland shook his head. "Doesn't ring a bell. Who is he?"

"Maybe you know the name, Braddock, Lee Braddock?"

Fowland pursed his lips. "Braddock? Sorry. No."

Magliore shook her head. "It was something somebody said about him. I just had an idea he might move in your circle."

"Now, this guy I do know." Fowland pointed to the photo.

"Christ, everybody knows Dennis Yates, Fowland. Unless you're telling me *he's* a kiddie-diddler?"

"No-no, not Yates. This guy, the General. Fowland was pointing at the man behind Yates and Braddock.

"Who is he?"

"He goes by the name Robert Owen, very secretive, wears disguises. Even I, the omniscient one—is that the right word?—don't know his real name. He's big in some kind of industrial thing. Tons of money. They call him the General because he dresses his chickens in toy-soldier uniforms. He had a bunch of outfits made by a tailor, told him it was for a production of the *Nutcracker Suite*. A real weirdo."

Magliore met that comment with a slow turn and a wry look. "You're sure this's him?"

"He's got one of those unique faces. One of a kind, you know?"

"But Braddock, you don't recognize at all."

"Can't help. I can ask around. Can I keep the picture?"

"Sure, I've got copies. See what you can find out."

"I'll probably encounter some expenses." He gave Magliore an unctuous smile.

She took money from her pocket and peeled off some bills, handing them to Fowland and holding up the rest of the money. "If you score with Braddock's name, and if the information pans out, you can have the rest of this."

CHAPTER FORTY-EIGHT

"So why are you telling me this?" Diane Porter said. She was on the phone with Mary-Margaret Yates.

"I want Dennis to get what he deserves. I've known about that girl almost since it happened. The way they were acting, and Marty finally told me to get it off his chest, but they both said it was Matt who killed her, but they made him out as a hero. They said the girl threatened them with a knife, Matt grabbed her, and she was killed in the struggle. Over the years, I asked them about it a few times, and their story kept changing, from her being stabbed with her own knife to her being choked or smothered or something, to her falling and hitting her head on the bumper of the car. I was always suspicious, and then I read about it in Matt's book—"

"Mackey showed you the manuscript?"

"I found it here, downstairs, locked in his gun closet. It's like a safe, a big heavy steel thing, but I know where he keeps the keys, the idiot. They raped that poor girl and then they killed her, and poor Matt was just a kid along for the ride. He had nothing to do with it, and they blamed him all these years. And now Dennis kills Marty."

"Why would he have done that?"

Mary-Margaret hesitated, then said, "He said he couldn't trust anybody any more, that everything was falling apart, and he thought Martyn was losing it. He said, 'I'm going to have to take care of that bastard before he does it to me.' He said, 'I can't take any more chances. I'm not going to sit here like a dumb sheep and wait for the axe to fall. I've got to get him before he gets me.'"

"Do you have any idea how he got hold of the manuscript?"

"No idea. And he wants to use me as an alibi. I'm supposed to say he was with me the whole day and that we went to the dinner together. It's not true. He left early in the afternoon, and I didn't see him again till he walked through the door of the meeting room."

"You're at home now?"

"Yes."

"I'll be there in fifteen minutes."

CHAPTER FORTY-NINE

Gianlucca, the Italian cook at Beulah's, enjoyed his Marlboros. With some trellis from his garage at home, left over from building his grape bower, and a discarded roll of linoleum that had been lying against the fence at the back of the gift shop next door to the restaurant, he had built a sort of terrazzo behind Beulah's that afforded shelter from the elements. Aldo, the second cook, had sealed things up nicely with duct tape, so the rain ran off the lino roof. It was ideal in the summer, and as long as you wore a coat, it was fine in the fall. Superannuated plastic bamboo placemats from Lee's Golden Garden (Chinese and Canadian specialities) helped keep out the wind, while exhaust from the kitchen vents kept the edge off the cold. The smoking shelter hadn't gone through a winter yet, but Gianlucca planned to buy an electric fan heater and run a wire through the kitchen window. Aldo donated the seating, half a dozen white plastic garden chairs, which had been his only furniture for a time when he moved into his apartment after his wife threw him out.

Roger Sammon and Stark were sitting in the chairs and talking.

"I knew I wouldn't like it Roger, having nothing to do. It hit me the first morning. I've been off work for months, but I was always thinking I'd be going back, and I had things to do to prepare for going back, to speed up the process of healing, to keep in shape, to keep my mind sharp, all that. But I woke up today and said, 'Okay. I have to go to the market and buy a few groceries, and after that, what?' After that, Roger, not a god-damned thing. No wonder old geezers sit and drool: gives them something to do."

"Chill out, Harry. I'm drowning in your self-pity. Get a job, for Pete's sake. You're young."

"Compared with whom? Maybe compared with you—"

"That's enough."

"I have no qualifications and no aptitude to do anything else. Maybe I could deliver pizzas."

"They'd be cold by the time you found the address, and you'd never get the change right."

"Thanks."

"What about a security job?"

"Walk around a mall and talk on a walkie-talkie?"

"I mean a security consultant."

"I don't know anything about security, Roger. I've been in Homicide most of my career. I don't know anything about locks and alarms and background checks. Or fraud. I might be able to lie myself into the job, but I couldn't do the job, and I wouldn't want to. I'm on the side of the shoplifters, Roger."

"You don't have any—hobbies or anything?"

"I could go into business as a male escort."

CHAPTER FIFTY

"Martha?"

"Fowland. I hope you're not phoning for a friendly chat."

"I have nothing, but that's something."

"Translate?"

"Braddock's not a puppy-lover. The guy is as square as you can get, or, at least, he was. You didn't tell me he was dead. Somebody shot him."

"Never mind. How do you know he's straight?"

"I have contacts in high places, my dear."

"Don't call me your dear."

"Sorry. This guy is a total cuboid. He's devoted to his wife, pillar of the Catholic church, all that. A very bad example for impressionable young children."

"You make me sick. I'm not paying you."

"Hey, you wanted information on this guy, and I got it. I can't help it he's a dork. I got the goods: you pay."

"I said I'd give you the rest of the money if you found out anything useful about the guy. You found out zip. Goodbye."

CHAPTER FIFTY-ONE

Ron Simms's enormous form rippled with anger, like a huge dog shaking off rain. Porter was afraid she'd get hit with the perspiration that ran down the man's face. Stark could have told Porter that this was an act to frighten young, inexperienced detectives. Porter would have recognized that if she hadn't already been nervous about this arrest that was going to make the front page of every newspaper in the country. At least she had covered herself and had gone to Peters first.

The evidence was circumstantial, but strong, and she had been able to convince Peters and later, the Crown. What she hadn't known was that Peters would normally not have accepted a circumstantial case for the arrest of someone politically connected—and especially one with such a high profile, touted to be the next leader of the official opposition, with prime ministerial potential. He normally would have demanded an ironclad case, with direct forensic evidence or an irrefutable eye witness. But he had some conversations with key party members, at least one of whom was in The Compact, and they had all indicated that Dennis Yates's cord had been cut. Abandoned in the political wilderness, and without protection, he was the ideal trophy for Peters' ambition. The news conference had been scheduled for early the following morning, and the arrest would be kept quiet until then, giving Peters time to prepare.

Simms said, "You're out of your mind if you think this case is going anywhere except to civil court in a false-arrest suit. You don't arrest a man of his stature in that manner. You should have given me the courtesy of my bringing him in voluntarily. Your career is in serious jeopardy. Where is Stark?"

"Detective Stark has retired from the service."

"I just spoke with him the other day; he didn't say anything about that. You don't start on a case a few days before you retire."

"It's my case, Mr. Simms. It was always my case. Detective Stark was assisting me."

"I want to see the Crown."

"She said she was going dancing."

"This is a travesty."

"Well, sir, I'm about to interview Mr. Yates, and you are welcome to be present."

"You cocky little pup. I don't know you. Don't do anything yet. I'm going to call Wallace Peters at home. You'll be walking a beat in Fifty-One Division."

"You can call the inspector if you like, sir, but he's fully apprised of the situation and in total support of the arrest."

There was a flash of surprise in Simms's eyes, but the big man kept his front intact. "We'll see about that."

CHAPTER FIFTY-TWO

"Stark, I'm bloody sorry. Please let me make it up to you."

"Martha, haven't you done enough?"

"You treated me like shit, Stark. We used to have a good thing. How could you—"

"Martha, bugger off."

"Don't hang up. I've got some evidence for you. I can help you get back on the force."

"I don't—" Stark hesitated, and then, with a shrug, he said, "Okay..."

"You asked questions about Lee Braddock because his name was on that list I gave you."

"What list?"

"The list of people Mackey was investigating."

"Braddock's name was on that?"

"Of course it was. Wasn't that why you were investigating his death?"

"I was investigating his death because he was dead. Why was Braddock's name on the list?"

Magliore sighed. "I thought I knew. There was something in the back of my head that said Mackey had said Braddock was into kiddie porn."

"What?"

"But I talked to a guy who—knows just about every pervert in the city. Apparently, they trade things back and forth. They even swap kids—it's disgusting. And this guy's never heard of Braddock. I showed him a picture of Braddock taken with Dennis Yates. He didn't recognize Braddock at all. But he did recognize some guy in the background of the picture he says is a notorious child-care worker."

"Child-care worker?"

"One of their nicknames for a pedophile."

After a moment's silence, Stark said, "Okay, so—you have some information?"

"Yeah, well that's it. Christ. What if Fowland is wrong?"

"Who's Fowland?"

"The pervert expert. Suppose he's wrong about Braddock, that Braddock managed to keep such a low profile... I had Fowland put out some feelers, by the way—that's a bad choice of expression—He couldn't find anything on Braddock. But Matt asked me about Braddock, and there he is in this picture with a notorious pedophile standing right behind him, as if he was part of the little group in the picture."

"Where'd you get this picture?"

"Our photo archives."

"And the caption didn't identify this other guy?"

"Nope."

"Let me get this straight, Martha. How do you figure what you just told me is going to get me reinstated on the force?"

"Not by itself, but don't you think there are links? Mackey is investigating Braddock because he's supposed to be a pedophile. Mackey is murdered. Braddock was in a picture with a known pedophile, and Braddock is murdered. Martyn Waterman wasn't married or seen with women. Who knows how he got his kicks? Was he another kiddie diddler? And he's murdered."

"I'd say you're so far off base, it's not even amusing. But at least your heart's in the right place—perversion. Goodbye."

CHAPTER FIFTY-THREE

Ron Simms was triply offended: he was being forced to endure an interrogation conducted by a rookie homicide cop, and a female at that; the assistant Crown on the case was also a kid and also a woman, although Simms was sure she'd be replaced by a more senior prosecutor as time went on; and he was offended for his client, who was not being accorded the respect and deference his position entitled him to, magnified by eminent counsel. He and Dennis Yates were seated at one side of a table in an interview room in police headquarters, Diane Porter and another detective Simms didn't recognize, and whose name had slipped by him, were seated on the other side. They were being recorded by audio cassette and by a video camera. Porter had introduced everyone for the purpose of the recording devices, and then Simms had looked straight into the camera and declared:

"I wish to state at the outset that my client will avail himself of his right to silence. I also wish to put on the record that I regard this entire procedure as pure harassment. All right, get on with it."

Porter gave Simms a saccharine smile. She read a caution to Yates, and asked him whether he wanted to say anything.

"He already told you I'm not going to say anything."

"Let me tell you what the evidence is against you, Mr. Yates. Then you might want to consult with Mr. Simms in private and maybe change your mind about giving a statement. All right?"

Simms waved a hand, "Get on with it."

"You had a motive for killing Martyn Waterman. With Matthew Mackey dead, Waterman was the only living witness to the rape and murder of a young girl in 1968."

"That's nonsense," Simms said.

"Let's move on." Porter said. "You had motive and opportunity."

Simms held up a fleshy palm. "That's precisely what we didn't have. We were with our wife preparing for an important political speech and then we were at the venue where the speech was delivered, forming a contiguous flow of events that precluded our being at Waterman's apartment at the time of his murder. We weren't there, we didn't do it, and you have nothing."

"That's not what Mary-Margaret Yates says." Porter enjoyed the snap of the heads of Yates and Simms at those words.

"What?" Yates said.

"She says you left the house in the afternoon, and she didn't see you again until you appeared in the meeting room at the Granite Club."

"The bitch is lying."

"Calm down," Simms said. He turned to Porter. "There is an estrangement between Mr. and Mrs. Yates. It's clear to me that in a state of heightened emotion, Mary-Margaret has imparted false information for the purpose of harming her husband. We were present with our wife on the afternoon in question—"

"That's your story, fine. Let me go on with mine, all right?"

Simms waved his hand.

"We have motive, we have opportunity, and we have means. We searched your residence—"

"You did *have* a warrant?"

Porter shook her head slowly. "We were invited into the residence by Mrs. Yates. She permitted the search. In fact, *she* called *us*."

"Bullshit," Yates snarled.

"Take it easy." Simms patted his client on the hand. Yates jerked away.

"In the residence," Porter said, raising her voice, "we found several weapons, including high-powered rifles, shotguns and shells, among them double-aught buckshot. We compared the wads, and these are the same make of shell as the one that killed Martyn Waterman."

"And how many thousands of those do you think have been sold?" Simms scoffed.

"Under the box of shells, we found a copy of a manuscript." Yates and Simms flinched. "A manuscript written by the late Matthew Mackey. Interesting that you had a copy of it when no one else seems to have. No comment? Okay. The clincher? Your wife says that you said that Mr. Waterman posed a danger to your well-being, and you were going to eliminate the danger. I'm paraphrasing. The Crown will give Mr. Simms a copy of the statement. I have to agree with Mr. Simms when he says that you and your wife are not on the best of terms. I don't think she likes you at all, Mr. Yates. Would you like to make a statement of your own, sir?"

"There will be no statement," Simms said.

"Very well. I'm going to leave you with your counsel for a short time, Mr. Yates, after which I will return to determine whether you have changed your minds about saying anything."

CHAPTER FIFTY-FOUR

Magliore had borrowed a camera from the photo department without signing for it. She drove her own car, a black '99 Honda Civic hatchback. Knowing her limitations as a driver, her impatience, short temper and her propensity for booze, she rarely drove on assignment. The car mostly remained in her parking spot at the paper. At the video store, she saw Terry Fowland on the sidewalk, leaning against the front of the building. She pulled on to a side street and parked illegally, almost at the corner of Yonge. She shoved the camera into her jacket pocket and ran across Yonge, arrogantly raising a hand to stop traffic.

"Is he still in there?" she asked Fowland breathlessly.

"He's still there. Blue suit, white shirt and tie. You can't miss him. You got the money?"

"I'll give you the money if anything comes of this."

"Hey, come on, Martha. You wouldn't even know about the guy if I hadn't called you."

Magliore grimaced, but pulled out her wallet and gave him two twenties. "That's all I can spare; I didn't bring the rest. You'll get the rest if I can make anything out of this."

"I want a thousand bucks."

"Fuck you, five hundred."

"What if I went in there and told him you were out here?"

"Then you wouldn't get a fucking penny, and I'd kick your balls into your throat, how's that?"

Fowland angrily shoved the bills into his pocket and strode off haughtily down Yonge Street.

The video store door had sheets of orange and blue polyethylene across it in diagonal stripes, as did the front window of the store. The door opened, and her quarry emerged wearing a slouch hat pulled low on his forehead, his head bent forward. He turned north, walking quickly up Yonge.

Martha tried to get the camera out of her pocket, but he was too far away from the storefront to make a picture of any value, so she abandoned the effort with a curse and ran across the street, dodging traffic, and got into her car. She made a U-turn and pulled straight out into Yonge, cutting off a taxi, eliciting a long horn blast. She hugged the curb, driving slowly and keeping her man in sight. He turned on to a side street, and Martha floored the accelerator, weaving across Yonge through north and southbound traffic, producing screeching brakes and more horn blasts. On the side street, she slowed again, pulling to a stop when the man went into a parking lot.

He drove out moments later in a black Buick, turned left and drove toward Bay Street, Martha following. She pursued him up Bay and on to Davenport, where he turned right and made his way to Rosedale Valley Road. Martha followed him on to the Bayview Extension and then the

Don Valley Parkway, then up the 404 to the 407, on which the man drove west to the 400 and turned north. He stuck to the passing lane and drove fast. Fast didn't give Magliore any trouble. She could not conceal the fact that she was proceeding at the same speed as the black Buick and, therefore, could be following the car.

At Barrie, the prey turned west on County Road 90. Another car interposed itself between the Honda and the Buick, and Magliore thought she would have to pass, but the intruder drove as rapidly as the Buick and afforded cover. They turned south on County Road 10 and drove through the town of Angus, and then she saw the Buick's turn signal begin to flash, and she slowed, pulling to the side of the road as the Buick made its turn.

It wasn't till she had stopped that Magliore had a chance to read the sign at the spot where the big car had turned: "Canadian Forces Base Borden." She allowed the Buick to get some distance ahead on the access road to the base. She drove fast down the road, coming eventually to a guarded gate. She took out her press card, and showed it to the soldier who had appeared at the side of the car.

"I'm here to the see the CO."

"Do you have an appointment with the base commander, ma'am?"

"Not exactly, but tell him it's Martha Magliore of the *Gazette*, and I have a pressing inquiry involving national security."

"I see," the guard said. He took her press card into the gatehouse, and a moment later, emerged and returned the card to her. "Okay, ma'am, I'll give you some directions—"

When she got to the building the soldier had sent her to, Magliore was greeted by another soldier who conducted her into the building and left her sitting in an anteroom. He gave her a copy of *Esprit de Corps* to read. She had just opened the cover when another soldier entered, one with a coat of arms on the sleeves of his jacket, shoulders like a football player and a complexion like polished mahogany. Martha had an urge to whistle.

"Ms. Magliore, Chief Warrant Officer Wilson. I wonder if I can be of any assistance to you?" He had a deep, mellifluous voice.

"Maybe. I want to see the base commander."

"I'm afraid he's tied up today. You don't have an appointment?"

"No—"

"You mentioned something to the gate guard about national security. I wonder if you wouldn't mind telling me what that concerns?"

Magliore was on the verge of launching into her "you don't want to mess with me" routine, but the soldier's smile and his intense brown eyes put a hole in her balloon before she could inflate it. From his smile lines to broad forehead to angular jaw, there was a thin layer of politeness, and an underlying menace. Magliore returned a weak smile of surrender. "I'm not going to get to see the CO, am I?"

"Not today."

Magliore sighed. "All right, look. I've got this—" She fished out the copy of the picture of Braddock and Yates. "I'm doing a story. I've been following this guy." She pointed at the man in the background. "And I followed him here to the base. I think he's involved in—criminal activity. And I'd like to know who he is."

The NCO looked at the photo. "Isn't that Dennis Yates?"

"The other man."

"You think he's involved in criminal activity, but you don't know who he is?"

"He uses an assumed name. I don't know his real name."

"And what is this criminal activity exactly?"

"It's the kind of thing, that, if you're accused of it, the accusation sticks even if you're cleared, so I'd rather not say until I know for sure."

"Don't you think that's a matter for us to investigate?"

"Oh, so you recognize him?"

"I'm saying that *if* he is on the base, it's likely that he's military personnel, and accusations of criminal activity should be investigated by military authorities."

"Well, I just can't tell you."

"I see."

There was a knock on the door.

"Come in."

A soldier entered and whispered to Wilson, who nodded and turned to Magliore. "The *Gazette* says you are who you say you are."

Magliore gave a slight chuckle. "You don't read the *Gazette*?"

"Sure."

"You don't recognize me?"

He shook his head and smiled. "I don't read columns very often. I'm afraid we're not going to be able to help you today. However, I'm going to take a photocopy of this picture, and—we'll see what happens. In the meantime, there are proper channels through which to conduct your investigation at the Department of National Defence. Thank you for your concern."

Magliore's protests were met with smiling silence. The chief warrant officer waited while she punched herself into exhaustion. He took all her blows implacably, unflinching. When she was finished with her fruitless verbal assault, Magliore was followed off the base by two military policemen in a jeep. As she drove through the gate, she gave them the finger. She retraced her route along Highway 90, driving slowly, distracted, thinking about what she should do next, cursing herself for not getting the licence number of the Buick. Wait, wait, what about that general she did the nice piece on? He'd told her any time she needed anything to give him a call. She knew a few other military types, too. A military tow truck passed her with its lights flashing. She watched it absently, nearly running into it when it pulled in front of her and braked sharply.

"What the hell—"

An arm protruded from the driver's side, waving at her to pull over. She turned on to the shoulder of the road and stopped. The driver got out, wearing battle dress. He marched smartly, head erect, toward Magliore's car. She rolled down the window and looked up as the man stood beside her car. There was something familiar—

CHAPTER FIFTY-FIVE

"Here's your coffee. Tea is better for you. I always have tea now, except at Bert's: he hasn't got a clue how to make tea. How come you stopped drinking tea?"

"How are you making out, Stark?"

Stark leaned his back against the kitchen counter. "Is everything going all right? That depends, doesn't it."

Porter smiled.

"Depends on what you're comparing it with."

Porter nodded and sipped her coffee.

The kettle was boiling. Stark poured water over the tea bags in a huge brown Betty pot. He covered it with a tea cozy in the shape of a cat.

Porter chuckled. "Where'd you get that?"

"What?"

"The cat tea cozy."

"Don't say 'cat'; she gets jealous." Stark pointed at Powder, who had suddenly made an appearance and was rubbing herself against Porter's ankle. "That's amazing. She's never done that before; oh wait, except with Jane. I guess she likes pussy. Jeez, why did I say that?"

"Stark, that's beneath you. The *new* you."

"Sorry. I'm not sure I like the new me much. He's boring."

"Stark, *we* all like the new you, so don't lose him, okay?"

"I haven't got much choice. With this head thing and a couple of other parts that aren't working too swell, it's either the new me, or no me. I'm getting used to it. Like, I really like tea now. My parents used to drink tea. So did I when I was a kid. This is Darjeeling. Good stuff. I've applied for a British passport."

Porter gave her head a shake. "Where did that come from?"

"My parents were English, so I can get a passport. A lot of paperwork, but fortunately I kept all the documents. I'm thinking about going over there."

"Can't you just go on a Canadian passport?"

"Yeah, sure. I just thought that with a British passport, I could work there."

"In England?"

"It's probably a fantasy, and the chances are I won't go at all."

"Take it slow. Why are you talking about working in England?"

"Being a former Canadian cop, I might, you know, be able to offer a different way of looking at things, maybe set up as a private investigator, or something."

"Nobody knows you in England. You've got contacts here. If you're going to be a private eye, and you're doing a good job as one already, you'd be better off here. Anyway, I'm not going to pay much attention to you right now," she went on. "What you think is a setback—personally, I think you're going to see it as the best thing that has ever happened to you—but. In the real world, I've got news."

"What news?"

"I've charged Dennis Yates."

"You got the DNA results?"

"Not with the '68 case. I've charged him with the murder of Martyn Waterman."

"What?"

"Hey, relax."

"Why the hell would he kill the guy who was going to make him prime minister?"

"Because Waterman was the only living person who could link him to the murder of the girl."

"What about the other guy in the car? The one Mackey didn't identify?"

Porter shrugged. "There might have been another guy, and maybe they already got rid of him, or maybe he vanished. Who knows. Maybe

Mackey made him up as a kind of guilt surrogate to take the rap for him. Maybe Mackey was the other guy."

"The guy's nickname was Number Two. Didn't you know anybody who was always called by his nickname, never by his real name, except by his mother?"

"So?"

"You've got to be a guy to follow the train of thought. Let's say somebody hung the handle Shithead on him, right? So, another joker then euphemizes Shithead to Number Two—bowel movement? You remember your mother saying, 'Do you have go number one or number two?'"

"We never said that."

"Well, anyway, you know the term, right?"

Porter nodded. "If he existed. Maybe Yates just hasn't got around to him yet. He got rid of the two guys we know were there, Mackey and Waterman. He's a shooter, a hunter. He's got a steel cupboard full of guns. He had opportunity. His wife said he told her to say he was with her that afternoon. And he had a copy of the manuscript hidden in the gun cupboard."

"Mackey's manuscript? How'd he get that?"

"How do you think?"

"Christ. Did you find the computer?"

"No. But the tech lads looked at the videotape. We did some measurements at the scene, so we could figure out the height of the killer. Six feet, same as Yates. But the most telling thing: you ever noticed the way Yates walks? He lifts his heels way up, so he's up on his toes with every step. He sort of—lopes, I guess you'd call, bounces on the balls of his feet. The guy in the tape walked like that."

CHAPTER FIFTY-SIX

"Why did you follow me?" Norton Fielding was frightening in his battle dress. He was a tall man and loomed over Magliore as he sat in the passenger seat of her Honda. He had a handgun and a big knife on his belt.

"I saw your picture—here." She showed him the photograph. "You're in the background, and I know a cop who's investigating Braddock's death. I told him a journalist called Matt Mackey was doing something about Braddock and a pedophile ring, and a guy I know who's—a pervert, told me he didn't know Braddock, but he recognized you."

"Who did he tell you I was?"

Magliore shrugged. "He didn't know your real name."

"So, who am I?"

Magliore looked at Fielding and shook her head. "I don't know."

"Have you got a tape recorder?"

"Yeah, right here."

"Thanks." He took the machine from her hand, removed the tape and put it in his pocket.

"I've got notes on there."

"I'll mail the machine back to you. I'll tell you this because I want you off my back. First of all, I'm more than aware of who Mackey was. I'm sorry he's dead, but I was glad when I no longer had to worry about him. I don't know who killed him, although I have an idea. He was looking straight ahead, through the windscreen. "Mackey was blackmailing me. He found out that I get pleasure in a way that sanctimonious society frowns upon."

He turned toward Magliore. "I don't have to tell you this, but I don't have sex with boys. I do have a weakness in that direction, but I have always been able to beat that weakness by using surrogates. My sexual partners are boy-*ish*, but over eighteen. Nonetheless, the publication of that information would ruin me. I paid Mackey money, but that was like—conscience money, like a fine he had levied on me for my transgressions. What he really wanted, and what I supplied to him, was information on a group I belonged to until recently, a political group providing various kinds of support, some of it not entirely above board, to Dennis Yates. That's all finished now, of course. Do you have a notepad?"

"Uh, somewhere." She pulled a pad out of an inside jacket pocket.

"Okay, here's my proposal. Would you be interested in a complete story, names and dates, on this organization?"

"Sure."

"Two conditions. First, you take up where Mackey left off. I won't insult you by offering you payment, but in return for the information I will provide you, I want your solemn undertaking that you will not pursue any further information about nor make public in any manner my inclinations. Is that agreed?"

Magliore's expression at first displayed reluctance, but after a moment, her look turned to one of resignation. Finally, she nodded gravely. "All right."

"Tell me what you told the chief warrant officer."

"I asked him to tell me who you were. I showed him that picture, and I told him I was investigating you on a criminal matter, but I refused to tell him anything more. I didn't say anything about—boys."

"Young men."

"I told him I didn't want to say what my suspicions were in case they were wrong."

"What did he say?"

"It was obvious he wasn't going to have a discussion with me on the subject, but I got the impression that the army would be having a hard look at your activities."

"They won't find anything. In the meantime, I want you to telephone the warrant officer—I'll give you the number—and tell him it was a case of mistaken identity, that you were pursuing the wrong man, and that you have no reason to believe the person whose photograph you showed him is involved in anything, and you apologize. All right?"

"I'll do what you ask, but I'm not going to be held to anything if I find out you're stringing me a line. You understand?"

"The story I give you will be one of the biggest you've ever had. I guarantee that. And you don't have a story involving me. I saw you with Terry Fowland at the video store. The idiot couldn't have been more obvious. You can't see in through the windows of the place, but you can see out. I didn't recognize you, so I asked the store manager, who got very nervous. He knew you immediately. When I left the store, I saw you run across the street and nearly kill yourself pulling out on to Yonge Street, and then I saw you follow me to the base."

"So, why did you come here? Why didn't you try to lose me?"

"I had to be sure you were shadowing me, and when I confirmed that, my best course of action was to drive to the base and disappear inside where you couldn't follow. The best way to lose you was to vanish into the depths of Base Borden. I didn't count on your being quite so forward. When I saw you enter the camp, and I determined you were being interviewed by the warrant officer, I decided the only thing left open to me was to confront you and make you the offer I have just made. And by the way, if you were to contact Fowland now, you would find he's lost his memory. Fowland is a very venal man, and very concerned about being blacklisted. He will be of no further help to you in matters concerning me. Now, before I start giving you names that will make your eyes light up, you'd better make that phone call for me."

CHAPTER FIFTY-SEVEN

With the arrest and arraignment of Dennis Yates—the news of which drew the journalistic troupe as a sack of peanuts attracts attention in the chimpanzee cage—DNA testing of the sperm taken from the body of Rhonda Wilton and carefully preserved since 1968 was given top priority by the police brass. Samples of Yates's saliva, along with blood from the body of Martyn Waterman, were to be compared, the expectation being that bodily fluids from both have been present in the girl's body. Diane Porter was publicly congratulated by the inspector, who hinted at a commendation.

As these proceedings were under way, Mary-Margaret Yates was in a suite in the Holiday Inn in Hamilton. She had entered the building wearing a black wig beneath a kerchief and a pair of large dark glasses. That she was a celebrity trying to avoid detection was apparent to any observer, but just who this famous person was defied determination. A man had registered in the hotel and had been assigned the suite in which Mary-Margaret now found herself. Entering the building, he had shown no fear of being identified, and had signed his own name on the register. While Bernie MacIsaac had been the creator of one of the country's best-known popular-culture personalities, he was unknown among the hoi polloi. Mary-Margaret was sitting on the bed wearing an almost-transparent negligée. Her body was trim and firm, and she was as proud of it, as Bernie—who was walking around the room naked—was of his. They went to the gym together three times a week, usually extending their vigorous exercise sessions to almost equally athletic bouts of lovemaking.

"Why are you pacing?"

"Things aren't cut and dried. The whole thing is on a knife edge."

"Relax, Bernie. All I have to do is tell the truth and he's gone. Dennis wasn't there, and he did try to get me to say that he was there."

"But you know where he was."

"Not for sure. I'm beginning to think that maybe he did kill Martyn."

"Jealous rage?" MacIsaac said wryly.

"He can use that gun. You've been hunting with him. And that cop made him really nervous. He did say he was going to have to take care of Martyn."

"Dennis?"

"He was nervous because Martyn is the kind of person who figures he can win by stabbing you in the back. I he didn't do it, why wouldn't he get the chick to tell the cops he was with her?"

"She is married."

"I know."

"And rich. I'll bet she's left the country."

"If Dennis was with her, he'd tell the cops right away. So, I don't think he was. But what happens if she does alibi him and he gets off? No insurance pay-out then."

"It might take awhile, but they'll pay. We may have to settle, but we'll get plenty."

"Why would they pay if he's still around to make a record?"

"His only alibi is he was having sex with a married woman. That's moral turpitude, and he's covered for that. His value as an artist has always been tied to his image as the ultimate family man, and because he has that impeccable reputation, the insurance company was willing to underwrite the policy—for a big bloody premium, mind you. And his reputation is even more important now, because the only audience he has is older people. That's why we didn't put him on the board. If he owned the record company—as he wanted—he couldn't collect on something he had caused to happen and was in complete control of. This way, if he got caught with his pants down, at least we get something out of it. That's why I had him sign a real contract with BM Recordings, guaranteeing to make a record every five years. One way or another, after this business is over, he'll be a useless commodity. BM Recordings' great investment will fizzle. The insurance company will pay."

"But it's not going to come out that he was with her if she goes to the cops and alibis him and they drop the charge."

"We'll make sure it comes out. And the crap about The Compact. I've made bloody sure I've covered myself."

CHAPTER FIFTY-EIGHT

Twenty minutes into the interview, it became apparent to Fielding and Magliore that they couldn't continue to sit in her car. An OPP car had passed by slowly in the opposite direction. If he came back, and they were still there, he'd likely stop, and Fielding didn't want that, so they left and found a roadside café. It took two hours to finish the interview, and Magliore gave her solemn word she wouldn't betray her source. She told him she had gone to jail twice in her career to protect her sources, and had never given one up. When they parted company, Fielding offered her his hand. Magliore hesitated, but in the end she wouldn't take it. Fielding shrugged and cautioned her a final, finger-wagging time that she had not a single fact to link him to any illegal activity.

Shortly after Fielding had gone, Magliore's cellphone rang, and the *Gazette*'s city editor, Paul Carbray, told her that all hell was breaking loose, that Dennis Yates had been arraigned for the murder of Martyn Waterman, and that they wanted her back there to do the story.

"Jesus Christ, Yates charged with killing Waterman? Holy shit, this is fantastic. Listen, Paul, with the interview I've just finished, combined with this thing, I've got the biggest fucking story of the year. In fact, it's probably the biggest political story in this country's history. That's amazing. I guess you couldn't get me a helicopter?"

"A helicopter? Don't be ridiculous. Where the fuck are you?"

"I don't know. Near Barrie. I won't be long. This little buggy of mine can hustle."

"Well, for god's sake, don't kill anybody."

When Wallace Peters and the chief and the mayor read Magliore's piece the next day, they went off like rockets. Diane Porter hadn't made them aware of the full political ramifications surrounding the case against Dennis Yates: that Martyn Waterman's murder appeared to be linked to two other killings, those of Lee Braddock and Matthew Mackey, and the common ingredient was The Compact, the identities of the other members of which were so strongly hinted at in Magliore's article, they could be inferred by any reasonably knowledgeable person. Two of them were key elements in the mayor's electoral machinery. One was a regular golfing partner of the chief.

This time, the inspector spoke to Porter in private, figuratively knocking her to the floor and jumping up and down on her head in hob-nailed boots for a full fifteen minutes, after which Porter was taken to a boardroom in a part of headquarters she had never seen before and compelled to brief a glittering array of brass who sat at one end of a long table, while she sat alone at the other end.

At the opposite end of the table was the mayor, in a shiny silver suit and a maroon turtleneck. Beside him, in a blue pinstripe, was the Crown attorney. The case was now to be under the direct control of Det. Sgt. Edward Henry, under the direction of Inspector Peters, who would be in frequent consultation with the Crown, who would personally handle the prosecution. Reports on a daily basis—immediately on any significant developments in the case—were to be provided to Deputy Chief Rawlins, who would keep the chief and the mayor fully apprised of the investigation's progress.

CHAPTER FIFTY-NINE

"Is this Harry Stark?"

"Gee. Judging by the sweet sound of your voice, maybe it should be. Who are you?"

"Colleen McLean."

"I already gave blood."

"Don't hang up. You have no reason to be pissed at me."

"I prefer 'pissed off.' Pissed, to me, means drunk, and I don't drink."

"I told you I was a reporter. I told you I was doing a story. You knew that anything you told me could appear in the public press. What's your grievance?"

"Come on. You misrepresented yourself. That's my grievance. Christ. You were supposed to be writing for a little country weekly, and the goddamned story appears in the Toronto *Gazette*."

"CP picked it up."

"Canadian Press doesn't pick things up from local weeklies. And even if they did, and if you'd published the next day, they couldn't pick it up till then, so how could it appear in the *Gazette* the same day?"

McLean sighed. "They picked it up from the Hamilton *Spectator*. I string for them."

"That's the lowest form of casuistry."

"Okay, I apologize, but you should have a thicker skin by now. Maybe I had you pegged wrong."

"Maybe you did."

"Wait. I didn't call to discuss journalistic ethics. I have some information I thought you might be interested in."

Stark said nothing.

"Well, do you want to hear what I have, or not?"

Stark opened his mouth to say 'not' but produced a mumble.

"What?"

"All right," he said with a sigh.

"I think you should come here."

"What the hell for?"

"I think that what I tell you will make you want to have another chat with Peter Mackey. And because I'd like to make up for my slight subterfuge, and make you dinner."

Stark hesitated, but finally, after a dramatic groan, said, "Why not. I can be there in a couple of hours."

"I'll be looking forward to it."

Stark wasn't supposed to drive until and unless his tests were clear, but he wasn't about to take the bus. He wasn't sure his old car would start, he hadn't driven it in so long, but it cranked over fine, and within fifteen minutes of McLean's phone call, he was on his way. Retirement had decreased to one cat the number of people he had to answer to. Powder had a big bowlful of dry cat food and plenty of water, and he'd cleaned the cat litter.

He arrived at the office of the Grandfield *Chronicle* at a quarter to two in the afternoon. McLean came out on to the sidewalk and indicated for him to roll down the passenger side window.

"What?"

"Park around the back. The parking places are marked on the wall."

She was waiting for him at the parking spot. She wasn't wearing the bulky roll-neck sweater she had on the first time, but a white blouse and a black skirt that ended above her knees. Her legs were attractively swathed in sheer black nylon and supported by high heels. Stark noticed that beneath her blouse, she was wearing something frilly. Her hair had been done. She wore it long, and it was swept up dramatically from her forehead. She gave Stark a smile that made something catch in his throat.

"You're late. Which way did you come?"

"The usual way. I had to feed the cat."

"Come on in."

She led Stark into the building, but instead of going through to the front, she went up a flight of stairs. Climbing a few steps behind her, Stark felt that thing in his throat again.

They entered her apartment. It had a similar layout to his own apartment, a fairly standard pattern for a long, narrow living area above a commercial establishment. But apart from the arrangement of the rooms, nothing in this place resembled Stark's. He thought it could easily have been featured in *Better Homes and Gardens* circa 1962: lacy things and curlicues and patterns and needlework, everything colour coordinated and carefully positioned. Magazines were held neatly at the ready in a piece of furniture intended to hold magazines in that manner. A row of canisters in a yellow-and-green flowered pattern ranged in ascending order along the rear of the kitchen counter, like tin soldiers ready for inspection.

Something with a delightful aroma was baking in the oven, but there was no evidence anywhere of any preparation of the dish. Had Stark been cooking a meal for McLean at his place, he would have greeted her in a stained apron, and the kitchen would have looked like a bombsite.

She directed him into the living room at the front of the apartment, and he took a seat on an uncomfortably firm couch with rounded cushions in a smooth, shiny material. He feared he might slide off if he didn't brace himself with his feet. He was ill-at-ease in the room; it was an atmosphere in which bad language would refuse to be spoken.

And then McLean sat opposite him, crossed her legs, and everything changed. The contrasting background of the prissiness of the surroundings magnified her sexuality.

"I'm glad you came," she said

"Nice place you have here," he said lamely.

"I can't stand it. Everything is as it was when I bought the paper from Tom Crosby's widow. It's her stuff. I'm only here to sleep. That's why it's so pristine. You should see my bedroom."

Stark imagined he saw a sparkle in her eye.

"I spend most of the time in my office downstairs. I have a little fridge and a coffee machine there, and even a TV, and I almost always eat out, or order in a pizza. The cleaners who take care of the rest of building keep this place dusted and wash the dishes. They look after the whole place, except my bedroom, which is off-limits—to them."

Stark cleared his throat. "Well, it's—nice. It is a little—"

"Stuffy?"

Stark nodded.

"One day I might get around to changing it."

"It makes you look good."

"It does?"

"Yeah, it—Listen, you said you had something to tell me about Peter Mackey."

"Down to business."

"Well—"

"I read about the arrest of Dennis Yates."

"I'm not sure he did it."

McLean gave him a quizzical look. "That's an unusual thing for a cop to say."

"I'd better watch what I say with you, eh?"

"This is off the record. Anything that is said here stays here."

"Right." Stark chuckled. "What about Yates?"

"Not him; his wife. Did you know she was Matt Mackey's cousin?"

"I thought Martyn Waterman was his cousin?"

"Related to the mother. Mary-Margaret is the daughter of Peter Mackey's cousin. I saw her first on Main Street, and I recognized her right away, of course."

"Of course," said Stark, smiling thinly.

"She's like a Canadian Yoko Ono." McLean pointed a finger at Stark. "That's a joke."

"Yes."

"So I saw her on the street, and I thought, 'What the hell is M&M doing here?'"

"M&M?"

"Surely, you've heard her called that? I followed her, and she walked down Elm and up on to Peter Mackey's veranda and knocked on the door. Then the old man came to the door, and when he saw her he greeted her like a long-lost daughter. He threw his arms around her and kissed her and the whole thing, and they went inside. So, naturally, I hightailed it to Mr. Chapman in the drugstore. He knows everything about everybody in this town."

She gave Stark a self-satisfied smile. After a moment, Stark said: "Is that it?"

"Well, yes. Here's the wife of a famous singing artist and politician who's been arrested for murder, and she comes to see her uncle whose son has been murdered. Don't you think there's—a connection, or something?"

Stark shrugged. "You could have told me on the phone."

"I know—" McLean blushed. "I just wanted to make up for the story I wrote. I realized it might have got you into some trouble."

"It did."

"I'm sorry."

"So, maybe I'll go see Mackey before dinner?"

"Your niece, cousin—whatever you call her—was here to see you."

"So what?" Mackey was drinking coffee liberally laced with Wiser's Special Blend. Stark had declined the addition to his coffee. "She's my second cousin, or third cousin or somethin'. But I'm like her uncle."

"She's close to you?"

"I don't see her that often. Who told you she was here?" Mackey was staring into his coffee cup when he started the question, but at the end of it, as he took a sip, his eyes flipped up and looked hard and suspiciously at Stark.

Stark stared back until Mackey's eyes flipped back down. A thought popped into Stark's mind, and he kept looking at the older man as he tried to fit the thought into things he knew.

"She's been here a few times, a couple of times, anyway, lately, hasn't she?"

"That nosy old bastard Chapman tell you?"

"There's nothing wrong with a niece visiting a favourite uncle, is there? It's nice that she'd do that, especially now, with her husband in trouble."

Mackey made a huffing noise.

"What about Martyn Waterman?"

Mackey froze for the briefest instant, and then, as if he'd just remembered something but wasn't sure what it was, he went quickly to the coffee pot on the kitchen counter and added to his cup, then filling the vessel with an equal amount of Canadian whisky.

"You want some more coffee?"

"No, I'm fine, thanks. Martyn Waterman is a cousin, too? Matthew's cousin. You told me that the last time I was here."

"Look, I can't stand around here all day yakking."

"Do much hunting? I noticed the camouflage vest and hat hanging in the hallway."

"So what? Sometimes. I'd like you to go now."

"A while ago, Mary-Margaret was here for quite a long time, wasn't she? Did she tell you something about Martyn Waterman, about an incident that took place a long time ago, in 1968? Did she tell you what Martyn Waterman and her husband, Dennis Yates, had to do with that incident?"

"I don't have to tell you nothin'. Get out."

"Take it easy, Mr. Mackey. I'm the police. I ask questions and you answer. Unless you'd prefer to go back to Toronto with me and have a longer chat at headquarters?"

"I don't give a good god-damn what you do. I'm not telling you nothin'."

"Was it the second time she was here that Mary-Margaret took something away with her? Maybe some SSG shells?"

"What the hell are you talking about? She didn't take any goddamned shells."

"Your son left something here, didn't he, Mr. Mackey. He left a copy of his manuscript here, didn't he?"

Mackey glared at Stark. The look was enough to confirm Stark's suspicion.

"Did you kill Martyn Waterman, Mr. Mackey? Mary-Margaret told you where he was and how to get to see him, and what you should do, didn't she, Mr. Mackey?"

Mackey was shaking his head at Stark's suggestions, his face screwed up like a baby being forced to eat something unpalatable. He slammed the cup down. "Shut up. I didn't kill that sonofabitch. I wisht I had killed the bastard, but I didn't."

"Calm down. You didn't kill him. Okay. I'm going to go now, but I want you to think about doing the right thing. Just think about it, okay? One more thing. In that car all those years ago, there were four people: your son, Martyn Waterman, Dennis Yates and one other. There was one other person in that car, Mr. Mackey. Can you tell me who that fourth person was?"

Mackey was breathing hard, leaning back against the counter. He turned slowly and looked blankly at Stark. He took a deep, shuddering breath, half turned and retrieved his cup from the counter and drained the contents in one swallow. He looked into the empty cup and raised his head slowly. His eyes were wet but blazing, and barely audibly, through clenched teeth, he said, "No."

CHAPTER SIXTY

"So, is she a good cook?" Porter asked.

"As long as she sticks to the chicken casserole. Apparently that's the only recipe she knows."

"And what about the other?"

"What other?"

"Well, you did stay overnight."

"So?"

"Never mind. I shouldn't ask."

"You shouldn't."

"It's just that you seem rather cheerful. Doesn't he, Bert?"

"I didn't notice. I have other customers to serve, you know." The other customer was Roger Sammon, who sat in a booth, thumbing through a magazine.

Stark spun his stool to face him. "Why're you up and around so early, Roger?"

"The Greek gaucho has a luncheon do for the real estate office down the street, so he's paying me to play waiter, and I've got to get over there in half an hour. Bert, give me another coffee, and try to pour it from the bottom of the pot. I need undiluted caffeine."

Stark chuckled and turned to face Porter.

"You know I'm just a foot soldier on the case now?" Porter said.

"What happened?"

"Did you read Magliore's article?"

"Nope."

"Stark, she blew the lid off the whole thing. It was all over the front page."

"I hardly read the papers, Diane. You know that."

"Well, you should have. She had everything on The Compact and Waterman's connection with it, and Braddock. And she did everything but actually name the other members. When the brass read that, they went bananas, so I've been relegated to spear-carrier, and Ted Henry has been made lead investigator."

"Well, that's not such a bad thing. Ted's not stupid. Don't let it bother your ego."

"I'm a bit relieved, really. It was getting a bit heavy."

"Where did Magliore get her information?"

"She won't reveal her source," Porter said, with mock gravity. "She told me she'd take that information to her grave."

"She's nothing if not melodramatic, Martha."

"But I figured it out."

"Oh yeah?"

"And I'll bet he was Mackey's source, too, and I'll bet Magliore either found some of Mackey's notes, or he'd told her more than she admitted."

"So, who do you think it is?"

"Fielding. The soldier boy. Remember we went to his house in the Annex?"

"Right." Stark nodded. "Why do you think it was he?"

"He's the only major one not identified in the article."

"I thought you said she didn't identify them?"

"She put in where they live and what they own and how old they are and who they know and so on, enough that people in the know would be able to identify them. The brass *and* the mayor obviously knew who they were right away, and that's why the case became suddenly the biggest thing around, and I got the shuffle. Peters went ballistic. I'm not far from believing that if I had gone to Peters and told him about the connection between Yates and Waterman and The Compact and Braddock's killing and Mackey's killing and so on, that Yates would not have been charged. The fallout from this is going to leave stains on everybody's tie."

Stark chuckled. "Martha didn't put Fielding in the piece?"

"No."

"Could be she forgot, or he slipped through the cracks."

"Somebody told her all the stuff she wrote about, and it had to be somebody inside. And somebody had to tell Mackey; my money's on Fielding. So tell me, why did you go to Grandfield? It's hard to believe you'd be interested in seeing that woman again after she torpedoed you in the paper?"

"She's very nice."

"Oh, now she's very nice?"

"She had some information—about the case."

"Stark, you're—retired."

"Relax. I had nothing to do, so I went down there. She thought I might get something out of Peter Mackey, the father."

"And did you?"

"I think so, yeah."

"And were you ever going to tell me?"

"You asked before I could tell you. I think you've charged the wrong guy."

"Peter Mackey told you this?"

"Did you know that Mary-Margaret Yates is Peter Mackey's cousin? But she calls him uncle."

"I didn't know. How'd you find that out?"

"Colleen told me."

"The nice woman? How did she know?"

"It's a small town, Diane."

"What does that mean, her being his niece?"

"Before and after Waterman was shot, she was seen visiting the old man. He's not that old, actually, and he's in pretty good shape, apart from the fact that he's a bit of a piss-tank. Anyway, she was there."

"So?"

"Mackey's a hunter. He knows guns. He had a pretty good revenge motive for killing Waterman—"

"You think Mackey's father murdered Waterman? Give me a break, Stark."

"I still can't see Yates as a killer. He doesn't have the balls. He moves only when somebody pulls the strings, and the guy who pulled the strings was Waterman. If he kills him, he collapses on the stage in a heap of string and wooden pieces."

"If revenge is a good motive, survival is a better one. He thought he was going to get nailed for killing that girl in '68."

"What's happened with the DNA?"

"It's supposed to come down today."

"If it pans out you'll have a case against him for killing her, with direct evidence. But the Waterman thing. Frankly, with what's happened, I don't think that's even going to get to court. Mary-Margaret put the manuscript in the metal cupboard."

"You think she killed Mackey?"

"No. She got it from Peter Mackey's house in Grandfield. The son had begun visiting his old man in the months before he was killed. He left the manuscript there, and Mary-Margaret found it."

"That's speculation."

"No, it's experience and highly developed instinct. Ask her what she was doing there. Tell her the old man gave her up. Chances are she took a box of the old man's shells and put them with Yates's. Look for her fin-gerprints on the shells. Better: look for the old man's fingerprints."

Porter shook her head. "I'll ask them to check."

CHAPTER SIXTY-ONE

The biggest setback to that point in Diane Porter's young career as a homicide detective occurred that afternoon when the results of the DNA testing were delivered. The semen found in Rhonda Wilton's body was from one person, and the DNA extracted from that semen matched the DNA of neither Dennis Yates nor Martyn Waterman.

Less than an hour after being shattered by that news, Porter was hit harder when Ted Henry asked that she join him in an interview room to speak with a Mrs. Anne Nevins, who lived on The Kingsway with her husband, a prominent accountant, their two teenaged children and twin

English sheepdogs. Mrs. Nevins was the intrepid and embarrassed bearer of bad news—good news if you were Dennis Yates. In a gesture of selflessness and duty, she had come forward, head bowed a little sheepishly, but later, as she found her feet, lifted regally to take her due medicine without flinching, like any good Bishop Strachan old girl. She had presented herself, in the company of two lawyers, Ron Simms, representing Yates, and Hedley Austin, representing her, to disclose the fact that she had been with Dennis Yates in a compromising situation during the time that Martyn Waterman was murdered.

Porter suppressed with anger the nausea that seemed to fill every cell in her body. In trying to frame her husband for Waterman's murder Mary-Margaret had ruined the detective. Porter expected to be transferred to Traffic in Etobicoke before the week was out. As well as furious at Mary-Margaret, Porter was angry that Dennis Yates was going to get away with a murder he did commit. Peters and company would see to it that Matt Mackey's manuscript was misfiled in the bowels of evidence storage, never to be seen again. There would be considerable public relations tap-dancing and backtracking, and a sacrificial lamb or two—Porter's name no doubt leading the list of candidates—would be slaughtered. And then a great silencing blanket would descend on all until the news vultures got tired of hanging around and another lame beast limped into view to draw their attention. Porter was also angry that, with the disclosure that Yates couldn't have killed Waterman, that Stark's belief that Peter Mackey was the killer took on greater weight. But if Porter suggested that, she was going to do no more than aggravate the situation and add to the ammunition against her.

Porter went to see Mary-Margaret.

"They're not going to release him?"

"There's no evidence against him, with the exception, that is, of the evidence you planted."

"What are you talking about? I want police protection."

"Why, has he threatened you?"

"He'll kill me."

"I doubt it. Just move out."

"This is my house, too. I don't want him in here."

"Jesus, what happened to the world's most perfect couple?"

"Go fuck yourself. I want police protection."

"Get a court order."

"Shit."

"You know, when I prove that you brought that manuscript and those shells back from your uncle in—wherever the hell it is—Grandfield, I'm going to charge you with obstruction and perverting the course of justice."

"The only pervert around here is Dennis. What are you talking about—my uncle?"

"You went to see him—two or three times."

"So?" She was pacing, puffing furiously on a cigarette. "I can't leave here. It wouldn't look good," she said mostly to herself. "What can I do?—Wait, wai-wai-wai-wait. I know. I know." She picked up the phone.

Porter watched her curiously.

She kept pacing and smoking as the phone must have been ringing on the other end. She smiled when somebody answered. "Hello, you. Listen. No-no, listen to me. He's getting out. She said he was with her.—I know, listen. I want you to get hold of that concert security outfit. You know—the ones we used in Peterborough. They're from here aren't they?—I want you to send them to the house. And a locksmith. I'm not going to be here alone with Dennis.—Yes, it's better if I stay here. I can smell a really big divorce settlement, everything to little me, a freezer carton under the Bloor Viaduct for Dennis."

CHAPTER SIXTY-TWO

Norton Fielding took a step backward when he opened the door and found Stark on the veranda, grinning. Fielding was nervous. His voice cracked a little when he asked Stark what he wanted.

"Just a couple of questions, Mr. Fielding. May I come in?"

Fielding turned and looked into the house, as if he were trying to remember whether he had left the kettle boiling.

"Mr Fielding?"

"You'd better come in—I suppose."

"Am I disturbing something? You seem a little—distracted."

"Eh? No, it's all right." They stood in the foyer. As on Stark's first visit, the inner doors were closed. Fielding exhaled, and, as if the release of air had cleared his mind, he seemed suddenly in control again. "What is it you want?"

"Well—" Stark gave a brief, thin smile, "—a number of things have happened since we talked last. Martyn Waterman has been murdered; Dennis Yates was charged in the death; and Martha Magliore has written an extensive and thorough exposé of The Compact—of which you were a member. We wondered what Martha's source was for the piece, and so we asked her. I found it interesting that no one who came even close to matching your identity is mentioned in the article. Martha agreed not to include any reference to you—and your activities. And it seems that you made a similar arrangement with the late Matthew Mackey concerning his book. But Martha had Mackey's notes, tape recordings and the like, in which your name is liberally included."

Fielding folded his arms defiantly, his expression betraying nothing. "What do you hope to accomplish with this nonsense? Get out. I have a bloody good mind to make a formal complaint to the police commission."

Stark phoned Porter from his car. "Diane, I went to see Fielding. He didn't exactly break down in tears and confess."

"Shit, I should have called you."

"Why?"

"Yates is out, he's off the hook. Some woman came forward and said he was with her in the sack when Waterman was killed."

"I told you."

"You didn't know he was with this woman."

"I told you he didn't do the killing."

"It's worse, though. The DNA test came back. The semen didn't belong to either Yates or Waterman."

"The third guy."

"Sure, the third guy. What good does that do? Maybe Yates will give him up on his deathbed."

"Not good."

"So, did you get anything out of Fielding?"

"Righteous indignation. He was visibly shaken when he found me at his door. He's nervous about something. My gut tells me he's the guy who talked to Martha."

"I'm frozen out, Stark. I can't go near it. I'm just keeping my head down and hoping Ted Henry can protect me."

"Have you spoken to Ted?"

"No."

"I would. If anybody's going to help you, it'll be Ted. Talk to him. He likes you, maybe he's even hot for you."

"Fuck off."

"Sorry. Listen, I'm going to try a reverse. I'm going to call Martha and tell her that I know Fielding is her source."

"Martha?"

"Stark?—Gee, the last time we spoke, you told me never to darken your doorstep again, as I recall. Let me guess, you want something? Mmm?"

"Martha, Martha. Things change. Life is all hills and valleys, isn't it? That was a very interesting article you wrote.."

"I *am* surprised you read it. Thank you."

"I've been talking to your source, and, he had illuminating things to say about why you didn't include any reference to *him* in your piece. When I read it, I didn't think it could have been an oversight."

"You don't know my source."

"Of course I do. Norton Fielding is a bit of an odd duck. I shouldn't think you and he would get along very well."

Stark could almost hear her thinking. Her next word rang out like a shot.

"Fowland."

"Mmm."

"It *was* that bastard, wasn't it?"

"I can't reveal my sources, Martha."

CHAPTER SIXTY-THREE

Powder was licking Stark's hair furiously. Stark pushed the cat away in his sleep, but the beast persisted, returning again and again until Stark swung his feet to the floor and sat on the edge of the bed, pressing his face into his hands. The cat leapt from the pillow as if given an electric shock. Leaving a short squeal in its wake, it ran from the room, and Stark knew that it would head for the kitchen to pace in front of its bowl until he fed it. If he wanted more sleep, he would have to shut the bedroom door, but he rose and stretched, made his way into the kitchen and dropped a couple of handfuls of food into the cat's bowl, Powder's head pushing his hand away.

Stark boiled water for tea and sat at the kitchen table, reading *Strangers and Brothers* again. The headache he had gone to bed with had disappeared. He had an appointment that morning with the neurologist. He was anxious to hear what the man had to say. Stark never wanted to delay bad news, nor good news for that matter. He had no patience for anything, and while he had always had difficulty delaying gratification, he could stand putting off pain even less. If he had a series of tasks to do, he always did the most unpleasant first, followed by the next most unpleasant and so on. He saw the fear of the pain as being part of the pain, a part he could avoid by getting over the actual painful thing as quickly as possible.

His appointment was at ten-fifteen, but if he could have gone to the doctor's office at that moment, he would have. As it was, he arrived half an hour early, and sat in the waiting room, reading *Chatelaine*s and *Canadian Living*s until ten-thirty-seven, when the nurse took him to the examination room, where he sat reading the *Compendium of Pharmaceuticals and Specialties* until ten-forty-two when the door opened and the doctor, a tall, lanky man in a green checked sports shirt and chocolate brown, wide-wale corduroys, practically fell into the room.

"Sorry to keep you waiting, Mr.—" He had to consult the file for the name—"Stark."

"That's all right," Stark said, smiling weakly. He didn't think it was a good idea to antagonize the man who held your life in his hands, even one who kept you waiting nearly half an hour and then couldn't remember your name, even after he had written a report that could get you a disability pension.

The doctor returned a professional smile and consulted the file. "Ah yes, good. Mmm hmm, good, yes. Okay, well, Mr. Stark, good news. Everything looks pretty clear, but I'm afraid your headaches will continue for some time. They'll get less intense and more infrequent as time goes on. But no hockey, no football, nothing in which you are at risk of receiving a blow to the head. That's out, at least for the next year or so. You can drive, do anything that you have always done, but keep away from anything where you might get bashed in the head. Don't do squash, for instance, but tennis would be fine. You should exercise. Start moderately, don't strain yourself. All right?"

CHAPTER SIXTY-FOUR

Terry Fowland's voice on the phone sounded wired, too up, too bright and bouncy. "Hi, Martha, it's Terry. How are you doing?"

"Fowland?"

"You got it." He burbled a laugh.

"You sonofabitch, you spoke to the cops, didn't you? How much did you get from *them*, you bastard?"

"I didn't talk to the cops. Why would I do that?"

"For the same reason you talk to me, you prick, for money. You told them about Fielding."

"Who?"

"What do you want?"

"I want to see you. I've got something for you."

"AIDS?"

"No, great information, really hot."

"Tell me on the phone."

"Too risky. No, you'd better come here. I'll be waiting."

There was almost always a line of cabs outside the paper, so it was rarely necessary to phone for one. Martha was going through the front door, about to gesture to the first cab in line, when Len Kraft, a freelance photographer, spotted her. Kraft knew Martha did juicy stories and rarely brought a photographer.

"Martha? Want a ride?"

"I'm going to take a cab, Lenny."

"I can drive you. I'm not doing anything."

"There's nothing in it, Lenny. There's no picture."

"Aw, come on."

Magliore shrugged. "Why not?"

It wasn't until they got to Fowland's house that Magliore realized she'd made a mistake letting Kraft drive her. "Damn it. Shit. Why didn't I think. I should have taken a cab, Lenny. You can't come inside, and I don't know how long I'll be. Now, I'm going to have to call a cab to take me back and wait in there for the bloody thing to come. Shit."

"Hey, no problem. I'll hang here. I've got nothing going on. Bertwhistle's running the department today, and he doesn't like me, so I was only going in to chew the fat with the guys. There's some interesting old places here. I might snap a couple of texture shots. Take your time."

Magliore rang Fowland's door bell. The door opened almost immediately. Fowland was standing nervously in the hallway. Magliore marched into the house so intent on lashing into Fowland that the thought didn't register that the man couldn't have opened the door and stepped back ten feet without her having seen him move. It wasn't until she heard the door close behind her that she realized somebody else was in the hallway behind the door. Norton Fielding.

Len Kraft was surprised to see Magliore come out of the house after only a few minutes, since she had implied she might be a long time. Two men came out of the house close behind Martha. Automatically, Kraft started snapping pictures of the trio. He was even more surprised when Martha got into the front passenger seat of a rather battered and ancient Volkswagen Jetta, and one of the men got into the driver's side; the other man got into the back seat. They drove away, Martha not acknowledging Kraft in any way.

"What the hell."

Except for a few moments of anger, Kraft didn't think any more about what had just happened. It wasn't the first time that Martha had left a photographer cooling his heels while she slipped out a side door with a subject. In fact, helping people evade the news media hordes was part of Magliore's stock-in-trade, gaining her grateful exclusive interviews. Kraft hurried back to the *Gazette*. He would have been eager to share the fact that he had been the subject of such abuse at the hands of *any* smart-ass reporter. That it was Magliore who had abused him would add immensely to the significance of the incident, and would be ever-accreting fodder for a story he would endeavour to embellish into an element of journalistic legend.

Amanda Dworkin entered the photo department as Kraft was telling the tale for the fifth time. He stopped when he saw her.

"Hi, guys. Has anybody seen Martha?"

"Yeah," Kraft said.

"Where?"

"I gave her a ride."

"Where'd you take her?"

"Some house in the Junction."

"What was she going there for?"

"She didn't say."

"Well, why did she go with you?"

"She didn't have a photographer with her, and well, she tends not to think in terms of pictures. So I figured I'd take her in case there was something to shoot."

"And was there? What was she doing there?"

"She went into the house and I waited outside, and then she came out with these two guys and they got into a car and drove off."

"She just left with two men without saying anything to you?"

"Exactly."

Dworkin shook her head. "Okay, where was this house?"

"She just gave me directions. I didn't pay any attention to the street name, but I can show you on the map."

Dworkin rarely worried about the well-being of Martha Magliore, but she was concerned now, because Magliore owed her a column, and her deadline had passed a half hour ago. Magliore never missed a deadline. And Dworkin was concerned because Magliore had left the photographer standing on the sidewalk, and driven off without so much as a wave. While it was true that she could become fixated on a subject and pass you in the hallway without acknowledgement, she wouldn't have forgotten that the freelance had driven her there and was parked on the street waiting. Magliore was pushy, brash and sometimes vulgar, but she was considerate of others at any level. Ignoring the photographer was a signal, Dworkin thought. If Kraft had been a little faster with his brain than his shutter, he would have followed Magliore. Dworkin trotted to the photo department. Kraft was telling his story yet again.

"I don't suppose you took any pictures of Martha and the two men?"

"Yeah."

"Where are they?"

"I haven't taken the film out of my camera."

Dworkin sighed. "Aren't you digital?"

"Yeah, but I still use film for my own work. I was just taking a few—"

"Just get me some prints as fast as you bloody well can, all right?"

"Right away."

Dworkin hurried back to her office and found Stark's card in her desk drawer. He'd told her to use his cellphone number.

"Hello."

"Detective Stark?"

"Who is this?"

"Amanda Dworkin, at the *Gazette.*"

"What can I do for you?"

"It's Martha Magliore. I'm worried. She's sort of missing."

"Sort of missing? When I said I sort of knew Martha, you thought *that* was an odd construction, but sort of missing, I think you've topped me."

"The thing is, you do know her. That's why I called you. I couldn't dial 911: they'd tell me to take a pill. She was seen getting into a car with two men. She hasn't filed her column. We had to fill with wire copy for first edition. She left her computer on, and the column is there, half written. That's not like her. And she left a photographer standing in the road without looking at him. I think she wanted him to follow her, and she didn't want the two men to realize he was with her. Maybe they were armed."

"I don't know how—"

"Look, I can't call the police—I know you are the police, but they wouldn't do anything until it's too late."

"I'll get somebody on it."

"We've got pictures of the two men."

"I'll send somebody around."

"Why don't you come?"

"I'm not minimizing your concerns; I wouldn't be of help in this. I'm going to send you someone, and she and I will work together on this. All right?"

Dworkin sighed. "Okay. When will she be here?"

"As soon as she can."

Stark phoned Diane Porter.

"Diane, can you do me a favour?"

"What do you want, Stark?"

"The editor woman at the *Gazette*—Amanda Dworkin—she thinks something's happened to Martha Magliore, who was seen going off in a car with two men—probably for a threesome," Stark put in wryly. "She didn't hand in her column today, and she ignored some photographer on the street or something. Dworkin thinks that was a signal to follow her. Do you mind running over there to the *Gazette* and having a word with this Dworkin woman?"

"Why don't you send a couple of uniforms?"

"I'm not a cop any more, remember?"

"I could send a couple."

"No, don't—"

"You've got the hots for this Dworkin woman?"

"She looks like death, only skinnier. No, I've been rough on Martha lately."

"Which she deserves."

"Will you do it?"

Porter groaned. "Sure. Dworkin? What was the first name again?"

Forty minutes later, Stark's phone rang. Powder was sitting on Stark's lap. Stark was in his undershorts. When the phone rang, the cat leapt off his lap, digging her rear claws into Stark's bare legs for purchase.

"Shit—ow—" Stark grabbed the phone. "Yeah."

"Stark?"

"Diane? That was fast. Don't tell me: she was in her office, pissed—as in drunk—when you got there?"

"She's not here. It's about the pictures, Stark. The photographer took shots of the two men? And one of them is Norton Fielding."

"I knew that sonofabitch was her source. So, she let the column dangle today. We don't have to worry about her. Diane, I'm sorry—"

"Stark?"

"What?"

"Fielding was carrying a gun."

Amanda Dworkin had been right about Magliore's actions. She had *intentionally* not looked at Len Kraft; it *had* been a signal. Unfortunately, Dworkin had been right about Len Kraft, too. Magliore hadn't tried to signal Kraft because she was afraid Fielding would shoot him.

Because Magliore hadn't signalled, Fielding had no reason to pay any attention to the idiot in the bush ranger get-up standing across the street. When Fielding had seen Magliore walking toward the house, he had assumed she had parked up the street. When they went out to Fowland's car, Fielding asked Magliore where her car was, and she told him a cabbie had dropped her off at the wrong house she'd thought was Fowland's place. Her story was supported by the fact that her car—the make and colour of which Fielding remembered—was nowhere on the street. The effect was to bolster Fielding's confidence that he had nothing to worry about. The police would undoubtedly eventually question him about Magliore, but by that time, no trace of the woman or Fowland would remain.

"Put your hands behind the seat," Fielding said when they got into the Jetta.

"How am I supposed to drive like that?" Fowland said with a frightened giggle.

"Shut up, and drive."

Fowland started the car and pulled away from the curb.

"Martha, please put your hands behind the seat," Fielding said. He spoke softly to Magliore, but snarled, with apparent disgust, at Fowland.

"I can't reach behind the seat."

"Just put them back as far as you can, Martha.—That's fine." Fielding wrapped one wrist with duct tape, stretched the tape across the back of the seat and wrapped the other hand. He passed the tape back and forth several times. "Go south on Keele Street," he told Fowland. When he had finished taping Martha, he ordered Fowland to turn on to a sidestreet and pull up to the curb. "Shut the car off and give me the keys. Don't move or I'll put a hole in your head." Fielding got out of the car on the street side and opened the driver's door. Fowland cowered. Fielding reached around Fowland's waist and stuck the end of the roll of tape to the seat back and passed the tape across Fowland's abdomen. He had to get into the back seat to complete the loop and get back into the front seat to pass the tape across the man's gut again. He did this three times before shutting the driver's door, resuming his seat and returning the keys to Fowland. "All right, get going, drive."

With his captives restrained, Fielding relaxed and allowed himself a smile.

"Why are you doing this?" Magliore asked.

Before Fielding could answer, Fowland said, "Listen, man, I don't know anything about you, not even your name—I know they call you the General. What does that mean to anybody? Nothing. I can't hurt you, man. Anything I told them about you, I'd be telling them about myself. Please, man, let me go. You can take the car, and you can do whatever the hell you want with her. I won't say a word. Please, man, please."

"Stop whining, you little shit. Just drive."

"You didn't answer my question," Magliore said, looking at Fowland with revulsion.

"What question?"

"Why are you doing this?"

"You told the cops about me."

"I didn't."

"You betrayed my confidence. I can't trust you. Sooner or later, you're going to tell them everything. I should have known. It didn't work with Mackey. He was going to betray me. We had an agreement. He came to me and told me if I gave him information about The Compact, he would keep my name out of things, even out of the book he was writing. And then later, he said he was going to put me in the book anyway, he was going to put—everything in the book."

"You killed Matt Mackey?"

"Oh god," Fowland said, half turning, causing the car to swerve into another lane."

"Watch where you're driving, you idiot," Fielding shouted.

"Oh god," Fowland said.

Fielding directed Fowland down Keele Street to Parkside Drive and on to the Lake Shore, on which they drove east to Cherry Street and then south to Commissioners Street, eventually pulling in to the weed-bristling parking lot of an abandoned factory.

"I own this," Fielding said proudly. "In the next couple of years, I'm going to resurrect this place. In the meantime, I use it for diversions. We won't be disturbed here. Pull up to that door," he ordered Fowland. "Give me the keys."

He got out of the car and put a key in a lock at the side of the wide overhead door. When he turned the key, the door rose. He got back into the car, handed Fowland the keys and told him to drive inside, where he took the keys from Fowland again, got out of the car, pulled a commando knife from inside his jacket and cut the tape securing Magliore to the seat, leaving the tape wrapped around her wrists. He told her not to move, went to the driver's side of the car and cut the tape holding Fowland in place. "All right, get out, both of you," he said, waving the gun in circles.

"You won't get away with this," Magliore said.

Fielding stood still and looked at her with mild disbelief. A deep, genuine laugh rose from his midriff.

"My god, you've never met a cliché you didn't like, have you, Martha? You're a caricature of yourself. I've read your stuff. Clichés—you even abuse them, twisting them around to do your bidding in convoluted constructions you think help bolster your absurd views. I've tried to be polite with you, Martha, but it's impossible. You really believe that I won't *get away with this.*" He emphasized the echo of her words. "But then, how could anyone get away with doing anything to you that you didn't want? You wouldn't permit it." He had started pacing, soldier-like, a few steps to the left, a few steps to the right. "Who made you reporters god? You force your moralizing into private places and then make those places public, and then you claim you're protecting society. If you left well enough alone, things would continue as they have for centuries and will for centuries to come, for centuries after meddling muckrakers like you have burned in hell."

Magliore watched the blood vessels in Fielding's temples throb and perspiration form on his brow. He gripped the gun tighter and thrust it toward her to emphasize his rant. She decided not to argue with him. She looked around. The building was the size of a football field, one big empty room, except for an office on one wall.

"What are you going to do?" Fowland whimpered.

"Shut up, and sit down, sit with your back against that girder."

"This floor is filthy," Fowland said, and Fielding shoved the gun at him. "Oh god." Fowland scurried to sit where Fielding had ordered.

"You, too," Fielding said to Magliore, "on the other side, with your back toward his." Magliore did as she was told, and Fielding wrapped duct tape around both of them, pulling their arms back at either side of the steel support beam. He continued to tape in a continuous strip, spiralling up their bodies, across their mouths and around their heads.

"Don't worry, you won't be here long. Tonight, we're going for a little drive. I have a little nightwork to do at my plastics factory, long after everyone has gone home."

CHAPTER SIXTY-FIVE

Porter knew she had dug herself a hole so deep it was unlikely she'd ever climb out of it. She'd be lucky even to stay on the force. She had no choice, and she had to act quickly. She had to move and at the same time call for help. Explaining in detail why a province-wide alert had to be issued for Magliore and Fielding and an unknown male would take her longer than it would to get to Fielding's house. She had to hope she could persuade Ted Henry with a précis. As soon as she got to the car, she called Henry on his cell.

"Okay, sarge, listen. I'm not supposed to be doing anything on my own in this thing, but—I'll explain later, but you've got to issue a province-wide alert for three people, Martha Magliore—"

"The writer?"

"Yeah, and Norton Fielding—he's one of the members of The Compact, you know—"

"I know who they are."

"And a third male, unidentified, all right?"

"Go on."

"Fielding has a gun. He and the other guy have abducted Magliore."

"How do you know this?"

"Sarge, it would take too long to explain. I'm on my way to Fielding's place now. I'll be there in a few minutes. You'd better send back-up. I think Fielding is our killer."

"What, of Waterman?"

"And Mackey and Braddock."

"Porter, get back to earth. Tell me more. Christ."

"Fielding and this other guy took Magliore away in a car, an old grey Jetta. I don't know what year, and I don't know the plate number. A photographer from the *Gazette* took pictures and I've seen them: Fielding has a handgun, looks like a Colt .45 semi-automatic."

"How are are *you* involved?"

"Stark called me."

"Stark? What's he been doing?"

"An editor from the *Gazette* called him. She had his card—from before. And Stark *knows* Magliore, and—he called me, because it was just a favour. I show up and talk to the editor, because she was convinced that something had happened to Magliore. I went, and I saw the picture of Fielding with the gun. I recognized him because we—interviewed him."

"I'm having trouble following, Porter, but on your word, I'm going to issue the alert and send back-up. Where is the house?"

"Forty-five Parry Street. In the Annex."

"Don't hang up. I'll be back."

Porter turned on to Davenport Road. She was less than a minute away from Fielding's house. She kept the cellphone against her ear, turned off the siren and flashers, made a left and a right and slowed to a crawl. She cursed. Stark's car was double-parked in front of Fielding's place. She stopped, turned her phone off, jumped out of the car and started running toward the house. Halfway there, she slowed to a walk. Stark was coming out of the house. Porter heard sirens in the distance, and it hit her that she couldn't let the back-up find Stark there. She started running again.

"Stark, back-up's coming. They can't see you here. I'm in enough trouble."

"I'll pull around the corner. Call me as soon as you get a chance. I'll wait."

Stark was nodding off when his cellphone rang. "Diane?"

"Yeah, what am I supposed to do now?"

"Let's think."

"Henry's on his way. How do I explain why I suspect Fielding of all three murders without saying 'Stark told me?'"

"Why didn't the photographer call the cops?"

"He said he was concentrating on the faces. Fielding was carrying the gun down beside his leg. You could only see it clearly in one picture. The photographer saw it, too, once he'd printed the pictures."

"All right. If I'd seen the picture, it would have been the first time I suspected Fielding of the killings. I told you I thought he was the source for Magliore's article. We said before that Mackey must have had somebody on the inside, because his accounts of The Compact's meetings read as if he had been there?"

"Right."

"So *we*, sorry, *you* didn't think about Fielding until you read Magliore. You thought Fielding might be Magliore's source and maybe Mackey's source at some point, too, but that wouldn't make him a suspect in Waterman's murder, so you'd have no reason to mention him particularly to Henry. Now, that's the truth, and it's perfectly reasonable. You'll have to stretch it a little and say you talked to Fielding and Magliore and confirmed that Fielding was the source."

"You never told me what Magliore said."

"She didn't give her source away on purpose, but she gave it away. You've just got to know how to play her."

"So, what should I do now? I don't want to be sidelined again."

"They'd better get this photographer to show them the house they came out of. See who owns that, whether there's anything lying around that might give a clue as to a place they might take Martha. Oh, shit."

"What?"

"I told Fielding she *had* given him up."

CHAPTER SIXTY-SIX

The trouble with covering somebody's mouth with a rectangle of duct tape is the person can loosen the tape enough to speak by wiggling his or her lips for a while. With lips that got as much exercise as Martha Magliore's, the loosening took no time at all. She and Fowland were still taped to the girder when Fielding left, after the creepy promise about the evening and his plastics factory.

"Fowland."

"Mmmhh."

"Wiggle your bloody lips, you can get your mouth loose." Magliore waited while Fowland tried. "Hurry up. Stretch your mouth, do a smile, do a frown, make a face. The tape will—"

"I've done it."

"Let's stand up."

"How?"

"Brace your back against the girder and bend your knees up, and then push up when I say—Ready?"

"Yeah."

"All right, push. That's it." They slid up the girder until they were standing. "Great. See, that's loosened the tape a bit. Now, I can reach your pockets—perish the thought—which means you must be able to reach mine. Can you?—Yes, I see you can. Okay, reach in, and not too bloody far, either. Wait a minute. I'll twist to that side. Okay, now, you should be able to feel a big Swiss Army knife. You got it?"

"I've got it."

"Okay, carefully, pull it out. Carefully." Fowland withdrew his hand slowly. There was a clatter of something hitting the floor.

"You idiot. Jesus." Magliore groaned.

"Shit, I'm sorry. Damn." Fowland's shoulders slumped.

"Shut up. I can see it out of the corner of my eye." She stretched her leg toward where the knife lay. "Damn, I can't reach it. It's closer to you, to your left. Reach your foot out. Can you see it?"

"No. I can't get my head around far enough."

"Okay. I can see it. Reach your foot out. Okay, not too quickly. Stretch your leg a little more. That's it. Good. Now, move your leg about an inch to the left. Okay, slowly pull your foot back toward the girder. That's it. That's it. Keep going. Great. I can reach it now. Let's slide back down. Slowly.—Okay, I've got it. Stand up again. Ready, push up.—All right, I'll turn it around—and hold it by my fingertips—and reach back. Now I'm holding it tightly, but only by my fingertips, so don't pull like it's a tug of war. The blade opens easily on this knife. Okay, now the blade is the most protruding of any of the thingies. So feel around gently until you find the thumb—whatever you call it—slit, slot—you know what I mean. I hope you've got a thumbnail—Great, you've got it. A little bit more. Okay, I've got it." Magliore rotated the knife in her hand slowly, gripped it tightly and began sawing at the tape. "Lean forward. It'll stretch the tape taut and make it easier to cut."

It took her twenty minutes to cut through the tape along her right side, his left. When she cut the last strand, they spun away from the girder, still attached along their other sides. They both grabbed at that tape and ripped it away.

"Let's get out of here," Magliore said, and they began running toward the big overhead door. When they got there, they realized the futility of their haste. "Shit. You can't open it without a key. All right, we'll have to forget the car. Come on."

Magliore hurried to a door beside the overhead. The locking bar wouldn't move.

"It's locked. There must be other doors." They ran around the perimeter of the building, encountering several doors, finding each as securely locked as the first. They were steel fire doors with bar releases, impossible for them to pry open even if they had had anything to pry with. They had returned almost to the spot they had started from, and came up against the wall of the office, which jutted into the interior of the building, the only thing that interrupted the rectangular space.

"Christ, let's look in this thing," Magliore said. They walked around to the front of the office; she opened the door and went inside, Fowland close behind. "What's the chances the lights will work? Can you find a switch? I'm sure the hydro's not on."

"Here's the switch," Fowland said. They were surprised when the lights did come on and more surprised by what they saw. They both recoiled.

"Oh my god," Magliore said.

"Wow, amazing," Fowland said.

"You vile bastard, it's disgusting. You're both fucking perverts. God. This is sickening."

The room looked like a huge children's playroom. There was a life-size wooden soldier in each corner; a massive toy drum, on its side, like a little dance floor in the centre; big rag dolls sat against the walls; there was an oversized toy box, pretend toys protruding from it. The walls were covered with a wallpaper of circus animals and clowns and acrobats. The ceiling was stretched with a net full of stuffed animals. There was a red-and-blue wooden train engine and two cars, each big enough for a kid to stand in. There were shelves full of real toys—trains, dolls, trucks, balls. It was a room every kid in the world would have loved. Magliore thought she was going to bring up. Fowland was spinning around, grinning, eyes wide.

"You like my room?"

They turned toward the voice. Fielding was in the doorway, smiling, the gun at his side.

"You fucking pig," Magliore said, striding toward Fielding.

"Gently, gently," he said, gesturing for her to stop.

Fowland came forward a few steps. "General, General, listen to me," he said plaintively. "This room—this room—General, I can get you chickens, the best: clean, pretty ones that would do a set-up like this justice. Not street kids, really excellent kids."

"Shut your mouth." Fielding held the gun out at a level with Fowland's head.

"All right. But why me, General. I wouldn't say anything to hurt you."

"You'd sell your own grandmother. How did *she* find out about me?" He waved the gun at Magliore. He turned to Magliore. "I'm impressed that you got loose. I should have searched you. The tape's cut clean, so you must have a knife. Very sloppy of me. I'd put a soldier on report for an oversight like that. I'll have to punish myself. You won't get out quite so easily this time, though." He held up two sets of handcuffs.

CHAPTER SIXTY-SEVEN

Stark was already at the counter, looking at the menu in Mo's Lunchroom on College Street, when Porter arrived in a hurry.

"These places used to be great until the yuppies discovered them. Look at the prices."

"Stark, listen."

"What did Henry say?"

"He wasn't impressed. I have to go see him tomorrow morning for the full dressing down. At least he's not going to clue in Peters. I don't think he is, anyway."

"He won't. So, what are they doing to find Martha?"

"Nothing."

"Nothing?"

"Well, they issued an alert. But wait. A couple of units went to the house where the photographer saw the three of them come out. Some dump in the Junction. Inside—get this—they found paraphernalia for every kind of sexual perversion you might imagine, and pictures, mostly of little boys. This guy's a sicko. It was all there, pictures, videos, all that crap."

"And Fielding knows this guy? Bingo. That's what they had on him. That's why he gave Mackey and Magliore information on The Compact. And that's why he killed Mackey and probably the other two as well, eh?"

"Could be. Anyway, they interviewed Fielding's housekeeper."

"What did she say?"

"She didn't have a clue where he might be. He has a cottage in Muskoka. They alerted the OPP, and they called back in fifteen minutes. They had a unit at the cottage that fast. It's going to stay there all day. Of course, they weren't there. He owns a big factory in an industrial area south of Steeles, over by Weston Road somewhere. A couple of units went there, but the people there hadn't seen him. They said he rarely goes there. They went to his office, and the staff said they didn't expect him all day. That's about it. With any luck, somebody will spot them, or the car. He doesn't know we're looking for him, you know. So, he's got no reason to be particularly cautious. Now, I guess we just wait."

Stark shook his head.

"And he's in the army reserve, a colonel or something. He goes to Camp Borden a couple of times a week, so they've been alerted."

"He's hardly going to take them to Camp Borden."

"No, but if he shows up there—"

"I wish there was something we could do."

"Well, I don't think there is."

"He's going to kill her—if he hasn't already, the sick bastard."

"Stark, there's nothing we can do."

"If I hadn't started her sniffing around, this wouldn't have happened."

"How did she know about Fielding?"

"I told her."

"You told her?"

"Yeah, I told her that we knew he was her source."

"No, I don't mean that. I mean, how did she know to go after Fielding in the first place, and how did she know he was a kiddie-diddler—that's assuming that he is a bird of same feather as this other guy. I don't know his name."

"I think I do. I think it's Fowland."

"Where d'you get that?"

"Martha. When I said we knew that Fielding was her deep throat, she spit his name out, accused him of being the one who told us about Fielding. My guess is that the other guy is Fowland."

Porter said, "There's a pay phone up the front. I'm going to look the name up."

"Why don't you just call information on your cell?"

"I can't remember the street name. I'll recognize it if I see it."

Porter came back nodding. "That's the guy, T. Fowland."

"Lot of good that does us. I wish I were still drinking."

"Why? What good would that do?"

"I could got get pissed and stay that way."

CHAPTER SIXTY-EIGHT

"Don't move," Fielding said. "I have to override the alarm system. Yes, turn the key and punch in the numbers 1,3,2,4. There we go, and now the door key. All right, let's go, get inside."

He pushed Magliore and Fowland ahead of him, handcuffed together. In the car, Fielding had handcuffed Fowland's left hand to the steering wheel. He had handcuffed Magliore's left hand to the seat frame, cutting the vinyl of the seat cover to expose the steel frame.

"Nice, eh?" Fielding said, gesturing with the gun at the wide expanse and vaulted ceiling of the reception area, the centrepiece of which was a long chandelier in narrow glass strips of varying length, like a cluster of icicles. The furniture was modern and stark, but attractively designed.

"It's all plastic," Fielding said. "I'm a plastics man, so that's natural. We don't make this kind of product, but it's all in the same family. Of course, they're bloody uncomfortable to sit on, but they're only for salesmen anyway. I rarely come here myself. I don't even have an office here. Not any more; I used to. All right, plastics, go through that door there. I'm going to give you a little plastics lesson."

They entered the production area. Fielding switched on the lights. A row of big machines ran down the centre of a long room, each with a bank of dials and buttons at one end. Glass-walled offices, a cafeteria and a games room paralleled the machines along one wall. Every surface that wasn't glass was brightly painted. Above the level of the machinery and the offices, a continuous strip of windows around the four walls must have provided a bright environment, Magliore thought. Somehow, the place reminded her of an Ikea store.

"Walk," Fielding said, and they preceded him past the machines almost to the back wall of the building. "Sit down," Fielding said, indicating a bench. "Okay, I promised you a brief lesson. Now, plastic is made from fractions of natural gas or crude oil, changed chemically into solid form. Now, there are two basic types of plastic: thermosetting and thermoplastics. Thermosetting plastics are fixed in a permanent shape and can't be softened. They're used mostly for dishes, furniture, that sort of thing. Thermoplastics, on the other hand, are soft when exposed to heat and pressure and harden when they're cooled. Thermoplastics are the most common type of plastic, and that's the kind we work with here. They're used to make auto parts, inflatable toys, insulation, pipes, shampoo bottles, shower curtains, food containers. You follow? Good. PVC, which is polyvinyl chloride, is more precisely the type of plastic we use here. Now, it's composed of macromolecules, and they're made up of carbon, hydrogen and chlorine atoms. PVC is created by combining ethylene with chlorine, which is produced from rock salt. It's fabulous stuff, you know, PVC. Now, you may not be aware of it, but of all the synthetic thermoplastics, PVC is probably the polymer in modern use that has the oldest pedigree. Vinyl chloride monomer was first produced by a chap called Regnault in France way back in 1835, and its polymerization was recorded in 1872 by another fellow, Baumann, who exposed sealed tubes containing vinyl chloride to sunlight." Fielding stopped speaking. His smile vanished. He gritted his teeth and poked Fowland violently with his foot. "Are you listening?"

Fowland started, as if he had been caught in a daydream by his teacher. He lifted his head quickly and recoiled against the wall at the sight of the gun, which Fielding had extended toward him. Fowland shoved himself back against the wall as if he were trying to push himself into it. "Oh, please let me go. I won't say anything. Please." His feet were scrambling desperately for purchase on the painted floor, he rose higher and higher against the wall. "Please—"

Fielding shot Fowland in the forehead. The noise was deafening. Magliore slumped to one side and vomited on the bench. Her bladder had given way. Her ears buzzed with the reverberating sound of the shot. She was shaking, gasping for breath, unable to move, expecting to die.

Fowland fell slowly to the floor, pulling Magliore toward him. Fielding reached down and unlocked the handcuff around Fowland's wrist, leaving the other end dangling from Magliore's arm.

"Now, where was I?" he said, grinning widely. "Oh yes, this wonderful product. Without plastics, we'd still be in the industrial era. We wouldn't have the products that have enabled us to leap to where we are today and continue to allow us to move ahead with mind-blowing rapidity. We wouldn't have any of our wonder weapons: we'd still be fighting wars by sending men out to die by the thousands. Medical developments would be fifty, seventy-five years behind. Nothing would be as it is. Well, as I was saying—the earliest patents for PVC production were taken out in the US in 1912, and pilot-plant production began in Germany and the States in the early 1930s." He paused and gave Magliore an avuncular, affectionate smile. "Now, Martha, the reason I want you to know all this is because you're going to be—well, rather intimately involved in the process in very short order. All right? I'm afraid I get a little carried away with the subject. Perhaps I'm going into too much detail. I can stop now if you like and—get on with the business at hand?"

"No—I'm interested. Really."

"Good," he said, pleased. "Well then. Do you have any knowledge of chemistry, or are you interested in it?"

"I am, yes."

"The raw materials for PVC are crude oil or natural gas and sodium chloride. The hydrocarbon raw materials are converted to ethene—ethylene—and the sodium chloride is electrolysed to produce chlorine. The ethene and chlorine are reacted to produce 1,2-dichloroethane—ethylene dichloride—according to the reaction: $C_2H_4 + C_{12} = C_2H_4C_{12}$. The ethylene dichloride is then decomposed by heating in a high-temperature furnace, and then other materials are added. Okay, I see you're getting a little fidgety, so I won't go on with the chemical details." He took a deep breath. "What I propose is—uh, perhaps I shouldn't go into it. It's a bit unpleasant. But let me say this: I'm going to see to it, Martha, that you live forever, in a manner of speaking, anyway. I'm afraid, though, that in order to reduce you to useable components for the extrusion process, I'm going to have to do a little—no—that doesn't have to concern you. Martha, I must say, you've been a very attentive student. I'm sorry that we haven't been able to get to know each other better. We might have had some interesting discussions." He raised the gun.

"Wait, wait, just—wait a little while, please. Let me ask you a couple of questions, all right. Please. I'm a little shaky."

"Questions?" Fielding brightened. "You want to know more? Well, we manufacture a number of products. The precise process we use here is patented. I devised it—"

"No—I wasn't thinking of that. Although that's—very interesting."

"I'm so glad you think so."

"I was thinking about why, well, you know, how this all got started? Not your plant. I mean—killing Mackey and Braddock and Waterman. Why? I mean, I know the general reason, but exactly why did you do it at the time you did it? I think I have the right to know, don't you?"

"Oh, I don't mind telling you. I guess I knew it was over, that it was not going to go on as it had been for many pleasant years, when Mackey confronted me. He wouldn't tell me how he knew about my—diversion. But I knew that he couldn't have just happened across the information. I kept it well hidden. At least, I thought I did." Fielding paused, slightly distracted. "I thought I was, how shall I say, impenetrable. My military training included covert operations. I was a sort of commando, and a bit of what you might call a spy, I suppose. In any event, I tried to keep Mackey quiet by feeding him information about The Compact."

"Yes."

"It's a group of very powerful men committed to a new vision for this country, a return to family values and to honesty and hard work and all the essentials that we have lost after years of socialism. We were very active behind the scenes—Dennis Yates was to be our Ronald Reagan—a pretty face, popular among core, middle-class voters, the baby boomers. We were going to run the country and put things right again."

"So, what happened?"

"After Yates was arrested, and all this business, it's finished."

"Why did you suddenly feel you had to kill Mackey?"

"From what Waterman said, the publication of Mackey's book was imminent. Mackey was going to renege on our agreement and include me in the book—things that would have destroyed me utterly. And it was apparent that his death was not long in coming, and I knew that the publication was to occur shortly before, or to coincide with, his dying. I saw an opportunity when Waterman told The Compact about the book, and strongly hinted that the only guarantee of safety for all of us was to do away with Mackey. Later, when I examined the book in Mackey's computer, I understood why Waterman was so concerned about its publication. When Waterman implied that Mackey should be dispatched, I protested vociferously to deflect suspicion, and then I killed Mackey. I'm trained for that sort of thing, you see." Fielding smiled.

Magliore felt sick.

"I rappelled down the side of the building from the roof, and dispatched the man with efficiency. Then I shoved every piece of paper I could find in the apartment into a duffel bag, which I then tossed from the balcony into some bushes below. I strapped the computer on my back and returned the way I had come."

He nodded as he recalled the events, and looked quite pleased with himself.

"By the way," he said, "I also jumped in front of a subway train to establish myself in the role of a victim in the list of dramatis personae."

"What?"

"I knew what I was doing. I know where the hot rail is, and I gave the driver plenty of time to see me and stop. I pretended I had been pushed, but I insisted it had been an accident. That sort of denial serves to bolster the view in others that one has in fact suffered the thing one is denying."

Magliore tried to look as if she were impressed by Fielding's cunning. "Wow. So then, please tell me, why did you kill Braddock?" she said.

Fielding lowered his eyes and shook his head slowly. "Lee and I knew each other for many years. We were friends. We had a common interest."

"Braddock was a pedophile?" Magliore said, regretting the words as soon as they spat out of her mouth. Fielding glared. The knuckles of his hand gripping the gun turned white.

"Prejudice is selective, isn't it?" he said. "The terrible tyranny of the majority. Were the ancient Greeks and Romans pedophiles? Well, I suppose they were, if you give the word the same semantic meaning as anglophiles, or bibliophiles, for instance."

"I wasn't being judgemental," Magliore said quickly. "I was just—trying to be clear on what you meant by common interest."

"Well, your bald inference was correct. We both loved young people, yes. We did." Fielding sighed. "When I did away with Mackey, I removed every piece of paper I could find in the apartment that had any sort of writing on it. I took anything that might have recorded information. Subsequently, I examined his notes, both written and in the discs and in the hard drive of the computer. And I discovered that Mackey's source about me, I'm so very sad to say, was Lee. He had been rather indiscreet, and Mackey had—quite accidentally—discovered his indiscretion. I suppose I can forgive Lee for acting badly in desperation—he had much more to lose than I: he was married and had children and grandchildren. In return for a promise that Mackey would not disclose what he knew about Lee, Lee offered him me. The fact that I am a colonel in the reserve and that I had been for many years a regular officer made me a more attractive target for self-righteous exposure, and Mackey agreed, intending to betray Lee eventually, I'm sure."

"Tell me about the book." Magliore might have been asking the question to buy more time, but she was just as motivated by journalistic curiosity.

Fielding chuckled. "It would take much too long." He looked at his watch. "I've taken too much time as it is. I'm sorry—"

"You didn't tell me about Waterman."

"You did include him in your list of my—accomplishments? Well, my dear, I didn't kill Waterman, I'm sorry. I had absolutely nothing to do with that pig's death. Oh, I would have enjoyed doing away with him, I must say, but I don't know who killed him. He had many enemies, but it's a mystery to me. And now, I'm afraid—"

"Police! Drop that gun now or you will be shot. Right now. Drop it. Drop it." The voice came from the other end of the room. Fielding and Magliore turned to see two uniformed policemen crouched in firing position, their guns trained on Fielding.

Fielding smiled. "They'd be awfully lucky to hit me from there," he said calmly. Magliore began to get to her feet.

"Don't get up," Fielding said quickly, turning his head to look at Magliore. He sounded concerned. "It'll be a lot safer if you stay down." He looked back down the room. "Where's that other cop? Oh, he's slipped over to the other side of the machines. Very cunning."

"Drop your weapon," the cop still in sight shouted. His voice was young and nervous, though he was trying to sound in command, masterly. "I will not ask you again. You will be shot."

Fielding turned his head again toward Magliore. "Well, you're going to have an award-winner out of this, Martha, aren't you. Lucky girl. Not only do you not get shot, but you get to write a Pulitzer prize-winner, or whatever they call it in this country."

"National Newspaper Award."

"Sad how ignorant we are of our own country's institutions."

The policeman's gun fired. Magliore dropped to the floor.

"Oh shit," she said.

"Very wise to duck," Fielding said. "He's just as likely to hit you as me. Goodbye, Martha. Make sure you spell my name right. And please, show a little understanding." Fielding began walking toward the policeman, firing his gun every few steps, aiming toward the officer, but over his head. The cop returned fire. On the third shot, he hit Fielding in the left shoulder, causing him to lurch backward and turn to the left, to face the wall. Another shot, this one from the other cop, who had crawled over the top of one of the machines, hit Fielding in the back of the neck, just below the edge of the skull. He staggered forward, his head smashing hard against the concrete wall. His knees buckled, and he crashed to the floor, his legs splaying out as his face landed. After that, he was still.

CHAPTER SIXTY-NINE

If he'd still been a cop, Stark would have arrested Peter Mackey, but because he no longer was, he couldn't see the point. Diane Porter, on the other hand, needed something dramatic to prevent being banished to some gulag in Scarborough. An opportunity presented itself in the disclosure in Martha Magliore's epic account of her abduction and near-death that her abductor, Norton Fielding, had killed everybody in sight except "Martin" Waterman. (She had continued to spell his name wrong, but this time the copy editor corrected it.)

Magliore's piece had occupied the top half of the *Gazette* front page, the space being taken up mostly by a five-column picture of Magliore sitting up in a hospital bed with a laptop on her knee and an (unlit) cigarette dangling from her lips—she had insisted on the prop. The story had turned to three full pages, two of which were illustrated by pictures of Fielding in uniform, Fielding's covered body on a stretcher, the exterior of Fielding's factory and head shots of Matt Mackey, Lee Braddock and Martyn Waterman. A third page, composed mostly of photographs, showed the interior of the vacant factory on Commissioners Street, including Terry Fowland's car and the playroom. Magliore told the paper about the building long before she told the cops, giving the photographers time to get there. They had paid a locksmith a thousand dollars to get them inside. The photographs included a police mug shot of Fowland, his house, and his covered body on a stretcher.

While Stark was content to let Peter Mackey drink himself to death in peace, he had no brief for the man, so that when Porter asked him to help, he was more than willing.

"You're sure Mackey did it?" Porter asked Stark. They were sitting in Porter's police car on the Danforth. Porter had been coming to Stark's place, but had seen Stark walking along the street. She had seen him from behind, and at first had not recognized him, identifying him only by his ancient duffel coat. It was a cold day, and Stark was hunched against the wind, but it was the walk that confused her: almost a shuffle, almost like an old man's walk. She had had to call Stark's name twice before the man looked up.

"How can you ever be sure somebody did it, unless you were there? He had motive, opportunity and the means."

"But no forensics."

"You'll have to ask Ident, but if they didn't present you with anything before, then I suppose we can assume there's nothing that points to an old man who lives in Grandfield, Ontario."

"So, what would you do? I mean, how can we prove he did it?"

"Search me. You'll have to get him to confess, I guess."

"Do you think he will?"

"If you press the right buttons he might."

"Like what?"

Stark sighed. "I think you should try to get the Crown to go for a deal, offer him a light sentence to a plea to manslaughter. That might work, especially if you throw in the idea that he did the honourable thing, avenging the death of his son."

"But he wasn't."

"Sure he was. He read the manuscript Matt had left at his place in Grandfield. That's where Mary-Margaret got it. Mackey thought his son had been killed by Waterman, or on Waterman's orders, because of the book."

"You're going to have to come with me."

"Are you going to go Grandfield and arrest the guy?"

"I can't go anywhere near the case. No, I mean you have to come with me to see Ted Henry."

"Jesus, what for?"

"Because you're going to have to explain the whole thing to him. He's not going to listen to me, besides I'd be giving it to him second hand. And you have to tell him you went there on your own, that I didn't know. All right?"

CHAPTER SEVENTY

"So, what's bozo-boy want now?" Bernie MacIsaac asked Mary-Margaret. They were in the big bedroom at the Yates house. MacIsaac was wearing purple silk pyjamas that belonged to Dennis Yates. "They interviewed him on the way into the House. He came loping up the walkway." MacIsaac imitated Yates's bouncy walk.

"Don't do that. It gives me the creeps."

"What?"

"That walk. What did he say in the interview?"

"Same crap as usual. You know, you listen to him, you hear all the words, but then when he's finished, you can't figure out what he just said. It's amazing. They really trained him well. So, what did he want?"

"He wants the house back."

"He can't have it. He wants his political career back, too, but he's not going to get that either. Talk is, the caucus has asked him to resign. He won't, but he'll never be renominated. You didn't tell him I was living here, did you?"

"No. And listen, this is *my* house. The only person who can say whether he gets back in it or not is me."

"Whoa, take it easy. I was simply giving you my support, that's all." Mary-Margaret was sitting at her make-up table. She had turned to face MacIsaac and jabbed in his direction with an eyebrow pencil to stress her words. MacIsaac strolled across the room, and tried to kiss her on the top of the head. She pushed him away.

"Don't. I'm not kidding, Bernie. Don't start presuming. Back away."

He went and sat on the bed. The big bedroom was Mary-Margaret's room. Dennis's room was at the opposite end of a long hallway. Almost as big, it had been the children's playroom. Mary-Margaret had pushed Yates out of the master bedroom years before, having a lock installed on it and a staircase built that led from the rear corner of the room to a landing with two doors, one to the outside and one into the kitchen. She had had the bedroom redone in white and mauve, with billowing drapes and sheers, everything festooned with flounces. The bed was a four-poster, with a white-satin-draped canopy. The carpet was mauve and deep and thickly cushioned. A mirror in the shape of a swimming dolphin stretched for most of the length of the wall opposite the bed. A large Andrew Wyeth watercolour of a battered barn hung in the centre of the wall to one side of the bed, and floor-to-ceiling windows ranged along the wall on the other side.

"Where are you going?" MacIsaac said. There was a mixture of petulance and irritation in his voice.

"Mmm?" Mary-Margaret took a drag on her cigarette. "Where am I going? None of your fucking business."

"Jesus, what kind of relationship have we got here, M&M?"

"Stop calling me that. My name is Mary-Margaret."

"Where the fuck are you going?"

"Fuck off. If you don't like it, you know what you can do."

"What the hell is going on?"

Mary-Margaret pivoted around to look at MacIsaac. "Bernie, we've never had a relationship. We have an arrangement. We've had the same arrangement for an awful long time. Three times a week always seemed enough for you in the past. And now, we also have a business relationship. My lawyer called. We're now officially partners. But only in business, Bernie. Only in business." She turned to face the mirror and resumed working on her hair. "It was fun playing Mummy and Daddy with you, Bernie, but I don't want you in here when the kids come home for

Christmas. And I don't want you just to move out of the bedroom; I want you out of the house."

"You manipulative bitch."

"Bernie! How could you?" she said ironically.

MacIsaac leapt up from the bed and charged across the room. Mary-Margaret saw him coming, and grabbed a pair of scissors from the make-up table. As MacIsaac reached for her hair, Mary-Margaret stood up and spun away from his outstretched hand. She swung the scissors and stuck him in the hand. He pulled the hand back, shouting in pain and fury. His other hand hit the curlicued wrought-iron back of the make-up stool, clutched it and swung it in an arc at Mary-Margaret. She ducked under the stool and stepped inside its arc, driving the scissors into MacIsaac's chest. He straightened to his full height and staggered backward, turned once slowly, and crashed to the floor, face down.

CHAPTER SEVENTY-ONE

Porter was an hour into her turn at interviewing Peter Mackey when Ted Henry called her out of the room and told her that Mary-Margaret was being held, and Bernie MacIsaac was in critical, but stable, condition in Sunnybrook. They put Peter Mackey in a cell and went to question Mary-Margaret.

"What am I doing here? He tried to kill me. I had to stop him. If I hadn't stuck him with those scissors, I'd be dead. I'm not saying anything more until my lawyer gets here. Is he dead?"

It took MacIsaac a week to recover, during which time, Mary-Margaret told the police that Bernie had been in a car with her husband and Matthew Mackey and Martyn Waterman on a night in 1968 when they raped and killed a street girl. MacIsaac's DNA matched the DNA of the sperm found in the body of Rhonda Wilton. MacIsaac was charged with first-degree murder.

The Crown decided they'd never get an attempted-murder conviction against Mary-Margaret, and the charges were dropped.

Peter Mackey was released.

Dennis Yates was also charged in Rhonda's murder, based on what Mary-Margaret said Dennis had told her of the event. She was to be the key witness in the case against both her husband and her lover. Bert

Bartram, the drummer and Mary-Margaret's erstwhile lover, came forward and said that both Yates and MacIsaac had told him what they had done that night in 1968. There was a grain of truth in that: Yates had once confessed to Bartram in a drunken moment of guilt-cleansing that he had done "something terrible" to a street girl. Bartram hoped that with Yates and MacIsaac and Waterman out of the way, he might get back in there with the now-very-wealthy Mary-Margaret.

The cases against MacIsaac and Yates were clinched when each accused the other, which meant admitting at least to being present on the night in question. They were both found guilty and given life sentences.

No one was ever charged in the murder of Martyn Waterman.

CHAPTER SEVENTY-TWO

"So, what are you going to do, Stark?" Diane Porter shouted over the noise in Stark's crowded apartment.

Stark had decided to hold his own retirement party, which he could limit to his friends. The group was small. Roger Sammon was there and Boris and Bert Boyd. Ted Henry was there; and Howard Case, Diane's partner/boyfriend; and Bobby Payne, the IT guy who had played such a big role in cracking the case. Diane had made Stark invite Martha Magliore. Jimmy Windsor, Stark's tenant, was there, and a couple of local shopkeepers and their wives. Porter had been only mildly surprised that Stark had invited no one else from the service.

"I'm going to England, Diane. Jimmy's sister, Gloria, is going to move in here. She loves cats, so she's agreed to look after Powder. It'll be very handy for Jimmy because his girlfriend is pregnant, and they'll have a built-in babysitter. Jimmy's hoping he'll be able to get free tickets from the kid to any concert or sporting event in the city."

"What!"

"Well, Jimmy's girlfriend is a Mohawk, right? So Jimmy's hoping the kid grows up to be a scalper."

"You asshole."

"Seriously. Ask him."

"What are you going to do in England?"

"Maybe nothing. I managed to get my British passport."

"You really think you're going to be able to make a living there as a private investigator?"

"Or something. Why not? I'll bet you they find me fascinating. They'll think I'm an American. I'll wear a trenchcoat and a fedora."

"Well, I'm going to miss you—like mad, Stark."

"Hey—no kissing."

Marquis Book Printing Inc.
Québec, Canada
2008